"...But when in life's battle the going is rough,
And weaklings would whimper and whine,
Just give me the chap who had courage to scrap,
Backed up to the last one-yard line."
THE ONE-YARD LINE - J.W. Marson

"Coming Through! A Book of Sports for Boys" Copyright - D. Appleton and Company. Published with the approval of the Boy Scouts of America, 1927

CONTENTS

DEDICATIONS

To my loving and supportive wife Kathy who
provides me strength every day.
To our children, Annie and John, whom I adore
and cherish more and more each day.
To my parents, Bernie and Ann Ethel, whose
courage provided my roadmap for life.
To my friend, David, who ignited the spark.

*"Any time you have an opportunity to make a difference in this
world and you don't, then you are wasting your time on earth."*
- Roberto Clemente, "The Great One"

BOOK ONE

The Heart of the Twentieth Century

CHAPTER 1

VERNA'S GIRL - EILEEN

Verna had three children. The youngest. My Mother Ann Ethel was born in Chicago. 1925. Brother Teddy and her sister Eileen were significantly older. Ann Ethel adored and idolized them both. They on the other hand tolerated her. All three loved and feared Verna.

Eileen married in the 1930's. She had two children. First RoseAnne. Then Bobby. Her husband died during World War II. I have never heard a word spoken about him. I don't think he died in battle.

By the end of World War II, Eileen and her two children were living in Chicago on one floor of the north side three-story brick apartment owned by Verna and my Grandfather Nat (another family member I never heard a word about). Unmarried. Teddy and Ann Ethel lived here as well.

I only knew my grandma Verna as a gray haired lady. Even with gray hair, she was dynamic. She had red hair in her youth. She passed the red hair on to Eileen along with all of her red haired attributes.

Eileen captured your attention when she entered a room. Smart. Tough. Brassy. Razor sharp tongue. Not vulgar. Quick.

She was about five-four with a nice slight build. A pretty face. Slender shapely legs. Pretty freckles (Like Verna). And, all that gorgeous natural red hair: Like Maureen O'Hara or Lucile Ball.

At home, she was a caged lioness. She was always walking. Usually with a cigarette. Sometimes with a drink. All business. A single, working Mother. No apologies. No looking back. Eileen went out. Verna raised the babies.

Fall 1948

It's Sunday. No work today. Ann Ethel. Sitting on a small black lacquered chair at her bedroom vanity. Twenty-three years old. Born legally blind. Looking toward the mirror. Through her own ocular fog she's learned to overcome. Eileen's reflection behind her. Ann Ethel is slowly brushing her hair. Combs, brushes, and assorted Channel perfume bottles rest in front of the vanity mirror. Nat King Cole croons "<u>Nature Boy</u>" on the radio...

It's about 5pm. Verna's Sunday dinner is competed. The girls are relaxing. Eileen is sitting on the bed next to a half packed suitcase. Both girls are nursing their drinks. Eileen wrinkles her nose. Asks.

"What the hell are you drinking?"

"It's called an 'Old Fashioned'. I read about it at work in Esquire Magazine."

"What's in it?"

"Here's the article."

Ann Ethel throws the magazine on the bed.

<u>Old Fashioned Cocktail Recipe:</u>
Place the sugar cube (or 1/2 teaspoon loose sugar) in an Old-Fashioned glass. Wet it down with 2 or 3 dashes of Angostura bitters and a short splash of water or club soda. Crush the sugar with a wooden muddler, chopstick, strong spoon, lipstick, cartridge case, whatever. Rotate the glass so that the

sugar grains and bitters give it a lining. Add a large ice cube. Pour in the rye (or bourbon). Serve with a stirring rod.

"Seems like a lot of trouble. Glass. Bourbon. Maybe ice. That's a drink."
Ann Ethel pauses. Stops brushing. Looks up. Turns to Eileen.
"Is Mother making you take me?"
*"I've been married. I've got **two** children. I've buried a husband. I work. No one makes me do anything."*
"So you want me along?"
"No."
"So?"
"So. Verna doesn't think I should take a trip alone."
*"What do **you** think?*
"I do what I want."
"I know you do."
*"I'm driving the whole time. I might as well have company. Even though **you can't** drive."*
*"You want me along? **You asked** her if I could come. Didn't you?"*
"Shut up."
Ann Ethel smiles. Eileen smiles.

They leave the next day. By now, Ann Ethel was working. She wasn't naïve. Still, she was in the shadow of Eileen. Exactly where she wanted to be. She was company for Eileen. She was thrilled to be along.

Eileen loves her new 1948 Pontiac Silver Streak Convertible. She is as adept as any man handling the eight cylinder four-speed "Hydramatic" automatic transmission. There is a floor mounted push lever to start the engine.

An AM radio, cigarette lighter, white leather interior, and dashboard clock escort the girls comfortably on their trip. Outside. The Pontiac has white-wall tires and slick silver hubcaps. The paint is the color of maroon dried blood. A dark red. Very glossy. Not showy.

Ann Ethel has plotted the route. On her lunch break, she walked down to the Chicago Public Library at Michigan Avenue across from the Art Institute to use their atlas. From Chicago. Straight south on highway 45 till it meets highway 51. Then right into New Orleans. Eileen will drive the entire route. They'll stop when she is tired.

They made their first night's stop just as they passed Cairo, Illinois. The next day, they drove through Memphis. Stopped for the night in Jackson, Mississippi. They'd gone about seven-hundred miles. About two-hundred to go. Piece of cake.

Each day seemed sunnier and warmer than the next. The roads were empty. Out of Chicago. Driving seemed like a vacation. It was hard to believe the destination could be better.

The morning they left Jackson for New Orleans was perfect. Light dew on the grass. Very slight breeze. About sixty-five degrees at Seven AM. Both girls were early risers. Working women. It would get warmer through the day.

Almost ten miles south of Jackson. Eileen was driving about forty-five miles per hour. On open highway. She saw ahead in the distance on her right what appeared to be two people on the road's shoulder. She slowed her car.

Eileen coasted by at about ten miles an hour. Drove past. She was trying to register what she saw. She continued to slow the car by gently applying the break. Stopped. The road was still empty. She put the car in reverse. Drove back about thirty yards.

Eileen hadn't been sure of what she had seen. Now she was. It was a lady. A Black lady. Young. Younger than Eileen. Maybe twenty? She was crying. There was something under her on the roadside. She turned off the engine. Behind the lady was a one room wooden house. Window frames where glass should be. No glass. No door either. Likely had not been painted in twenty years. If ever. Eileen spoke to Ann Ethel first.

"Ann. Wait in the car."

Eileen moved out of the car. Walked to the prone lady slowly. The lady was wearing a white cotton dress. Apparently nothing else. No undergarments. No shoes. As she neared the lady, she could see that the lady was hunched over a small child. A girl. Maybe five years old? There was blood on the road.

"What happened here?"

The lady did not speak. She hugged her child. She cried. Eileen tried again.

*"What **happened** here? Are you OK?"*

The lady looked up. She sniffed deeply to compose herself. She did not stand.

"I own this land. Just me. No man. Just me. Just me and my baby."

"Yes?"

"I work the land. This here's my house. I can't be watching after my baby. She ran near the road. A car hit her. Never even slowed down."

"Let me see."

The lady stood. She had blood on her dress. The girl's leg had been hit. It was crushed inward. Likely hit from the side. Not full on. Still crying softly. Exhausted from trauma. The little girl was bleeding slowly. The cut was dirty. Mud and gravel matted. Blood seeping out. The lady had not bandaged nor washed her. She was just holding her. Eileen thought. It wasn't fatal if treated. But untreated, she might die.

"Did you call the police?"

"I don' have a phone."

"Can I take you somewhere to call the police? And, a doctor?"

The lady stood. She wasn't crying anymore.

*"No Ma'am. Ain't no policeman gonna stop **here.** Ain't no doctor gonna come **here**. To **them**, we iz just trash along the road. Ain't no-one cares about us."*

"Them?"

"Sorry to say Ma'am. White folk."

"I care. I'll take you to a doctor or a hospital."

7

"You ain't from here. Is you? No hospital near here gonna let us in. Colored hospital is two, maybe three hours away."

"Colored hospital? What the hell? Ok. I get it. I have an idea. Can you get your girl in the car? Ann, get in the back seat. What's your name?"

"Ginger ma'am. My baby's name is Lila."

"I'm Eileen. This is my sister Ann Ethel."

"Nice to meet you Miss Eileen. Nice to meet you Miss Ann Ethel."

"Yeah. Get in the car. Sit Lila between Ann Ethel and yourself. Ann, take one of your scarves. See if you can wrap the leg and stop the bleeding. Get a coat or blanket out of the trunk. We are going to need it. Ann, wipe some of Lila's blood on to your dress."

No questions. They all obeyed Eileen. She was in charge.

"OK Ginger. How do we get to the hospital or doctor where 'the White folks' go"?

"Drive back the way you came. You passed it comin out of Jackson. Big brick building. On this road. Bout twenty minutes by car I guess. They ain't gonna let us in. You'll see."

Eileen snapped back.

"You'll see."

Eileen didn't speed. She drove calmly. She saw the large gray wooden sign in front of the dandelion yellow brick hospital.

Magnolia Arms – Hospital and Medical Care
Established 1861.
By President Jefferson Davis to service the armies of the
Confederacy.
All Welcome!
City of Jackson – _The_ Capital of Mississippi

The wooden front door was freshly painted in light blue. A small hand printed sign hung with tied cord on the door knob. Black ink on white background. Two words. Meaning clear.

Whites Only!

Eileen noticed the state flag of Mississippi and the Confederate flag of Stars and Bars flying in the sunshine in front of the hospital. She noticed the red, white, and blue forty-eight star American flag was not present.

Eileen slowly drove the circular gravel road that surrounded the hospital. It was her preference not to make a grand entrance through the front door. In the back, there were two doors. The window of one door was printed in stencil.

"Emergency Entrance – Colored Not Allowed!"

On the other.

"Colored Workers Entrance"

Eileen stopped the car behind the hospital in front of the two doors. No-one was around. Eileen thought this was good. The less people, the better.

*"OK. You are **all** going to do what I say. No questions. Are you ready?"*

Ann Ethel and Ginger nodded. Eileen continued.

"Ginger. Hold the coat Ann gave you around Lila. Try not to show that she's hurt. Carry her along if you have to. Hide her under your dress if you can. It's Ok if you can't. Ann Ethel. Pretend you are blind. Keep your sunglasses on."

*"I **am** blind."*

"You know what I mean."

"OK"

Ginger. With your other arm, wrap it through Ann Ethel's arm. Like you are helping her walk. Like you are her guide dog. Understand?

"Yes Miss Eileen."

In her entire life, no White woman (or man) had ever spoken directly to Ginger. She had been "spoke at". But she had never been "spoke to". This was new.

She knew she was in danger. She'd be beat or worse for coming through the door of the White man's hospital. This was becoming the most exciting day of her life. And she knew. Without help. Lila would die. Or, be a cripple the rest of her life. She wasn't scared.

Eileen led the three to the Emergency Room door. White entrance. She stopped just outside. She had her purse over her shoulder. She took a deep breath. Held it in. Puffed out her cheeks. Than exhaled.

"This is it. Are you ready?"

Ann Ethel said with a slight smile.

"Yes Miss Eileen."

Eileen burst through the door with the others in tow. At the top of her lungs, she screeched in a pretty fair southern accent.

"*I need a doctor! I need one. Let's go! My sister was hit by a car. She needs help. NOW!*"

A nurse came running. Eileen's presence overpowered her.

"Let's go. Where have you been? Who's your manager? Get my sister into an examination room. Now!"

The nurse stammered.

"But…"

Eileen yelled back.

"BUT WHAT?!"

"That…I mean…her…She can't come in. She's…You know…She's colored. I'll get fired."

Calmly. Dripping with southern charm.

*"She's our maid. My sister is blind. Y'all see what I mean? She takes my sister around. **You** had a colored maid right? Didn't she take you around when you were young? Well. This one comes inside. **Has** to.*

People get used to it. It's an exception. I'm not happy about it. Daddy's got lots of money. You with me?"

Ann Ethel was listening to every word. Later when she told this story, she swore Eileen had mastered the southern accent right then and there.

The nurse stood and thought. Eileen went on the offensive.

*"**Let's go!** She's going to bleed out right here in your waiting room. You don't want that. You don't know my Daddy. Trust me. **YOU DON'T WANT THAT!"***

"Follow me."

They were in. A private room. Waited a few minutes for a doctor. Eileen knew. This was the point of no return. If the doctor was a Klan member, it was all over. If the doctor had compassion, there was a chance.

There was a light knock at the door. It opened. In walked the doctor. He looked to be about sixty years old. White thick hair. Trimmed salt and pepper beard. Round-rim glasses. About six feet tall. A little extra stomach. But not too much. Distinguished now in his white hospital-issue coat. Likely very handsome in his hey-day. In a warm, refined southern accent.

"Hello. My name is Jeb. You can call me 'Doctor Jeb'. That's what all the folks around here call me. What's all the yelling about?"

Ann Ethel thought to herself.

"Jeb. Of course it is. What else would it be? We're dead."

Eileen didn't miss a beat. The doctor walked in. The nurse tried to walk in after him. Eileen stood between them. Gently pushed the nurse back out to the hallway. With a thick drawl.

"Sorry honey. Sister is shy. Just wants the doctor."

At that Moment. Ann Ethel ad libs. She lets out a loud groan. Eileen. Not expecting help from inside the room whirls around. Stares at Ann Ethel. No more groans.

The nurse was taken aback. But, she didn't fight it. She didn't want **any** part of Eileen. The nurse left. Eileen closed the door.

No southern accent now. Pure Chicago (north side). She stared right at Jeb. She spoke clearly with intensity.

"OK Doc. Here it is. My sister wasn't hit by a car. We found this poor thing and her daughter on the side of the road. The little girl was hit by a car. Before you ask. No, it wasn't us that hit her. You can go check my car if it makes you happy.

We've got our vacation money. About $500. It's all yours. Cash. More than you probably make in a month or two. Am I right? The door is closed. Nobody says a word. You take care of the girl. The money is yours. We walk out the back door - the same way we came in. You never see any of us again."

It seems as though the room was silent for thirty seconds. It was probably only about five.

"Let me see the girl."

Under her breath. Ginger gasped.

"Jesus Hallelujah."

It took "Doctor Jeb" about thirty minutes to patch up Lila. The scarf had stopped the bleeding. He applied disinfectant. He checked her leg bone. It was broken. He didn't need to operate. He knew what to do with his hands.

She was young. Still growing. He didn't want a cast. He applied a splint and a bandage. He gave her some medicine to swallow. He gave the bottle to Ginger to take home along with some gauze bandages. When he was done. He addressed the room.

"Young lady (Ginger), *you'll have to look after your daughter now. Can you do that? Keep the wound clean? Change the wrappings. Make sure she takes her medicine? One spoon in the morning. One spoon in the evening."*

Ginger nodded. She could not speak. A White doctor was talking to her. She could barely raise her head. She looked to Miss Eileen. Eileen just nodded to her.

"She's going to be fine. She might have caught an infection through the open wound. She might have bled to death. She might have survived. Had a crooked leg her whole life.

Jeb paused for a Moment. He glanced in Eileen's direction for a Moment. With approval in his tone. Turned back to Ginger.

As it is, she might have a very slight limp as an adult. Barely notice-able. There's nothing anyone can do about that."

He turned to Eileen.

"As for you. I don't want your money. That is a lot of money. I don't want it. I was a medic in the Great War. I was a trainer of field doctors in World War II. Both times in Europe. The duration of both wars. I've seen my share of squalor. I treat the wounded. I don't care what they look like. War teaches you that."

Eileen was respectful.

"If we'd come in the front door, been honest, would you have seen us?

He took a Moment to answer.

"Me. 'Yes'. This hospital. 'No'. You never would have gotten to me."

He paused. Smiled. Rubbed his chin.

"That was quite a stunt you pulled. You've got guts. Could have used you in France. When you leave, you'll have to go out the way you came.

Mother, you'll have to keep your daughter away from people for a while. Anyone sees the bandages or the medicine, they'll think you stole them."

That was it. Crisis over. As Eileen prepared to walk out. She turned to the doctor.

"You're OK Jeb."

"You're OK too."

"If I were a little older…"

Jeb blushed. Smiled slightly. Jeb is happily married. He's not the type to flirt (or worse) with women. Particularly not at work. For a Moment. He enjoys the compliment Eileen has paid him.

"And if I were a little younger…"

Eileen drove Ginger and Lila back to where they found them. Eileen handed Ginger twenty dollars. Ginger hesitated.

"For Lila."

She accepted the money. They didn't hug. Eileen didn't want the emotion. Ginger would never have considered it. Ginger spoke.

"Can I ask ya somthin Miss Eileen?

"What's that Ginger?"

"You and Miss Ann Ethel got education? You real smart. Know just what to say and do. You talk to men folk like that where you come from?"

Eileen smiled.

"Yes. We both went to school. College too. Not sure how smart we are. We say what we think we need to. We don't back down. Our Mother taught us that."

"Miss Eileen."

"Yes"

I am going to get Lila into school. Get her some college. Send her away. Near you maybe. I never would have thought about it ain't it been for y'all. I think something good come out of today."

"Good luck Ginger."

"Miss Eileen."

"Yes."

"Thank you."

"You are welcome."

"Miss Eileen."

"Yes?"

"Jesus loves you."

"I don't know about that."

"God bless you and Miss Ann Ethel."

They never saw each other again. The girls left for their New Orleans vacation.

CHAPTER 2

SAINT JOAN OF ARC - IN JACKSON

"*M*ister. *Doctor Jeb?*"
"*Yes? Who is it?*

One week since Dr. Jeb had patched up Lila. Ginger was hiding behind a tree. Next to the hospital parking lot. Dusk. Nobody saw her. She didn't know if Mister Jeb would be there. She waited quietly. When she saw him leave the hospital, she quietly approached him.

"*It's me suh. Ginger. You fix'd up my baby Lila.*"

"*Yes. I remember.*"

Dr. Jeb looked around.

"*How did you get here?*"

"*I walked suh.*"

"*From where? How long did that take?*"

"*Down the road some. I figure about three hours to get here. I'm not sure.*"

"*Why? Where's Lila? Is she OK?*"

"*Lila's at home. You fix'd her real good. I have a friend watchin over her. She's safe.*"

"*Why did you come? It's not very safe. For you.*"

"*Mister Jeb. Doctor Jeb. I wan ask you a question.*"

"*Yes Ginger.*"

"*I don't make no money on my land. It's mine OK. But, ain't nobody here pay me a good price for my cotton. I know White folk's get more for their cotton. I can pay the tax. I can buy a little seed. I buy some food for Lila. That's about it.*"

"*Yes?*"

"*I want to know if I can work for you here at the hospital. Any job? I'll do any job you ask. Don matter how long it takes. I want to know if you'll help me sell my land. You can even jus have the land. If you'll give me a job, we'll just leave the land. It don matter. Miss Eileen talked about schoolin. I ain't gonna never get Lila no schoolin stayin on that land. I can sees that now.*"

Doctor Jeb looked at Ginger. Not a mean stare. Just looked. He was thoughtful. Ginger was wearing the same white dress he'd seen her in before. It was clean save a little dirt from the road at its bottom. She was clean too. Jeb noticed details.

"*You walked three hours to ask me this? For a job? To sell your land?*"

Expecting failure. Ginger turned her head to the ground.

"*Yes suh.*"

"*Well. Well. I might just be able to help you. I'm not sure. Would you like to take a car ride with me?*"

"*No funny stuff Mister Jeb?*"

"*No funny stuff Miss Ginger.*"

"*Yes suh. I would.*"

Ginger got in the back of the doctor's car. They drove about fifteen minutes into Jackson. They pulled into the circular drive-way of a stately red brick home. He honked his car horn. A Moment later, bounding down the front outside stairs came a smiling woman.

Similar age to the doctor. Ginger thought she looked beautiful. She wore a simple light blue house dress. Flat white canvas shoes. About five foot-six inches tall. Thick black hair. Not long. Above her shoulders. Covered her ears. Nice bangs. She radiated.

She wore a silver medallion on a chain around her neck. It bore the likeness of a lady. A saint maybe. Ginger wasn't sure.

Jeb got out of the car. He escorted Ginger out of the back seat.

"Ginger. This is my wife Simone. Simone. This is Ginger."

Simone held out her hand to shake.

"It's nice to meet you Miss Ginger."

Ginger hesitated. She took Simone's hand. She didn't speak. Her mind was reeling. She believed this was the first time a White person had ever intentionally shook her hand. Ginger had never heard a voice like Simone's. It sounded a little like the Cajuns she knew at the seed store. But not exactly. Jeb continued.

"Honey. Ginger is the young lady I told you about. The Mother of the little girl I treated last week. They came in with those crazy northern women. Ginger came to see me today. Walked three hours along the road to come see me. No appointment. Just walked.

Ginger wants a job. Wants to move off of her land. Wants to give her daughter a better life. Maybe some schooling. Is that right Ginger?"

"Yes suh. Thaz bout it."

"What do you think Simone?"

Simone was smiling. She loved her husband very much. She loved him the minute they met. Simone sensed Ginger's discomfort. She walked up to Ginger.

"Walk with me."

She looped her arm under Ginger's shoulder. Arm in arm, they walked slowly behind the outside of the house. Ginger was light headed.

"I will tell you a story. Would you like that?"

Ginger nodded.

"I am French. I am from Rouen. Northern France. Do you know Rouen?"

"No Ma'am."

"Rouen is where Saint Joan of Arc died. Do you know Saint Joan of Arc?"

"No Ma'am."

"*This medal that I wear. This is Saint Joan. She was burned at the stake by the English many centuries ago in my village of Rouen. For this reason, she is my patron saint. She is the patron saint of Orleans. She led the French in mighty victories against the invading English including the battle of Orleans. Just a young girl. She was mighty. She feared nobody. Honored God.*

Saint Joan said.

(Simone spoke in French.)

'Aide toy, Dieu te aidera.'

Do you know what it means?"

Ginger was baffled. She just shook her head side to side. No. Simone smiled warmly.

"*Loosely translated. It means. **'Help yourself and God will help you.'** Joan is the Patron Saint of soldiers, martyrs, and women that fight in battle.* **<u>Any battle.</u>** *Do you understand?"*

Simone was no longer smiling. She was serious. Not threatening. Serious. Ginger nodded slowly. Simone continued. Her voice gaining and losing strength. She was now transfixed.

"*The Great War. The German armies attacked my village. They attacked my family's farm. Stole our food. Slaughtered our cows. Burned it down. They murdered my parents. They left. I was seventeen.*

I had a husband. His name was Laurent. We had a young baby girl. Madeline. Laurent had been away fighting the Huns. They killed him. He was captured. They murdered him. Just like they murdered our cows.

I was hiding with my baby on our farm when the Huns came. They did not see us. We were alone. A young Mother. A small child. No money. No food. **<u>I would have done anything to protect my baby.</u>** *Do you understand?"*

This time when Ginger nodded. She really did understand.

"*Through the kindness of people in the city, my baby and I survived. Finally, the Americans came. I worked at their hospital. I met Jeb. I fell in love. When the war ended, he left. I was broken hearted.*

Than a letter came to the hospital a few months later. This medal I wear was in the package. It was his present. He sent a smaller one for Madeline too. He wanted me to know she was welcome.

He sent for me. Come to the United States. Be my bride. Bring your daughter. We had never even held hands. He sent money for the trip and boat tickets. We sailed to New York. Passed through Ellis Island. He was waiting for us. We got married in New York City the day I landed. Saint Patrick's Cathedral. A small Catholic church. We never lived a day in sin.

Jeb was working in a military hospital in New York City patching up soldiers. When his time was up, we moved here to Jackson. Jeb's home town. He set up a practice. We've been here ever since."

"Where's your baby girl now?"

"The Second World War came. Madeline volunteered. She was serving in London. She was killed in the German blitz. The United States sent us a letter. They sent us a medal to honor Madeline. It is inside our house on the wall. I am very proud of Madeline. A gold star still hangs in our window."

Simone stopped walking for a Moment. She did not shed a tear. She stepped back from Ginger."

"I do not cry for my daughter. She volunteered. Like Saint Joan. She is a hero. Ginger?"

"Yes Ma'am."

"Jeb see's something special in you. I think I see it too. How would you like to live in our house? You and your little girl. To the outside world, you'll be our maid. Jeb will find you real work at the hospital. I'll watch over your girl while you work."

"Yes Miss Simone. I would like that very much."

Simone smiled. Ginger smiled. They walked back to the front of the house. Jeb was sitting on the porch quietly smoking a pipe. Before the ladies reached Jeb, Simone reached into the pocket of her dress. She pulled out a small silver chain with a tiny medal. Saint Joan.

"This was Madeline's. I carry it in my pocket. I'd like you have it. A fresh start. You know? It's good to believe in something."

Simone walked behind Ginger. She gently put the chain around Ginger's neck. Tears were streaming down Ginger's face.

Post script: Jeb bought Ginger's land. Provided a fair market price. He turned around and sold the land regaining his money. Jeb opened a savings account at the Jackson Farm Bank & Trust for Ginger.

The hospital approved funding for a new laboratory for Jeb. Along with it, they approved the money to hire an assistant and a laborer to clean the lab. Jeb asked the hospital to only provide money for the laborer. He told them.

"Save the money on the assistant. I can handle the job."

The board was thrilled.

Jeb hired Ginger as his laborer. He trained her as his lab assistant. Together. They kept the lab clean.

Simone tutored Lila at home. They would not send her to the Colored school. Starting at the age of ten. In addition to the tutoring, he expanded her education. Jeb hired Lila as Ginger's assistant laborer with the board's approval. No-one questioned the hiring of an under-aged Black girl as a servant.

Lila and Ginger were both on the hospital payroll. Lila received school learning from Simone. She learned medical training from Jeb. She had no social life. Neither did Ginger. Jeb put all of the money the hospital paid Ginger and Lila into Ginger's bank account. Jeb paid for all of Ginger and Lila's food, clothes, and necessities.

When Lila turned eighteen, Jeb contacted a doctor he knew. A professor at the University of Chicago. The professor had been trained by Jeb in Europe during World War II. They were now old friends. Colleagues.

Jeb explained the unique circumstances surrounding Lila. His friend arranged a scholarship with room and board for Lila. She would enter the prestigious University of Chicago in pre-med.

Lila graduated Phi Beta Kappa. She entered the University of Chicago's Medical School. Graduated with honors. Trained as a surgeon. Her specialties were Gynecology and diseases specifically afflicting women.

Lila completed her residency at Rush Presbyterian Hospital in Chicago. Even with her stellar credentials, young Black women were not in demand. Not in the medical community.

Lila received only one job offer. To open a women's practice for a small hospital. Edward Hospital. In Naperville, Illinois. A farming community. About ten-thousand people. Originally settled by the Napers one hundred years prior. Forty miles southwest of Chicago.

Wearing the small Saint Joan of Arc medal Ginger gave her when she left Jackson at eighteen, she accepted. Lila moved to Naperville. She began her practice at Edward Hospital. She would work there the rest of her life. Growing her practice and reputation as the tiny community grew.

Jeb and Simone had Ginger tested for high school aptitude. She passed with flying colors. Jeb told Ginger.

"It's time for you to take care of yourself now. I want you to go to college."

Jeb was on the board of trustees at Millsaps College. Founded in 1890. Located in central Jackson near the Foudren business strip and the state capitol. A private school - not directly controlled by the Governor of Mississippi. Millsaps had a progressive reputation. Millsaps graduated its first woman in 1902. In 1965, Millsaps was the first all-White college to integrate in Mississippi.

In 1967, Bobby Kennedy spoke at Millsaps. He encouraged young Americans to give back to their country. Enrolled as a student. Ginger was in the audience.

Ginger graduated with a Bachelor of Science degree in Biology. She minored in English. Ginger earned her Masters and PHD in research science at the University of Mississippi at Oxford. There were now two doctors in Ginger's family.

Ginger moved back to Jackson. Moved out of Jeb and Simone's home for good. She settled on the Millsaps campus. Bought a small bungalow. Ginger finished her years happily. A tenured professor at Millsaps.

Ginger's determination. Jeb and Simone's bravery and kindness. Saint Joan of Arc's encouragement. Ginger often wondered how her life and Lila's would have turned out if Miss Eileen and Miss Ann Ethel had not stopped their car.

CHAPTER 3

EILEEN MEETS JOSEF

The rest of the ride to New Orleans was far less eventful. This was an incredibly unusual trip for so many reasons. "**Good**" women just **did not** travel without their husband, family, or escort for vacation. They certainly did not drive to New Orleans (of all places). Only Verna's children could have done this (and remained respectable).

Today. We would call Eileen's trip a "fling". For Eileen. The vacation was a stress release. An opportunity to leave the job, children, and Verna's apartment behind. Meet a man. Have a little fun. Come on home to the real world. As always, Verna would watch the children.

New Orleans, Louisiana and Orleans Parish (Parish, not county) is located about nine-hundred miles south of Chicago. Essentially bayou swamp land. Driving into town. The first thing you notice are the cemeteries. Most dead aren't buried. They are interned in chalky white mausoleums. They stand upright like marble apartment buildings creating cities of New Orleans past.

Water is everywhere. Lake Pontchartrain. The canals. The Mississippi River. The mouth of the Gulf of Mexico. The water surrounds New Orleans. The city is below sea level. Decades later, the world would stand by. Watch as New Orleans was deluged. Devastated by Hurricane Katrina.

Louisiana is truly an "American" state. It is the sum of its parts. Originally settled by French Acadian Creoles and Cajuns. From 1763 on, Louisiana would find itself... in Spanish control... French control again... American from the Louisiana Purchase... Seceded from America as a member of The Confederate States of America... and following the Civil War, a state in the union of the United States of America.

Through the port of New Orleans, Louisiana would add to its French and Spanish influenced populations by accepting waves of immigrants from the Caribbean bringing their own infusion of culture, food, religion and lifestyle. Centuries of slave trade also brought Africans to Louisiana. The oleo of life produced by blending these diverse cultures on bayou swamp land is simply unique.

Eileen drove the girls into a city unlike anywhere they had ever been. It was dirty. It was humid. It was exotic. It had a unique aroma.

Ann Ethel watched. Books were Ann Ethel's constant companions. They lived in her head. Everywhere she went. Favorite parts memorized. For a reason she could not explain. As they entered the city of New Orleans, Ann Ethel whistled and said aloud.

"I am the Ghost of Christmas Present. Look upon me! **_You have never seen the like of me before!_***"*

It was a line from Charles Dickens' "A Christmas Carol". It just popped into her head. Nothing she was seeing reminded her of Christmas. But, she was certain. Even with her limited vision, she had **never** seen the likes of New Orleans before. That was for sure.

Startled. Eileen asked.

"What?"

"Nothing. Just thinking to myself."

In Chicago. In the fall. When leaves are burning. The smell permeates everywhere. Moving by car with the windows rolled up. You can't escape the scent. When you smell it. Your senses know instantly. Fall. Chicago. Leaves. "Bear weather". Winter is coming.

Compared to Chicago, fall in New Orleans is still warm. In greater New Orleans, it seems as though all of the aromas that have followed the Mississippi River south meld together over the Parish.

Peppers. Spices. Hard labor. Bogs. Bayous. Beer. Simmering crawfish. Gumbo. It's not acrid. It's unique. On Bourbon Street. Sex. Urine. More alcohol. More cooking. Street vendors. Musicians. Street revelers. And **sweat,** born from an evening's successes and failures add to the Crescent City's aroma. Each morning, Bourbon Street is hosed down. It doesn't help. The smells are centuries old.

The people spoke in foreign languages. Riverboats traversed the Mississippi. Jackson Square at night. In the French Quarter. Narrow streets with French names like Toulouse and Carondelet house three-story buildings with black wrought-iron balconies. Each with a small hanging garden. Jazz and Dixieland flow from open and closed doors.

It is the birthplace of Louis Armstrong. Sidney Bechet. Antoine "Fats" Domino. Mahalia Jackson. Pete Fountain. Jelly Roll Morton. One American city with the rightful claim: "The birthplace of American Jazz".

Unlike Chicago, few buildings are very tall. There was no way to moor a skyscraper into the bogs of New Orleans securely.

They stayed at the Hotel Monteleone on Royal Street. They visited the Garden District, the antique shops of Royal Street, and the French Market by day. They drank at the Sazerac Bar in the Roosevelt Hotel at their leisure.

Our girls dined on Eggs Owen for breakfast at Brennan's. Supped on Red Beans and Rice for lunch at Tujague's. Enjoyed Bananas Foster for dessert at the Court of Two Sisters. They ate Oysters Bienville and Turtle Soup at Antoine's. They sipped Chicory and dunked Beignets at Café du Monde on Decatur Street. On St. Peter's Street, while sipping Hurricanes at Pat O'Brien's piano bar, Eileen met Josef (French: Pronounced Jo*sef*).

New Orleans was a Jim Crow city. New Orleans and the Deep South were strictly segregated. Josef was not "Colored" nor "Negro" (the term today is African-American). Had he been, Eileen never would have met him. He would not have been allowed to enter the restaurants frequented by the girls (Not through the front doors). He was not Mulatto (the term today is bi-racial) nor Latino. But, he was dark. Not working the fields tan. He **was** dark.

Josef was the color of Mahogany. His face was handsome. Not model cute. Not pretty. He had thick wavy black hair. His six-foot frame bore no bulging muscles but showed a wiry strength. No fat. Not an ounce.

Josef came by his darkness through centuries of blended races and nationalities in Louisiana's St. Martin's Parish. Born, not in a hospital but in his Mother's bedroom. No official records existed of his exact age or birth date. He seemed about seven to ten years older than Eileen. No-one ever knew for sure.

Josef received no formal education. Never spoke English till he was in his twenties. And then, not so much. Like many Louisianans, he spoke a form of Creole his French decedents would not have likely recognized. He bore the same last name of an 18ᵗʰ century French colonel. He received no dowry, estate, nor value from the honor of the name. There is no evidence that any relationship existed. He was generally Catholic but not practicing. He was rural poor in a state that bred poor. Back home. Shoes were a luxury and rarely worn.

When he met Eileen, Josef was poor but employed. He was the head chef at Andre's famous French Quarter Cajun Restaurant. A number of years before, Josef's boyhood friend Andre left St. Martin's Parish to look for work in New Orleans. He was as poor as Joseph. Cut from the same Cajun cloth. Andre got a job in a French Quarter cafe assisting a bus boy. He was the lowest form of restaurant worker. He took out the trash.

Andre was promoted to bus boy. He sent for Josef. Josef took out the trash. Josef lived with Andre. His friend worked his way up the ladder. Bus boy... Captain... Assistant Chef... Chef... Head Chef. Each time Andre moved up, Josef moved up with him. Always one position behind. When Andre opened up his own restaurant. Josef became the head chef. The restaurant was a hit.

In broken English and in his native tongue, he spoke few words. Josef could cook. He had stamina. He was a workhorse. People respected him. When he directed, workers listened. He commanded his kitchen.

I'd like to say that Josef and Eileen met that faithful night at Pat O'Brien's. Fell in love. Married. The rest, as they say "is history". This of course was not the case. But, what a picture the two must have made the night they met.

Eileen. Flaming red hair. Bright white skin glowing from humidity and drink. A million freckles. Long elegant legs. Positively a knock out in her tasteful flower print summer sun dress with a modest (but not too modest) V neck front. Eileen didn't need to dress provocatively to lure men. Her looks and personality took care of that.

Josef. Dark skin and dark hair. A simple white button-down shirt. Neat – but not pressed. Black tie – No pattern. Ivory off-white pants and summer white jacket. In Chicago, he would have stood out from the crowd. In New Orleans, he blended in comfortably.

Both. Completely in control of themselves. Confident in who they were. They had a fling. And what a fling! Eileen enjoyed more intense gratification on this short vacation than she had experienced – well, ever.

Ann Ethel swore there were very few words shared between the two when they met. Living in New Orleans, speaking just a little

English was not a handicap. It would not have made Josef shy or self-conscience. Eileen made the first move.

"Will you light my cigarette?"

It wasn't just an affair. Nine-hundred miles away from home. Eileen opened up to Josef during the vacation. Eileen was normally a good social talker. But, this was different. She shared her feelings with Josef. This she never did back in Chicago. Never with Verna. Never with Teddy. Rarely with Ann Ethel. Josef was a good listener.

When it was time for Eileen to return to Chicago, Josef was passionately in love. He didn't tell her. He knew. He also knew telling her would scare her away. She wasn't ready. No formal education? Josef was smart.

Eileen on the other hand said goodbye after one final morning of passion. Eileen was not a stranger to sex or even temporary pleasure. Something was different. One last long lingering kiss. One last chance to put her hand on his face and caress his cheek. One last chance to feel a shaking she had never known.

She just said goodbye and drove away with Ann Ethel. She was sated and exhausted. She was spent. She had not given a second thought to love. She stirred inside the whole trip home. If Eileen had thought about it, she would have deemed: Love and happiness are not the same thing. She was happy.

I've often been asked where Ann Ethel was during all of the flinging. That's my future Mother we're talking about. A gentleman (or son) never tells.

CHAPTER 4

THE OVERCOAT

Seasons change. Eileen and Ann Ethel went back to work. Winter came to Chicago. The wind blew in off of the lake. The Bears were in season. Truman beat Dewey. Europe was still digging out from World War II. Stalin was unrelenting. Asia was falling to Communism. West Germany and Japan were now our allies. The United Nations and Israel were beginning.

At Verna's north side apartment, there was a knock at the front door. All guests were introduced to Verna before entering the fortress. Bobby called.

"Grandma. There's a man at the door. He's not wearing an overcoat. He looks cold".

Verna was born in the United States. She did not have a European accent like so many of her friends her age. Her voice was crisp. Her English. Impeccable.

"Tell him to go away."

"He's hard to understand. He's asking for Eileen."

"I'll be right there. Ask him into the parlor."

Verna looked at Josef who was happy to come in and get warm. November. Fall in Chicago was colder than any winter Josef had ever experienced. Verna served (no wasted words).

"What do you want with Eileen?"

In his best Creole-Cajun-English, Josef volleyed right back.

"I want to marry her."

Silence.

There they were. Two people that had never met. He knew about Verna. Verna did not know about Josef. Neither had met the likes of each other before.

Verna had the advantage. She was used to Eileen's suitors. Who, she had easily dismissed. And yet, she had not encountered anyone so direct and apparently sincere. He wasn't from the neighborhood. That was evident.

Two strong people who had survived on their iron wills for so many years looked at each other. Not a look of hate or anger. No fear. Not a look of glee or joy either. A look by two people that could not be more alien to each other sizing up the seriousness of the situation…and each other. Verna spoke calmly.

"Why?"

*"I'm **very** much in love with her."*

"Bobby. Tell your Mother to come downstairs."

Eileen was not a petulant teenager. She was an adult. While she would not sass Verna. She did not like being summoned. She came down the stairs and turned into the parlor next to the doorway. There was Josef.

There is an eerie combination of tenseness and uncertainty for Eileen at first. She is used to being in control of her own situation. Like a Hitchcock heroine, the situation has radically and quickly changed for Eileen with no warning.

There are no words. She does not rush to hug him. She is taking him in. Eileen moves slowly around the room. Ever the caged lioness, she is smoking a cigarette deliberately as she moves. She never takes her eyes off of Josef. It is not an intimidating stare. It is a stare of contemplation. Like a math student presented with a new equation. Never before seen.

Josef is patient. He is out of his element. He is happy for a Moment of calm. They all are. Verna speaks first.

"Bobby. Leave the room."

He is happy to do so. To Eileen.

"I will leave too. Speak with each other. Call me back."

This is a subtle nuance. In the past, Verna would never have left the room. Particularly not with a stranger (to her). Josef was certainly a stranger. She would have stayed to cross-examine the suitor. Or, Eileen.

She trusts Eileen. She trusts herself more. She's the Mother. She's the landlord. She's the baby sitter. She's the boss. Verna senses something. She walks out and leaves the two together.

With a puzzled look, Eileen asks Josef directly.

"Why are you here?"

"I've asked your Mother if I can marry you."

Eileen attacks.

*"If? **If?!** Don't you think you should have asked me first?*

Eileen's presence is **back!** Josef is a little put off.

"I have come to see you. I have practiced your ritual of respect. Do I ***need*** *to ask you?"*

He pauses. He realizes Eileen has not expressed an opinion. He also realizes he has not asked her directly. He softens.

"Eileen. I have come for you. What is your answer?"

There is no hesitation.

"My answer is no."

Josef's legs weaken ever so little. He takes one step back and unconscientiously sits down on the wing backed chair behind him. Eileen is gaining her balance as Josef is losing his.

"Where is your overcoat? Don't you know you're in Chicago now?"

"I came straight from the Union Train Station. I do not own a coat."

The discomfort is gone. They are talking again. Josef asks softly.

"Why don't you want to marry me? Don't you love me? I love you."

Eileen is careful not to answer his second question about love. He has never before expressed his love for her. Eileen has never once thought that **she** was in love with him. At least she has not allowed herself to think of it. She has certainly never said the words aloud to anyone much less Josef.

*"I did not say I do not **want** to marry you. I said **will not** marry you."*
Josef is clearly confused by this answer.
"What is the difference?"
For possibly the first time in her life, Eileen let's go. Completely loses control.

*"**I** am Jewish. **You** are Catholic. **I** have two children. Will **you** be their Father? Where will **we** live? Will **you** move to Chicago? What would **you** do here? **You** barely speak English. Are **you** asking me to move to New Orleans? Are **you** asking **me** to move from **my** Mother's home?"*

Eileen is scared. She is on shaky ground. She **never** loses her composure. Now she has. Josef stands. He walks past Eileen. As he leaves the parlor. He turns to her and says.

"I will stay here in Chicago."
That is all he says. And he leaves. Eileen is stunned. When her late husband died. They sat Shiva (A Jewish mourning ritual). Eileen did not cry. No-one had ever seen Eileen cry. After Josef left, Eileen sat in the parlor chair. She cried. Not hysterically. She was inexperienced with this new demonstration of emotion. Her body gently shook. Head held by one hand to cover her eyes. She cried quietly.

A month went by. Eileen did not hear from Josef. It was December. Snow was on the ground. The wind came off the lake. The trees were bare. Eileen had come to grips that she would not see Josef again. She was uncertain how she felt about it. She was leading her normal life. She worked. She had a few casual dates when she wanted.

There came a knock at the door. Repeating the scene, Bobby answered. Josef started.

"May I see Eileen?"
Bobby responded.
"Wait here (outside).*"*
Verna came to the door and ushered Josef into the parlor. He still did not have an overcoat. Bobby got Eileen. She came downstairs. They looked at each other for a good few minutes.
"I'm going back to New Orleans."
"Why?"
"To buy an overcoat."
Eileen smiled. Josef left.
The winter passed dragging into April as it is known to do in Chicago. May brought pleasant breezes, flowers, and made the beautiful neighborhood trees alive again. Radios could be heard from open windows including Verna's announcing a Cubs game. Jack Brickhouse makes the call.
"Branca looks in for the sign from Campanella. It's two and one on Cavaretta. Cubs up by two in their half of the fourth. Here's the pitch..."
Bobby pulls himself away from the radio to answer the knock at the door.
"May I see Eileen?"
This time, Bobby shows Josef directly into the parlor. He dutifully tells Verna. She instructs Bobby to get Eileen. Bobby does so and runs back to the radio. Verna does not go into the parlor.
Eileen enters. Josef is wearing an overcoat. **Over** his suit. The temperature is nearly eighty degrees outside. For Josef, It must have seemed significantly warmer. Inside and out. Josef is sweating noticeably. Eileen puts her hand to her mouth to cover her smile but does not laugh. Josef starts.
"Will you marry me?"
"Yes"
"I cannot live in Chicago.
"I know"
Will you come to New Orleans?"

"Yes"

"I love you"

"Yes I know. I love you too. Josef?"

"Yes?"

"What took you so long?"

Josef smiles.

Eileen calls for Verna. Verna does not need to be told. Josef asks Verna. Verna does not look at Eileen. She does not have to. She agrees. It is done. Almost. There are rules. Verna speaks.

*"You will be married in the fall. You will be married at Temple Shalom. We will have a reception at our apartment following the wedding. All of our family and friends will be there. Anyone missing the wedding of my daughter to this man will no longer be a friend **or** a member of this family. They will be dead to me."*

Now it is done.

Everyone came to the wedding. None of the family nor friends dared utter an unhappy word about Josef and his few Creole speaking family members that attended.

CHAPTER 5

THE GUMBO VAT

Eileen and Josef moved to New Orleans after their wedding. They lived in a wooden shotgun house on Dauphine between Esplanade and Barracks. On the edge of the French Quarter.

A shotgun house has a few rooms running from front to back. One hallway running through the middle. A living room next to a bedroom next to a bathroom next to a kitchen. There are no basements. The house is elevated a half floor on wooden posts. I remember only a few things about the house from my visits in the 1960's:

The kitchen had wooden slats on the floor. Food or dirt could be swept or washed between the slats. A giant steel Gumbo vat sat on the steel cross-bars of an old industrial-style stove on top of the wooden slats in the kitchen.

Josef stirred and added ingredients. I was just a kid. Josef's hair was thick but white then. The vat itself had to weigh eighty pounds. My guess is that it never got fully washed. Maybe rinsed.

The vat was the focal point of the kitchen. Friends and relatives sat in the kitchen at an old wooden table. Josef stirred. Added ingredients. Concocted delicacies.

Smoking. Drinking. Laughing. Warm. Softly humming jazz or Cajun melodies.

I think the secret to those delicious old gumbo and jambalaya recipes (in Josef's head) was that old vat. Ages of flavor blending from one dish to the next (year over year) with the bayou water that flavored the spices. It simply can't be replicated.

There was an old noisy waist-high electric cooler of chilled small Coca-Cola bottles in the kitchen. It wasn't a refrigerator or a freezer. It was specifically there to cool the Coke bottles. I loved Coke. I was in awe. I had never seen a house with its own cooler. Eileen could see I was surprised the first time I saw it. She stated proudly.

*"Coca-Cola was invented in the late 1880's in Georgia. Before every home had electricity. Today. **In the south!** **All** of the best homes in Louisiana have **electric** coolers of Coca-Cola in their kitchen."*

And finally, an 8 ½ x 11 black ink picture of Franklin Roosevelt circa 1933 drawn by artist A.M. Orlick hung on their hallway wall. FDR was drawn on wood with a shiny shellac that had turned yellow over the years. Many years since Roosevelt had died. Many more years since this picture was made.

There FDR was. Watching over the old shotgun house. This picture would hang everywhere Eileen lived as long as I knew her. (When Eileen passed away, I asked Bobby for the picture. I have it still.)

Eileen and Josef opened Josef's Restaurant in the French Quarter located at 327 Rue Bourbon just down the block from Galatoire's and the Royal Sonesta Hotel. Josef's occupied a brick walled mansion and courtyard.

The building had once served as the residence of Jefferson's Davis's Secretary of the Confederacy, Judah P. Benjiman. A lawyer, Benjiman escaped capture after the Civil War. Lived out his life in England. Council to Queen Victoria. An advertising piece intended for mailing is the only relic I have from Josef's.

__Josef's - The Diners' Club... Famous for French Cuisine__:
__House Specials__
*Oyster Bienville * Stuffed Chicken Perigourdine for Two **
*Shrimp Josef * Lobster Thermidor * Frog Legs Richelieu **
*Pompano Ponchartrain Amandine**
__Josef's Sauce__...Delicious on shrimp, steak, and other foods too
numerous to mention.
Send Money-order or check. $.65 per Pt. $1.30 per Quart.

Josef ran the kitchen. Eileen managed the books and the restaurant. It was very successful for about fifteen years. Then it became too much for Josef. He retired.

Eileen liked to work. She did not want to be home during the day. She took a new job. The finance office of the New Orleans Police Department.

Managed insurance payments, benefits, and pensions for the officers and police staff. Black or White. Rich or poor. When in need. When the paperwork, red tape, or politics got to be too much. They all came to Eileen.

She sorted out the issues. Took care of her people. **Her people**. Anyone that asked for help. Verna's influence. They never forgot her.

Eileen and Josef lived a fabulously happy life together. There are no scripts for a widowed Jewish Chicago Mother of two marrying a poor Louisiana Cajun. Having it work out well. They wrote their own story.

CHAPTER 6

THE GREEN WAVE

Part One

After the wedding, Eileen's daughter RoseAnne went to college. She never lived in New Orleans. Earned her Masters and PHD. Became a college professor. Married and started a family of her own.

Bobby made the move with Eileen. He was a typical Chicagoan teenage boy of his time. He was a rabid sports fan. Played all of the sports at Senn High School. Dated. Did well in school.

He wasn't sheltered completely. After all, he was being raised by Verna and Eileen. To be safe, he knew to stay in his Jewish Chicago neighborhood. He could use his fists if he had to. He was brave. Not big. Then came the move.

Bobby did not outwardly blame his Mother for the move. He was more protective than scared. He was much like Anna Leonowens' son Louis in "The King and I" ("Anna and the King of Siam").

Louis accompanies his widowed Mother Anna from European London to Asian Siam (Thailand today) in the 1860's. Anna is on her way to being the Siamese King's children's governess (and falling in love with the King). The two countries (England and Siam) could not have been more different.

For Bobby who had never been out of Chicago, New Orleans must have seemed like Siam to Louie. Or, like OZ to Dorothy. Everything was different. Food. Climate. Language. Music. Sports! There were no Chicago Cubs. No Chicago Bears. No professional sports of any kind for him to follow.

No Jewish boys. Nobody his age there had ever met a Jewish boy. Finishing high school in New Orleans was rough. He got the hell beat out of him by the local boys. For being a Yankee. For being new. For not having a group to run with. For speaking differently. For being Jewish.

The Black boys that lived in and around the French Quarter did not beat him up. Much of the kitchen, hotel, and general labor staffs in the Quarter were Black. So were the musicians.

Work was different than Jim Crow. They coincided. Even if Blacks could not use the same entrances, Blacks and Whites moved around each other in very close proximity. Almost as though choreographed.

Josef was a chef in the Quarter. Bobby spent a lot of time with Josef. It meant he spent a lot of time around Black kids. More than if he had been in Chicago. They ate together when no one was looking in the backs of kitchens. They played catch in the alley when they were supposed to be taking out garbage. They were kids. Jim Crow was for adults. White Adults.

Eileen was his life tutor. He survived. He went to LSU for undergraduate school. Tulane for his Masters. He learned to love college football. He learned how to speak like a local. He learned to drink in the Quarter.

Similar to Alabama's "Crimson Tide", Tulane's nickname is the "Green Wave". It's supposed to represent a torrent of unrelenting Tulane force. In the Quarter, it more closely described what came out of amateurs who could not manage their drinking.

By the time Bobby graduated from Tulane, he had fully acclimated. Being Josef's son helped. Living in the French Quarter helped. He was a young man of New Orleans now. He'd earned his stripes in a town that only trusts their own. Bobby was trusted. He trusted them.

Only I called Bobby "Bobby". Everyone else called him "Bob" (Drawn out: "Bawb") or "Mr. Bob". It was the south. He would never move from New Orleans – Or his Mother.

Verna's home had been Kosher. No shellfish. Not in New Orleans. Bobby could eat as he pleased. He enjoyed the gulf and bayou seafood. Weekend crawfish boils meant millions of the little crustaceans boiled in spice with Andouille sausage. Peel. Twist. Suck. Eat. Repeat. Wash it down with JAX or Dixie beer.

He chose his career wisely. He opened a PR firm (Public Relations). He would go on to successfully manage the campaigns of many mayors, governors, and judges. He managed not to get caught up in the graft or scandals that historically saturated Louisiana politics like a fine mist before and after Huey Long. Bobby was always quick to remark that no-one from Chicago's "machine" wards should be commenting on Parish politics.

Bobby's career and life were moving right along. When the National Football League (NFL) granted New Orleans a franchise in the 1960's, Bobby became the press box announcer for the Saints. Eileen was a season ticket holder. They drove to the games together at old Tulane Stadium.

Eileen and Bobby were at Tulane Stadium when the Saints beat the Cowboys for the first time. Archie Manning was a rookie. Eileen was a charter member of "Archie's Army." She'd sit in the stands with her girlfriend. Sip her cocktail. And they'd scream with the crowd.

"Throw the bomb Archie!"

Most times Archie did throw the bomb. Or run for his life. The Saints were not great during the elder Manning years. But they were fun.

Bobby helped promote the first New Orleans Jazz & Heritage Festival. Mahalia Jackson. Duke Ellington. Pete Fountain. Al Hirt. Fats Domino. The Preservation Hall Band. At the newly built Superdome, Bobby managed the local radio PR for Muhammad Ali's fight with Leon Spinks.

New Orleans hosted the 1984 World's Fair. Bobby provided media coverage. Each year, Bobby attended the Mardi-Gras balls and Sugar Bowl galas sponsored by his favorite Krewes. Rex, Venus, and the Elks Krewe of Orleanians. Eileen always dressed up and attended. Bobby brought a date.

He bought a home in Metairie. I once asked Bobby what he thought about the Oliver Stone movie "JFK" and Jim Garrison. In a nutshell - not much. Bobby was **all** New Orleans. He didn't want to talk about him. He felt anything that linked New Orleans with the President Kennedy assassination disgraced New Orleans.

After Josef passed away, Eileen retired and mellowed. Around 2000, Bobby finally married. Yvonne. From Thibodaux, Louisiana. A wonderful women. A beautiful and proud widow with her own large Louisiana family.

An afternoon wedding and reception. Held on the second floor of <u>Andrew Jaeger's House of Seafood</u> on Conti Street. The French Quarter cafe owned by Bobby's long-time friend. Following, the small party walked to Pat O'Brien's garden, fountain patio. The same Pat O'Brien's Eileen had first met Josef. It was the last time I saw Eileen. She passed away peacefully a few years later. Joined Josef once again.

Yvonne moved into Bobby's home. It was his office. It was a confirmed bachelor home. Bobby said it looked like a tavern. Eileen said it was decorated like a whorehouse. It took Yvonne about a year. She re-decorated the house. Turned it into a lovely home. He could not marry as a younger man. The tie to Eileen was just too tight.

Part Two

August 28, 2005

"Bob. I'm scared."

"I'm having a drink. Would you like to join me?"

"What good will that do?"

"It won't hurt. Come sit by me. There's nothing we can do."

"It's dark out. But, not like night. It's a dark green and gray."

"Yes."

"It's day time."

"I know. I have a watch."

"It's loud. Don't you think it's loud? It's not supposed to be this loud. It sounds like my son Bubby's motor boat out on the bayou. It sounds like his boat is right there in the next room."

"Well. It might just be. Soon."

"That's not funny Bob. Not at all. Not funny."

"I'm sorry. Come sit."

"The phones are out. Our electricity is out. I can't get a hold of anyone in Thibodaux."

"They're OK. Too far from here. There is nothing we can do. Nowhere we can go. We're stuck together. What do you think?"

Yvonne pauses. She turns to Bobby. For the time in two days she smiles faintly.

"I sure wish I hadn't spent the money to redecorate this. What did Eileen call it? House of no-good. What are you drinking?"

"Vodka with a lemon peel. Neat (no ice). Want one? Got to use the fruit up now that we have no power. Still can't bring yourself to call this old home a whorehouse can you? That's what Eileen called it. It's the retired teacher in you. You're too nice and proper. You want me to make you one?"

"OK. Make me one too."

There was a swimming pool in the back yard. The storm threw the pool water completely out. Trees, tree branches, and assorted other garbage now occupied the deep and shallow ends where water had once been. Bobby's patio pool chairs and table were blown into a park about one-hundred yards behind the house crashing into dozens of small pieces before resting against a black wrought iron fence.

Water was coming into the house. Not at a fast rate. Slowly. Their living room had a small recessed sitting area. Only about six inches down. Not even a full step. Yvonne had ripped out the ugly 1970's shag red carpet and installed fine cherry wood flooring. Just one of the many improvements. Now, water was running onto the wood. Clean water. Like a bath. Filling up the recess slowly but surely. So far, the rest of the house was dry. The roof was holding.

It was pretty simple. There was nowhere for the water to go. It had found its entry point. It would fill up the recess. Then if the water kept coming in, spread to the rest of the house.

Bobby lived on Taft Street in Metairie. The good news? His house was situated perfectly for its proximity to New Orleans and the eye of the storm. It seemed to be on just the correct sides of both the levees and Lake Ponchartrain.

Taft Street on his block was flooded. But not deeply. Not like other blocks. The water in front of his house ran from the street over the curbs and seemed to be resting for now. Puddling on the small square lawns in front of Bobby and his neighbors.

Occasional cars tried to pass the streets pushing the water closer to their houses. All that could be seen were their headlights. All that could be heard was the whoosh of the street water being moved. There seemed to be debris flying everywhere. More chance of being killed by a flying lawn jockey than the flood.

Bobby and Yvonne were smart enough not to sit by their windows. They huddled on a sofa they'd pushed to the middle of the house. They sat in near darkness. One candle lit. Their eyes acclimated.

There was no fear of running out of food or drink. Bobby kept a stocked liquor cabinet. Yvonne kept a stocked pantry. Drinking water might be in short supply. Not the essentials.

"Bob. Are you glad we married?"

"Funny to ask me that now. Is there someone else I should know about? Some Thibodaux Romeo?"

"Yes. But that's not what I asked you."

"Hmm. You want me to talk about my feelings?"

"I do."

"I love having you in my life."

"Not what I asked you."

"I'm glad to have someone to go to the Saints games with."

"Not what I asked you."

"You're a pretty good cook. Easy on the eyes."

"I'm a **great** cook. Better than your sainted Mother **and** Father. And I know what I look like. Your no prize you know."

"Jews don't have saints. What was the question?"

"Arghhhh."

"Yes."

"Yes what?"

"Yes."

"Say it."

"I love you. I'm glad we are married. I'm glad you saved me from a life of meaningless pleasure."

"That's all I'm asking."

"What about me?"

"What about me what?"

"Your turn."

"Oh go on Bob. You know how I feel?"

"Sorry. No good. Have another drink?"

"I better."

"You were saying?"

"You're the first Jew I ever met. No horns. Still. Something was tempting. I have to say."

"What was that?"

"I figured any boy that still had Sunday dinner with his Momma couldn't be all bad. You know I raised my family. All those boys. They're grown up now. Buried my husband. It was a good marriage. I retired from teaching. I was a little lonely. Still alive. Wanted something. Wasn't sure what."

"Me?"

"Naw. OK. Maybe. Remember how we met?"

*"As I recall, you put up a billboard on the Causeway between Veterans and Esplanade with **your** picture on it to get my attention."*

"Close. You joined a dating service. I thought you had all of the young ladies you could handle?"

"Guilty. I knew there was a retired teacher out there – just for me."

"Seriously. I know why I joined the dating service. Why did you?"

"I was lonely too. I wasn't expecting success. I just needed to change my life. You were the first girl that I met by arrangement."

"Do you remember where we met?"

"I need another drink. I do. Food court. JAX Brewery Mall. Ugh that food was bad. You wanted to meet in public. Can't blame you."

"That's what you remember? The food court?"

"I don't remember much. That day wasn't that important to me."

Yvonne frowns. Bobby continues.

"It was a sunny fall day. We walked. Out of the mall. Past Jackson Square. Through the Cabildo. Just walked and talked. Seemed like we went down Royal Street. You bought a small lead figurine of General Andrew Jackson for one of your sons at Le Petit Soldier Shop.

You were wearing a white pants suit with a flowered top underneath. Very fetching. A sun hat. Dark large sunglasses. You had your late husband's wedding band on your right hand. Wore a silver locket your sons had given you around your neck. Did we have a drink, some grilled

*Oysters, and Turtle Soup at Arnaud's? You took your sunglasses off inside. Your hair **and** your eyes were a dark brown. I do believe we held hands in public. You know. I really can't recall. It just wasn't a big day for me."*

Yvonne's eyes are damp. She says softly.

"You remember."

"I'll never forget."

Katrina came. **It** left. The politicians came. They made promises. **They** left. Hard to say which were louder – or did more damage – Katrina or the politicians. Katrina provided New Orleans an ominous new meaning to the Tulane nickname "Green Wave".

Yvonne and Bobby rode out the storm reminiscing as the rain and wind howled. Surrounded by the ruin of New Orleans and the Gulf Coast, they were incredibly and randomly fortunate. Water stopped at their living room recess. Their pool was badly damaged. The rest of the house was unscratched and dry.

The loving couple sold their house on Taft in Metairie. With the proceeds, they built her dream house in Thibodaux. They moved. About an hour or two from New Orleans. They've lived happily ever after.

Until. Bobby drove into New Orleans one day years later. He got lost. His city. **Lost**. Couldn't find his way home. Yvonne knew. Bobby had Alzheimer's. This confirmed it.

He promised he'd never forget their first meeting. He has. Yvonne has never forgotten. Katrina didn't get Bobby. Nature did. Yvonne takes care of Bobby. Their love story continues.

CHAPTER 7

"WHO IS THAT HULL? A GOLD JET?"

Winter January 1967 – Evanston – Saturday Night – Mom and Dad's Date Night

About 4pm. Dad would drive over to north Campbell Avenue. A short drive from our house. Pick up Verna. Verna would make dinner for the two of us. Mom and Dad went out. It was the same every weekend.

"Nat. What would you like me to make for dinner?"

"How about pancakes?"

"I don't know. Do you think they're any good? Would you really like them?"

"Oh grandma. You know they're the best. Please make them."

"OK. As it happens. I brought the ingredients with me. Your Mother never has any food in this house."

I imagine. Every eight-year-old boy loved his Grandmother's cooking. I sure did. Verna made silver dollar size pancakes. Ours was a very small kitchen. The stove was right behind the kitchen table.

Verna stood between the stove and the back of my chair. She never had to take a step. Helping after helping. Just slid the pancakes onto my plate reaching over my shoulder. My plate was

47

never empty. She ate standing up at the stove. The freshness. The smells. "Hmmm".

Frying pan warm. Thin and flat. Soft in the middle. Crunchy on the sides with browned edges. No syrup. Sugar sprinkled on in healthy servings. Not powdered sugar. Real sugar. Served with a large glass of whole milk. The pancakes just kept coming. Finally.

*"No more. **Please**."*

This brought on the weekly response.

"You didn't eat so much. Maybe they were not so good this time?"

I would give her a hug. Assure.

"They were great grandma. Best ever! May I please be excused?"

The rest of our routine was set. Verna watched the "Lawrence Welk Show" on our big black and white Zenith TV. After Lawrence Welk, if I was lucky, we'd watch the Black Hawks on WGN. If, they had an away hockey game. The Hawks only aired away games on TV. If the Hawks were at home, we listened on the green Zenith radio with the gold dial and round knobs.

Verna. On the couch knitting. I was on my hands and knees on the floor. Wearing out the knees of my pajamas. Playing with my hockey cards. I'd line the cards up into teams. Play imaginary games. The cards became creased and wrinkled. The better the player. The more action. The more creases on the card.

Almost every player in the NHL was from Canada. The best players in the world. Montreal seemed to get the best of the best. The 1966-67 Montreal Canadians were loaded. Those French names.

Jean Beliveau. Bobby Rousseau. Henri Richard. Yvan Cournoyer. Jacques Laperriere. Jean-Claude Tremblay. Jean-Guy Talbot. Serge Savard. Claude Provost.

The Black Hawks had one great French-Canadian player. Pierre Pilote. We had one great player from Czechoslovakia (Slovakia and Czech Republic were once one country called Czechoslovakia). Stan Mikita. The other great Black Hawks were Canadian too.

They had American sounding names. "Mr. Goalie". Glenn Hall. And **Robert Marvin Hull**. **"The Golden Jet"**. Verna hears the TV.

Announcer Lloyd Pettit's voice grows progressively louder with increased excitement with each advancement in Hull's rink-long dash.

"Hull picks up the puck behind his own net. He moves forward. Crosses his blue line. Beats Terry Harper.

He's at full speed. Crosses the red line. Dekes and beats Talbot.

Beats Rousseau at the Montreal blue line. Laperriere is skating toward Hull. Bobby winds up. He shoots. Full slap shot.

There's a shot ... And a Goal!!!

Unassisted! Hull! The Golden Jet has scored!

The Black Hawks take the lead!"

Lloyd Pettit's voice is practically hoarse. He is screaming through the TV. I'm jumping up and down in our living room.

"Who is that Hull? A gold jet?"

Laughing. I respond with the excitement of an eight-year-old boy.

*"Grandma. Not 'gold jet'. Bobby Hull. **He's the** 'Golden Jet'. He's the best player in hockey. He plays for Chicago. The fans love him. He's really fast. Like a jet. Has a great slap shot. Scored fifty goals in one season. He'll be a Black Hawk **for-ever.**"*

"Why golden?"

"His hair. He's blond. No helmet for him."

"His name is Hull? Is he from Chicago?"

"He is now. I'm pretty sure he's from Canada. His brother Dennis is on the Hawks also. He's got a good slap shot too."

"Hull is an interesting name in Chicago. May I tell you a story after your game?"

"Sure grandma. When you put me to sleep. OK?"

The Hawks won. Beat the Canadians! Both Hulls scored. Grandma and I shared a bowl of Carmel Corn. It was time for bed. She tucked me in. Sat on the edge of my bed.

"*Nat. Do you know who Jane Addams was?*"

"*Is she in '*The Addams Family*'? I love Lurch! 'YOU RANG???' He's so funny.*"

"*No Nat. Not on '*The Addams Family*'. Not on TV. **Jane** Addams.*"

"*No grandma. Who was she? A friend of yours?*"

"*Yes Nat. An old friend of mine. She was much older than me. I was just a kid when I started to work for her. She was a great person. Founded Hull House in Chicago. A pioneer.*"

"*A pioneer? Like Davey Crockett?*"

"*Not exactly. A different type of pioneer. A pioneer for women.*"

"*Why did women need a pioneer?*"

"*Back then, women and men had different rights. Did you know? When I was young. I wasn't allowed to vote?*

"*Why not?*"

"*Not just me. No women could vote till 1920. The 19ᵗʰ Amendment.*"

"*The Amend-what?*"

"*We'll talk about that another time.*"

"*So who was this Hull woman?*"

"*Not Hull. Addams. She founded Hull House. She won a Nobel Peace Prize for her work. I worked for her.*"

"*Did you win a noble prize too?*"

Sigh.

"*A Nobel Peace Prize. No. It is a very prestigious award. Just Jane Addams. Not me. She deserved it. Hull House helped women get on their feet. It wasn't so easy back then. Women were second-class citizens. Less school. Worse or no jobs. It was a social center. A place to go for women in need.*

If you were a poor immigrant girl, your prospects were not good for the future. Maybe be a maid. Maybe an underpaid factory job sewing. These girls needed help. We didn't want them to turn to a life a crime. Sometimes that was their only choice.

I was fortunate. My parents came to America. Found good jobs. Invested well. Saved well. Gave me and my sisters a good education."

"What did you do at Hull House?"

"At first. I just sort of hung around. I was young and single. That didn't last long. Jane Addams barked at me.

'Don't just stand there. Do something or get out of the way!'

I looked around. I saw a group of young girls. Maybe sixteen. They were foreign. Italian and German I think. They did not know how to read. They were in a small circle. They were trying to pronounce letters.

I sat with them. I read to them. Showed them the book. The letters. I kept coming back. Kept helping the girls. It was exciting."

"Were you a teacher? Were you paid grandma?"

"No honey. I was a volunteer. I just wanted to help. I got older. I eventually married your grandpa Nat. You never met him. He was a nice man. But, he did not like me helping at Hull House."

"Why not?"

"He was sort of an old-world person. He thought poor should stay to themselves. Thought nationalities and religions should stay in their neighborhoods. He didn't think women needed any help. Be a wife. Have babies. Tend to the house. That was Nat."

"Did you like Nat?"

Verna smiled.

"Yes. I loved Nat. Men of that era thought just like he did. It was not unusual. Nat made me very happy for many years. Still. I had my secrets.

I kept working at Hull House right along. Three or four hours a day. I made sure our house was in order. Nat never knew. It was harder when Eileen came along. She had school. In the summer. I'd drag her with. Oh she hated it at first. Her friends were at the beach or park. She was with me.

"Where did grandpa Nat think you were at? When you left the house?"

Verna smiled again.

"Knitting lessons. You know. I'm a pretty good knitter."

"I know."

"Well. I wasn't getting lessons. I was giving lessons. At Hull House. I'd sneak food. Books. Medicine. Clothes. My wool. And, my knitting *needles all in my big knitting bag. I'd knit sweaters for the Hull House girls. Gloves. Mittens. Scarves. Whatever they needed or wanted. Didn't take me long. I was pretty fast.*

These girls needed help. They didn't have nice clothes. Didn't know how to wash themselves sometimes. It was hard on Eileen at first. She got a hold of it after the first few times. Realized these girls were trying to better themselves. She wasn't scared. Came to like going there.

By the time your Mother was born, Eileen was a regular volunteer. We had moved to the north side. I owned a building then. Eileen dragged Ann Ethel down to Halsted Street. Actually, all Eileen had to do was ask Ann. She'd follow her anywhere. Quite the pest your Mother. Your Mom pitched right in. You would have been proud.

Eventually. Eileen grew up. Had kids. She worked there. When she had free time. She still went with Ann Ethel."

"Do you remember any of the girls?"

Verna Paused. Thought for a Moment. Decided to continue.

"I do. Before Eileen was married. Before Ann was coming. An Italian girl. Her name was Gina Marie. She was about the same age as Eileen. About sixteen. Very dark hair. A skinny girl. Poor. Not much food in her house. Dark skin. Dark eyes. Always clean. Dark circles under her eyes. There was a sadness about her. She spoke English. Not often. She was shy.

One particular day. Gina Marie came into Hull House. Her yellow dress had blood on it. She wasn't cut or bleeding. She was crying. She was scared. She had a fresh black eye.

A few minutes later. Her Mother arrived. Eileen was with me. Gina Marie was one of the girls Eileen was helping. We had never met her Mother before.

Ann Marie yelled at her Mother in Italian. Her Mother was crying. I could see her Mother had bruises on her arms. She had been grabbed. She had a purple bruise on her cheek too. Slapped or hit hard I thought.

"Was Gina Marie fighting with her Mom? Is that why they were both bruised?"

"We didn't know. It didn't seem that way. It seemed like the Mother wanted Gina Marie to come home. She was holding out her arms. Motioning to the door. Both speaking Italian. Very fast. Very loud. We couldn't understand much of what they were saying. They were going back and forth.
'*Enzo! Babbo! Padre!*'
*'No Gina. No! Enzo. **No!**'*
*'Si! Mamma. Si! **Padre!**'*
Suddenly. A man ran in. His arm was bleeding. He was holding a glass oil-lamp. It was cracked. Broken. Jagged edges. A little blood on it. **His blood**.

The man had a wild look in his eyes. His clothes were disheveled. Shirt untucked. Men did not typically leave their homes without a proper jacket and tie. No matter how poor. Something was definitely wrong."

I usually fell asleep during grandma's nighttime stories. Not tonight. I was riveted.

"What grandma? What was wrong?"

"Gina Marie pointed and shouted at the man.
'*Enzo! Padre – Brutto! Babbo – Brutto!*'
Her Mother's expression changed. She stared at Enzo with horror."

"Who was the man? What was she saying?"

"Gina Marie was saying that the man, Enzo was her Father. Padre. Father. She was saying her Father was bad. Brutto. Her Mother wildly ran toward Enzo. With both hands, Enzo violently threw the Mother to the ground.

Enzo marched toward Gina Marie. He slapped her face. Hard. Jarred her teeth. He grabbed her arm. He was hurting her. Leaving his wife on the floor. Turned to walk out the door dragging Gina Marie by her arm behind him. Gina Marie was frantically scared. She did not want to go. Her Mother was yelling from the floor.
'*Smettila! Smettila!*'
Stop it! Stop it!"

Verna paused. I practically yelled.

*"What happened next? **What?**"*

Again. Verna paused. Deep in thought. Serious.

"I'm not sure I should continue. You're not old enough."

She was not smiling. Looking back. I don't think she meant to tell me this much. The story was rushing out of her.

"Grandma. Don't stop now. I want to know."

Pause.

*"Enzo turned to the door. I picked up a chair. A heavy wooden desk chair. I was young. I don't know where I got the strength to lift that chair. I hit him over his head. I hit him hard Nat. As hard as I could. **With everything I had. I hit him.** The Father started to fall. Eileen grabbed Gina Marie. Held her and hugged her as Enzo fell at her feet."*

I could not believe it. My eyes were like large saucers. I begged her.

"Go on! Go on! Don't stop."

Verna sighed.

*"OK. Here it is. All of the story. Nat. I'm going to tell you something. Only Eileen knows. Nobody else living. I've kept this secret all of my life. My son Teddy. Your Mom - my daughter. Your Dad. They don't know. My parents didn't know. My husband didn't know. **NOBODY! Do you understand**? You can't tell **anyone** what I am about to tell you."*

This was the Verna Mom had told me about. Stern. In control. Commanding. I had never seen her like this before. I nodded.

"I understand. I promise."

*"I killed him. Right there. I hit him over the head. **I killed him.**"*

There was no smile. There was no *"I'm just kidding – good story huh?"* Verna was serious. If she felt some relief in sharing, she didn't show it.

"Did you go to jail? Grandma?"

"No I did not. We were the only ones in the room. Eileen. Me. Gina Marie. Her Mother. Her Father – dead on the floor. The room had a door which led to the street. The door they had come through. The curtains were

down over the windows that shown onto Halsted Street. Hull House was a busy place. Someone would be coming in any Moment."

"Yes…Yes???"

"Eileen looked at Gina Marie. Still hugging her. Supporting her. Holding her up. Gina Marie's Mother was in shock. Dazed. Eileen spoke calmly.

*'Gina Marie. Tell me what happened. **Tell me now**! Did your Father. Padre. Did he hit you? Did he hit you hard?'*

Gina Marie looked down. She nodded. Eileen continued.

'Today. Did your Father. Did he visit you? Did he visit you in your bedroom? Did he touch you? Is that why he is still in his home clothes? You can tell me.'

'Si. Yes. He come. He hit mamma. He hit me. He grab me. He touch me like I am Momma. Before too. I don't sleep anymore.

*Today. This morning. **He come again!***

__No more!__ I took the lamp. I hit him. The lamp – it broke. I shout.

"I am not yours! You cannot have me again."

I run out. I don't know where to go. I come here.'

I stepped up to the two girls. Stroked Gina Marie's hair.

'You did the right thing. Coming here was the right thing.'

I looked around. I knew time was short.

'Give me a hand.'

I grabbed the Father's arm. Eileen grabbed his other arm. Gina Marie and her Mother grabbed his legs.

'This is it. We're going to throw him onto the sidewalk outside. Look out the curtain. When no-one is coming. We're throwing him.'

We opened the door. We threw. Like he was a sack of potatoes. Right out to the sidewalk. We cleaned the room. Hid the chair. Changed Gina Marie's dress. I sent for Jane Addams. Spoke with her privately. Told her what had happened.

She sent a messenger for the police. When the police arrived, they found Enzo on the sidewalk. This was a rough neighborhood. By the time the police got there, neighborhood kids had stripped him like he was a car. They took his shoes. His socks. They took his shirt and pants. His belt. His watch. The few dollars he had in his pocket. He just laid there. Dead.

In his underpants and T-shirt. He was humiliated. Humiliation was too good for the Bastard. Doing what he did to his wife and child. **His child!** *She was just a child."*

Her voice trailed off. I had never heard my Grandmother use a bad word. Before or since. She was talking. She was trying not to cry. It's as though I wasn't there.

"If Enzo had been found inside Hull House, it might have served as an excuse for the city to shut us down. The male politicians were not pleased with us.

Worse. Men had all the rights then. If it came out any of us hit him. No matter what **he** *had done, a judge would have sent us to jail. If he had lived -* **Not him. Us!**

These were fine women. They did not deserve to be abused. They needed to be judged by their character. Not by their dark Italian skin color nor their gender. America wasn't ready for that. Jane Addams, Verna, and Eileen were ready.

Being a husband or Father did not give Enzo the right to be a monster. If Gina Marie had walked out of Hull House with Enzo, her life would have been **over.** *I'd hit him again if I had to. I don't regret it. Do you understand what I am saying?"*

I nodded. She continued.

"Gina Marie and her Mother waited inside with Eileen and me. Jane Addams spoke to the policemen on the sidewalk.

'It's very unfortunate. This man was robbed. Right here. Outside Hull House. We understand two men hit him over his head and took his things. They worked fast. Ran away. We did not get a good look at them. You wouldn't see women involved in a crime like this. Petty theft - Leads to death. So sad.'

The policemen wrote notes. Nodded. They had Enzo's body taken away. A robbery of a poor Italian man on south Halsted. By the looks of it. A vagrant. In this neighborhood. This was not news. A daily occurrence. This was not police-worthy. A case was never even opened. It was over."

"What happened to Gina Marie and her Mother?"

"They couldn't go home. They stayed at Hull House. Gina Marie's Mother helped Hull House for the rest of her life. Learned to speak English. Gina Marie worked on her studies. She got her high school degree. Hull House paid for her college education.

Gina Marie entered the Rockford Female Seminary. The same college Jane Addams attended. At the time, it was all women. I believe they allow men now.

Gina Marie did well. She went on to earn her law degree. She worked for years defending young women in the Hull House neighborhood. Later, President Eisenhower appointed her a judge. Your Aunt Eileen stayed friends with Gina Marie for a number of years. I worked at Hull House off and on till it became difficult for me to commute there when I got older."

Verna looked at me in bed. I'd finally conked out. Sound asleep. Verna kept speaking knowing I was asleep. With a sigh. Softly.

*"Nat. Please. **Never** let skin color get in the way of doing the right thing. **Never** hit a woman. **Never** allow a woman to be hit. Please."*

CHAPTER 8

A "UNIQUE TALENT"

"*I think you're old enough to know this now.*"
Blank stare.
"*I think you're old enough to know this now*" my Dad repeated.

It was the 1980's. I was twenty-eight. Married. Working. I had just returned back to Chicago from a Los Angeles business trip. While there, I visited my Aunt Helen and Uncle Davey in Glendale. Aunt Helen is my Dad's older and only sister.

It was my first time to their house. Not large. Lovely. Tasteful. Picture a contented, retired movie star's house in the 1940's. It was airy. Built for comfort. An honest personal style. Large ceiling fans. Small swimming pool. Expensive. Yet. Not built on ego nor meant for lavish entertaining.

Glendale is described as the "Jewel of Los Angeles". It was easy to understand. Nice quiet bungalow houses with orange trees. Wild Bird of Paradise flowers planted everywhere.

I knew my grandparents had retired in Glendale to be near Davey and Helen. My question which prompted my Dad's surprising response was.

"*Papa Will (his Dad) was just a newspaper delivery man and type setter for the old Randolph Hearst newspaper 'The Chicago American'. How did he end up retiring in Glendale? Now that I've seen Glendale, it seems* ***a bit*** *over his head."*

I added *"**a bit**"* a little too condescendingly. Dad continued.

"Your Grandfather had a unique talent."

I waited for the big finish. He paused with a sense of stage presence.

"Will could add large rows and columns of numbers and calculations in his head!"

Too quickly and too hurriedly. I replied unenthusiastically. Unimpressed.

"So?"

The look on his face. His reaction told me. He was disappointed. I should have gotten it. I was nowhere close to getting it. This was the "how could I raise such a dopey kid?" look. To my Dad, this wasn't school. **This** stuff... **this** was important! He went on.

"So? So he could add large columns in his head. Always accurate. Get it?"

As if repeating himself would bring it to light for me. I just stood there. It didn't bring it to light. I just felt stupid.

"What does this mean?"

Dad began. *"Will was born in Leeds, England. Poor. He worked his way over to America. Transported in a ship's steerage deck. That's the boat's basement. With the baggage and the livestock. The poorest travelers were put there.*

He came alone as an older kid. Probably about sixteen. His Mother came later. I'm not sure if his Father ever came. Broke. Jewish. A strapping five foot-four inches tall. Will wound up on Chicago's West Side. There. He did ***everything.***

He was a jockey. Semi-pro baseball player. Played for the Bantam Hat Company at old Mills Stadium. Played against old Negro League barnstorming teams managed by Rube Foster.

Buck Leonard played. He was just a kid. Rube and Buck never made it to the White major leagues. They both eventually were voted into Baseball's Hall Of Fame for their contribution in the Negro Baseball League.

It's a shame Buck never played in the majors. First baseman. They called him the 'Black Lou Gehrig'. He was great. Funny… Satchel Paige called Lou Gehrig 'the White Buck Leonard'. True".

"Better than Ernie Banks?"

"As good. Different. Buck was stocky. More like Harmon Killebrew. Could drive the ball a country mile.

I met Buck Leonard once. At the Hall of Fame in Cooperstown. You were there. He said he remembered Will. __My Dad!__"

An amazing sense of pride was building in my Dad's typically mellow voice. The mention of Buck Leonard seemed to bring him far away for a Moment.

"Remembered speaking with Will".

Dad continued. But, he was somewhere else now…

In Bernie's memory…

The infield has very little grass. It is a combination of hard dirt and finely grated concrete. A little broken glass. There is a steel wire backstop. About eight feet tall. About eight feet across. The outfield is grassy. Not finely mowed. Not too high. A fence with a few faded signs on the rickety wooden outfield fence.

"Uncle Sam Needs You!"

"Drink Coca-Cola – Thirst Knows No Season".

"Chevrolet – Man's Conquest of Time".

"Genuine Bull Durham Smoking Tobacco - The Standard for Three Generations".

It is a perfect seventy-two degrees. Very light breeze. A few cottony clouds. Watching the Black barnstormers take batting practice. The two ball players stand next to each other behind the backstop. They are alone in a crowd of players preparing to do battle.

Will is older than Buck. Small. Wiry. He wears his slightly loose, faded, worn Bantam Hat baseball jersey with pride. By comparison, Buck is a kid. About five foot-ten inches tall. He is nearly

two-hundred pounds. A slight belly is misleading. He is all muscle. Practically bursting out of his slightly too small gray jersey. A
very strong, dark Black man in a very white world. In his day, his
presence might have scared most White men. Not Will.

"How are you doing Buck?"

"Doing fine Mr. Will. Doing fine."

"Just call me Will."

"Thank you Will. I'll do that."

"Where are you from Buck?"

*"A little place down south. Rocky Mount, North Carolina. It's pretty.
I like it a lot."*

"Why did you leave?"

*"Needed to. Wanted to. Love baseball more. Can't do nothing but
work the fields down there. Not a fit life."*

*"You're just starting out. I've been watching you. You've got a great
future. Widen your stance against curve ball pitchers. Don't take such a
big cut. You're over swinging. Take a smaller step to the pitch. Or else,
they'll stop feeding you fastballs."*

*"That's good help Will. Thank you! You think you can make it in
baseball? Get to the White Majors?"*

*"No Buck. This is my last stop. A hard-working guy on a semi-pro
team. I'm not going any farther. Not young enough. Not good enough.
You. You're good. And young. Maybe someday the majors will open up
for you. It'd be nice."*

"Real nice. I'll just see where it all lands. How'd it go for you yesterday?"

*"I rode nine ponies. Three winners. Didn't get thrown. Cashed a few
tickets too. Horses were with me I guess."*

"That where you got that shiner?"

*"No. Got that last night. Went fifteen rounds with 'Bruiser Baines'.
He had twenty pounds on me. The 'boys' asked me to hold him up for the
first fourteen. Put him away. K.O. in the final round. I did it. Could
have put him away in two. Saved the bruises."*

"Looks like he caught you at least once."

"Yeah. More than once. He tagged me good. But, I can take it. Came home with fifty dollars. Gave it to Mother. She saw my face. That was it. I'd been boxing a while. Under the name. 'Little Willie Green'. I was moving up. She didn't know. Last night. First time I got nicked. Mother knows now. She put an end to it. I'm done in the ring."

The two made an odd couple talking at this oasis. A baseball diamond. It wasn't a very nice diamond. Didn't matter to them. They were no more than a foot from each other as they chatted casually. As if they were next door neighbors speaking over a fence.

"Want to know something Will?"

"What's that?"

"If we were back home, we couldn't be talking like this. Kind of makes me sad. Another reason I like to come up north."

"Yeah. Not everybody here likes me either. You pay no mind kid. You're going to make a lot of money in baseball. Me. I'll make my money OK. Just not in this game. Don't let anyone take that food out of your mouth. You hear me?"

Buck nodded. They shook hands. Something else you might not have seen in that era. Except behind a baseball backstop. Buck left to take his batting practice. Will watched with admiration as balls flew over the fence four-hundred feet away. Rattled off the train track on the other side.

Dad seemed to come back into focus. I could see he'd taken a detour. He didn't say where. He picked right up.

"Will met my Mother Goldie. They married. They had my sister Helen and then they had me. I was born in 1921. Will was working on the inside at the newspaper by then.

He was a great Dad. He took me to all of the sporting events. Dempsey-Tunney. Six-day bike races. Cubs, Sox, Bears, Hawks. Football and base-ball All-Star games. Soldier Field. The Stadium. Wrigley. Sox Park. And of course, we went to the local horse tracks. We went everywhere and saw everything." Dad was beaming.

"He was friends with all the sporting types. He didn't need tickets. Everyone seemed to know him. I didn't think about it. It was the 20's and 30's. I was a kid."

I grew up on these stories. I loved them. I had heard them all before. I still loved them. Dad ran out of a little steam. I gently asked.

"I'm still not sure I get Papa Will's special talent".

"Right. Will was a newspaper delivery man. He drove a horse and buggy. Every day, he delivered his papers to the newsstands, bars, cigar stores, candy shops, diners, and drug stores throughout the city. Early 1900's Chicago. Get it?"

Disappointing by the minute. *"Still no clue".*

Dad sighed.

"Do you know which sport used to have more paid fans than any other sport in the United States?"

"Baseball"

I said with some authority.

"__That__ would be wrong. It was horse racing. Know why?"

"People love cute horses with funny names?"

I said with a smile (I should have just shut up.). Not so much as a smirk. He continued.

"More people attended daily horse races than any other sport to bet the ponies. Hundreds of race tracks all over the country. Still, most people worked during the day. Or, they could not afford the time nor train fare to get out to the racecourses."

I knew Dad was driving somewhere. I could tell we were close. And yet... I still didn't have it. My blank stare told the tale. He blurted out.

"For God sakes, your Papa Will was a collector for the mob! Organized crime!"

Now when your Father starts a sentence with *"For God's sake"* and he is not inclined to exaggeration or hyperbole, the best thing to do is to look impressed. Of course, I laughed. Not good.

His stare froze me. Never once in my life did my Dad spank or hit me. He didn't have to. The stare was the argument ender. It was the discipliner. He just told me this thing that he'd held back for all these years. I laughed. Now. I was sorry.

"How? Dad, how is this possible? Papa Will never weighed more than 135 pounds in his life. Who would turn money over to him? And why?"

Dad was like Perry Mason in his final argument to the jury. Fast paced. But not too fast. Sense of urgency. But not so much that the point was rushed. Just enough to convey the truth. The obvious truth only he understood. That all would understand once he unraveled it.

"There were hundreds of race tracks throughout the country. Each track ran about nine races multiple days per week. Every race had different purse sizes. Every horse had different odds to win, place, or show in each race. The odds on each race as well as the payoff were different and multiplied in difficulty if bettors played trifectas (Betting three horses in one race to win, place, and show.).

There were few cars or telephones. Few houses even had electricity. Where do you think the locals went to bet the horses? You got it. The local newspaper stands, pubs, groceries, drug stores, and cigar stores. All of Will's newspaper stops housed bookies.

The customers were betting pennies, nickels, dimes, and occasional dollars every day. Workers, bums, housewives, drunks, Grandmothers, cops, business owners, rich and poor and even clergy. They all bet. Chicago was a wide-open city and nobody thought the worse of it.

*There was your Papa Will. He could take the bets from the bookies for his bosses. He could calculate the odds. He knew what was owed. He knew what to pay out. Day after day. Race after race. Shop after shop. Bet after bet. And…Here comes the important part. **He got a piece of every bet.***"

Now I **was** impressed. I knew my Dad had a gift for numbers. Now I knew where it came from. But still. I asked. This time with great respect.

"Why didn't someone just take the money from him? He wasn't a big guy."

Dad continued as if on cue.

"He wasn't the money man. He wasn't the muscle. He was just the collector operating between the bookies and the mob. The mob trusted Will. Who would be stupid enough to mess with him?

On top of everything else. Having been a jockey. Will knew a thing or two about the races. Will was a likable and connected fellow. He always told me. Every slate of races had one fixed race. Do your homework. Be prepared. Know which race it is. Be disciplined.

Bet only one race per day. Life will be good and profitable. Not only was Will taking a piece of the action, he was cashing his own tickets too."

He went on.

"He really did work for the paper. The newspaper delivery horse and buggy job was real. But, it was a front too. By the time I was born, Will had made his money. When the 'roaring twenties' came, Prohibition, automobiles, telephones, and new players in organized crime changed everything.

It was time for Will to get out and get out safely. I'm not really sure how he did that. Got out safely. But, he did.

Will tucked his money away. He wasn't a Rockefeller or a Carnegie. But, he didn't lose his savings in the stock market collapse of 1929. Imagine. He thought gambling was safe and playing the market was risky."

Papa Will passed away peacefully in Glendale. Dad idolized Will. It upset Dad when Davey and Helen moved to Glendale. It broke his heart when Will followed. Meeting Mom went a long way to healing his wound. But, he never fully recovered.

CHAPTER 9

CHRISTMAS EVE:
A SURPRISE UNDER THE "GREAT TREE"

This is the one and only experience Will kept from his son Bernie.

1920 Winter. One week before Christmas
The <u>Chicago American</u> Newspaper. Deep inside the building. Will is on break. He's balanced on two posts of a four-post wooden chair. Leaning back against the wall. Constant activity rushes by. Head down. Reading. Will is oblivious. There is a gentle kick at Will's chair. Not enough to knock him over. Just enough to gain his attention.

"Hello Frankie."

"Hello Will. How are you doing today? What are you reading?"

"An old <u>Saturday Evening Post</u>. Ring Lardner. 'The Real Dope'. Jack Keefe's moved on from the White Sox. From '<u>You Know Me Al</u>'. He's taking on the Kaiser in The Great War. It's grand."

"Your guy Benny Leonard looks pretty good. I won a bundle on him last week."

"Frankie. What brings you down to the paper? Talk literature and boxing?"

"Fraid not Will. Boss has a job for you. Wanted me to tell you."

Will straightens himself up and stands. He knows not to threaten Frankie. He is serious. Shows concern.

"Why didn't he tell me himself? Everything OK?"

"Oh yeah. No problems. With you. This job is more in my area. Know what I mean?"

Will nods. Frankie is in enforcement. Will points down the hall.

"Let's talk in one of the offices. The newspaper can be loud. And, busy with people."

The two enter a small office. No windows. Wooden desk. A couple of wooden chairs. Large sheets of newspaper sections all over the wall and floor. Red pen circles through each. Edits.

"What's going on Frankie? This has to be important for a day visit."

"It is. Remember 'Dress Up' Al Shires? Over on the south side?"

*"Sure. We ran a lot of business together. Particularly at Washington Park. A lot of winners. For **everyone**."*

"The boss knows. Will. He knows you've always been straight with him. Collecting or handling bets. You still got friends in good places. You know what the Eighteenth Amendment is?"

"Sure. Who doesn't? Prohibition. For legal joints. Why?"

"That's right. The boss is moving into bootlegging in a big way. He's using his gambling outlets to expand his business. He figures the money is going to be massive. He also figures if he doesn't move on it, he'll get pushed out of his gambling interests. Follow so far?"

"So far."

"So far is good. 'Dress Up' Al. He used to be a pal of yours. Right?"

"I didn't invite him to my wedding. But yeah. A good business contact. That's the second time you've mentioned Shires."

"Will. You're always to the point. Shires has his own booze distributorship. He's running for a gang out of New York. Last week. He hit one of our places. Hit it hard. Scared our customers. So scared. They're thinking of changing suppliers. Can't have that Will. It'd be the beginning of the end. Can't get pushed out."

"I'm listening."

"Boss needs to hit Shires hard. He needs your help."

"Frankie. You and I go back a lot of years. You know me. I'm no muscle. Never killed a person in my life. Don't carry. Wouldn't know how. Why me?"

"Boss figures we can't get close enough to make a dent without making a big noise. He needs a fresh approach. Knows you and 'Dress Up' are OK. He trusts you. You could get close."

"What happens if I say 'no'?"

"That would be the end of our association. For you. Might prove harmful at home or work. Who can tell? You've been enjoying our protection for a long time. Now you need to pay back."

"Frankie. You trust me?"

"You've always been straight with me."

"Can you give me a few days to think about it? I need to get my head around this. Come back to the paper in three days."

"Three days I can do."

Six days before Christmas

Will told Goldie he was going to work. He didn't. He went to the Chicago Public Library on Michigan Avenue. He needed to think in peace and quiet. About 4pm. Will walked over to Marshall Field and Company on State Street. Didn't buy anything. Just walked up and down the stairs. From the first floor to the thirteenth. Back down. About two hours in the store. About 6PM. Will went home.

Five days before Christmas

Marv is the editor on the <u>Chicago American</u>'s "Chicago Beat" desk. A long-time friend of Will's. Will stands outside of Marv's office. He raps on the door window. Sticks his head in. It's the first thing in the morning.

"Marv. Got a second?"

"Will! Will! Will! For you. **Anything!** *Pimlico. Second race. Fifteen-to-one odds. 'Sally's Dream'. How did you pick that one? Seventeen-hundred big ones. I won seventeen-hundred! The week before Christmas. I am a hero at home! Bought the wife a new fur coat. Still had money left over."*

Marv is smiling from ear to ear. Will smiles too. It is a short, weak smile. Marv is sharp. Used to fast conversations. Recognizes Will's got something on his mind."

"Marv. I had a hunch. Glad it paid off for you."

"Will. You get hunches about once a month. This is the tenth or eleventh time you've given me a tip that's paid off this year. I don't know how you do it."

"Just remember. It's between you and me. No-one else."

"I promise. Will. It doesn't look like you came in to talk about the ponies. How can I help you?"

Will makes sure the door is closed. He pulls a chair very close to Marv's. He's speaking in a very soft tone."

"Marv. I need two favors from you. You can't ask me 'why?' OK? If this works. I'm going to give you the scoop of the year. You'll be in print a day before the other city papers. Would you like that?"

"If it doesn't work?"

Marv was smiling. Will did not return the smile.

"Enjoy 'Sally's Dream.' He's the last pony I'll ever be handicapping."

Serious now.

"What do you need Will? Just name it."

"First favor. I need to meet with someone you know at the county morgue. I need to meet today. It's got to be someone you trust. But. Is not all together trustworthy. Willing to make a quick fifty."

"It's cold in the morgue. I got the guy. He's one of my guys. What's your second request?"

"Same request. The Coroner's office. Know anybody?"

"Yeah Will. I know a guy. You OK?

"I'll know in a couple of days."

"I'll make the calls. Come back in an hour."

Will stops by Marv's office exactly one hour later. Marv waves him in. He hands Will a piece of paper. Two names. Two addresses.

"They're expecting you."

"Thanks. I'll have a scoop for you in a few days."

Four days before Christmas.

Schulien's Tavern. West Irving Park Road. On bar stools. Still wearing their overcoats. They hardly look at each other. Smoking cigarettes. Drinking cups of hot coffee. Soft voices.

"Frankie. Tell the boss I'm in."

"That's good Will. Very good. How are you going to do it?

"You'll know. It will be in our paper. Then all the others. Headline. Proof. Soon. In a few days. You won't miss it."

"Boss don't want no publicity."

"Don't worry. You're back is covered. I need your help on a couple of things. And I have one condition."

*"**You're** giving me a condition? Tell me what you need."*

"I need about Two-hundred dollars. Twenties and tens. Need to grease the wheels a little. No-one knows. Just buys me some access I'll need."

"What else?"

"I need you to get me into Marshall Field's. State Street. A job. Seventh Floor. Restaurant. Walnut Room. Clean up staff. Need keys. Keys for the whole store. Not just the seventh floor. You've got people in Fields. I didn't think that it would be difficult for you. It would help me a lot. I'd be around for a just for a few days. Won't make any noise for you or the boss."

"OK Will. So far. Sounds pretty easy. I can get this done today. Anything else?"

"No."

"What's the condition?"

"It my last job. Last of any type. We walk away from each other. You double-cross me, I'll have the details of every gambling outfit in the city in

the press in less than twenty-four hours. Even if you kill me. I'll have the story positioned. It will all come out. See?

I won't double-cross you. I'm about to kill a friend of mine. That should be good enough. If I give that up, I'll go to the chair. Do we have a deal?"

"We do."

Three days before Christmas

Will takes the Halsted Street bus to the south side. Gets off at Archer Avenue. Walks a few blocks east to the corner of Cermak and Wentworth. Turns right on Wentworth. He is in Chinatown. On the west side of the street is a Funeral Parlor. <u>Chang's</u>. 2417 S. Wentworth.

Will does not go in <u>Chang's</u> front door. He walks up the stairs adjacent to the funeral parlor. There is a flower shop on the second floor. On the third floor landing. There are two office doors. He knocks on one. Neither have writing on their doors.

A pretty middle aged Chinese woman meets Will. She is older than she looks. She has aged elegantly. Her name is Grace. It fits. Her English is fair. In the outside foyer.

"May I help you?"

"Hi Grace. Remember me? It's been a long time. Al is expecting me."

Grace is cautious. Looks behind Will. Motions Will into her office. Then smiles.

"Sure Will. Nice to see you. How is Goldie?"

"All good. Thank you. And the Chang family?"

"Very well thank you. I'll let Mr. Shires know you are here."

Grace bows. Turns. Leaves down a dark hallway. She is gone only a minute.

"He will see you now. Please follow me."

Will does as he is told. Will has a steel trap mind. He has the inner fortitude to go with it. He's been in tight situations before. Yet. He knows. This is different. If this meeting goes bad, he'll have to go to plan "B". He does not want to do that. He enters Al Shire's office. With a confident smile.

"Dress Up" Al Shires has a richly deserved nickname. He's a violent gangster. He has a solid machine to do his work now. On any given day, Al dresses as though he is having dinner with a McCormick or some other city elite. From his polished wing-tip shoes to his ruby ring. Al is dapper. He is **dressed up**.

His office is decorated neatly. Sporting memorabilia. Photographs. Boxers. Jockeys. Baseball players. A fielder's glove. Boxing gloves. Even a saddle with silks. They are Will's silks. All of the sporting equipment in Al's office once belonged to Will. Gifts to a friend from a time gone by.

Shires worked his way through the south side neighborhoods of the slaughter houses. With each step up, his wardrobe and diction improved. He is a self-made man. Will understands this. They understand each other.

"*Al. How are you? Still hiding out in Chinatown I see. I always meant to ask you. Why Chinatown? You're not Chinese.*"

Al is smiling. It is genuine.

"*Will. How are you? It's been a while. I miss our meetings. I miss my winnings! Why Chinatown? Simple. Nobody would think to look for me here. I have a public legit business office in Bridgeport. The police and reporters assume I run my operations from there. I let them assume.*

*Confidentially. This building is mine. It's in the Chang's name. The funeral parlor. The florist. Other activity. The Changs work for me. I made them fifty-fifty partners in all Chinatown activity. All! They are **very** reliable.*"

Al continues. Not smiling.

"*Will. You sounded pretty serious on the phone. I don't hear from you for a year. And, you have to see me in a day?*"

"*Al. Are you carrying?*"

The question surprises Al. Al opens up his suit jacket. Right side. Revolver. Left side. Revolver. Al's guns are custom made.

The "Pearls". Pearl handles. Initials in gold. In certain circles, he is famous for the "Pearls". They are his calling cards.

Will in turn shows his. Nothing on the right. Nothing on the left. Will does not carry. He never has. Al knows. After the mutual display.

"Why Will? You've never asked before. You know I'm usually with my pair. I know you don't carry. Why ask now?"

"I need you to trust me."

"I'd trust my fortune on any bet you name."

"I need you to trust me with your life."

Al does not talk. He likes Will. They like each other. He is a man of strength. He is used to dealing from a position of power. There are very few people Al would have let get so close to him without first being searched. Without a guard in the room.

"I was sent to kill you."

"By who!"

Will is calm.

"You know who."

"Why?"

"You know why too."

"Yeah. I know. I can gut this out."

"Al. Have I ever given you a bad tip? You can't out last them."

"Why are you telling me? Why didn't you just kill me when you walked in?"

"First. You are my friend. Second. I am not a killer. If I killed you today, I'd had to kill Grace too. I'm not a killer Al. Lots of things. Tough to be a 'Limey' with no money. No prospects. I've made my way."

"So what are you going to do? If you don't kill me, they'll kill you."

"I've thought about that. I have a plan."

"Let's have it."

"You're going away. Leaving Chicago. Leaving Christmas Eve. You'll never come back. Never be in the public eye again. I know you have millions stashed away. You'll have a day to collect it.

Quietly settle your affairs. You can't tell your family. You can't pack **anything**. *Can't tell* **anyone.** *Nothing can indicate you knew you were leaving on Christmas Eve. Otherwise the plan will fail. We'll both be sunk if that happens.*

You'll have to change your name. Pick where you want to go. I suggest California or Nevada. Get far away. You can tell me Christmas Eve. Are you in? If not, you won't make it till Christmas."

"I'm in Will. You are a good friend."

"Listen closely. Christmas Eve day. 1PM. Come to Marshall Field's on State Street. All of Chicago comes to Field's at Christmas. No-one will notice you. Come alone.

Drive your own car. Registered to you. Valet park it. Put the parking stub in your wallet. Wear nice comfortable non-descript clothes for your trip. No monogramed shirts, socks, cuff-links, or tie. Nothing. No jewelry that can be traced to you after Christmas Eve. Bring 'the Pearls'.

First stop. Seventh floor. Make a dinner reservation. The Walnut Room. 6pm. That night.

Second stop. Thirteenth floor. Finance office. Open a line of credit. Use your real name. Bridgeport business address. Use real references including a real bank account. Something that can be verified honestly after the fact.

Explain you want to shop that day **on credit.** *Your reasons are personal. The credit manager will be cautious to extend you credit prior to a background check.*

Remove two-thousand dollars from your wallet. **Ask for a receipt in** **your name.** *Explain. You'll leave the cash as collateral. You'll be happy to have the manager keep the cash in his safe till your references are completed. He will agree. He will write you a letter of credit that you will use in the store.*

Next stop. Go shopping. Buy a suit. Have it tailored while you wait. Pay extra. Buy all of the accessories. Tie. Cuff links. Shoes. Socks. Belt. Undergarments. Buy yourself a new watch. A new ring. Get receipts **in** **your name** *for everything you buy."*

"In my name?"

"In your name."

"6PM. Walnut Room. You'll be seated by a hostess. She's stunning. You won't notice. No conversation. Don't work the local talent! I'll be working there. You don't know me.

You're going to be given a piece of candy as an appetizer by your wait-ress. Also stunning. No small talk. A chocolate. It's going to make you sick. You won't have to fake it. It will be drugged. It will take about fifteen minutes to kick in. You'll get nauseous. You won't pass out. It won't kill you. Signal your waitress. You'll be helped to the bathroom.

Two days before Christmas

Will spent the day and night at Marshall Field's. Field's was truly a palace. Starting at the corner of Dearborn and State. Heading south and east. Marshall Field's occupies some thirteen floors on seventy-three acres.

In 1907, a cast bronze clock with green patina was erected above each store corner on State Street. Nearly three quarters of a ton in weight a piece. The green clocks with black roman numer-als remain iconic symbols of Field's and the city of Chicago.

Louis Comfort Tiffany was commissioned to build a mosaic ceiling in the store's south rotunda. It was a prestigious and prof-itable job. The ceiling contains over one and a half million glass pieces.

In 1907, L.C. Tiffany presented the store with a private gift. A porcelain cat statue. About one foot in height. The cat had real sapphire eyes. It was coated in liquid 24 karat gold. Over the years, the gold color would fade to a brownish hue. The statue had an undetectable false bottom. And, an engraved greeting from L.C.T to M.F & Company.

L.C. Tiffany filled the statue with precious gems and gold coins. When moved, the cat sounded as though it were filled with broken glass. The statue was placed in the store president's office of John Shedd.

Each sales department features wares from the finest manufacturers and artisans. From all over the world. At every price point. The jewelry department features Tiffany gems. It rivals the finest jewelers in New York, Paris, and London. The book department occupies an entire floor. It is the largest of its kind in the world. The toy department sells toys from every continent.

Folk lore has it. Field's restaurant business started with Mrs. Hering's chicken pot pies. The original South Tearoom opened in 1890. Became the South Walnut Tearoom so named for its dark brown walnut interior. By the 1920's, the Walnut Room was a destination for Chicagoans and visitors.

The focal point of the Walnut Room at Christmas time is the "Great Tree." A full forty-five foot tall Balsam Fir. Decorated and lit. The tree itself rests through a hole in a six-foot stage. The stage surrounds the tree on all sides. Designed for safe support and balance.

Marshall Field and Company is the largest retailer in the world. Their slogan. "**The** store of the Christmas spirit".

Christmas Eve 11am

Al stops by his Chinatown office on Wentworth. He leaves two envelopes with Grace. Al cannot leave the envelopes with his wife. She would open them. Grace will do as told.

The first envelope. Hand written on the front.

Grace – Open on Christmas morning. Not before!

The second envelope. Hand written to Al's attorney.

Moshe Levin – Attorney at Law – Open upon my demise.

Grace's envelope is a deed to 2417 S. Wentworth. It also contains the licenses to the funeral parlor and florist. A letter of transfer is included. The Changs will now own the property and all of the legal businesses contained within. It is an incredibly generous gift. They now own one-hundred percent.

The Changs will own and manage the less-than-public Chinatown businesses previously owned by Al as well. This does not need to be addressed in his letter. It is understood. Loyalty rewarded.

Mo Levin's envelope contains Al's <u>Last Will & Testament</u>. All of Al's earthly belongings are deeded to his wife. She'll have to travel downtown to claim his car. She will be taken care of for the rest of her life.

Al's estate is sizable. In reality, his wife will get about half of the cash value. She'll never know this. One-hundred thousand dollars in large bills are sewn into the lining of Al's old wool top coat. The coat he'll wear Christmas Eve to Field's.

Over one-million dollars has been wired to a bank in Santa Monica, California. The money is transferred to a movie studio shell-corporation under Al's new alias name. A stock brokerage account is established with the money. The twenties are about to roar. His new bank account will not raise an eye. Just more seed money for another studio.

To his <u>Last Will and Testament</u>, there is only one other nota-tion. From Al's office, four items are to be delivered to Will at the <u>Chicago American</u>. Will's presents to Al. Returned with deep appreciation. A worn leather saddle with silks. A pair of smallish boxing gloves. A used Reach leather baseball glove. An Austrian made twelve carat gold ring with a single half carat ruby faceted with six corners. The words "Dress Up" are engraved on the inside of the ring.

Christmas Eve 1PM

Al drives from Chinatown to Marshall Field and Company. Only a fifteen-minute ride. Valet parks. It is a brisk twenty degrees out.

The sidewalks and store are filled with Christmas revelers. Lightly snowing. No accumulation. Al will spend the rest of the day as directed by Will.

Christmas Eve 6PM

Al Shires arrives at the Walnut Room promptly at 6PM. Bags in hand.

"I am Al Shires. I have a 6PM reservation."

Al is met by the hostess. Bridget. A beautiful young Irish, red-headed hostess. With a heavy Irish brogue. She is directing traffic at the front of the very busy line.

"Yes Mr. Shires. We've been expecting you.

Angela. Seat Mr. Shires at seat twelve in our special section."

Angela is Italian. Taylor Street, south side Italian. No foreign accent. A south-side accent. Statuesque. Dark black hair. Dark eyes. Olive skin. Beautiful. Al notices that all of the employees at Field's seem to be young and beautiful. He wonders to himself why he hasn't come to the Walnut Room more often. It's too late now. Angela brings Al to seat twelve.

"Your server will be Sonja. If you need anything at all. Please call for Angela."

Al is polite but reserved. He sits alone at his table for two. Next to a walnut brown post. Half-way near the tree. Half-way near a hallway that leads to the kitchen. On any other day, he would have asked Bridget or Angela or Sonja to join him at their break. Not tonight.

Sonja. A pretty blond waitress with a Polish accent brings Al his menu.

"Make I take your order?"

"I'll have the planked pork tenderloin with vegetables and apples."

*"Would you like coffee with your meal? **Irish coffee** with your meal?*

His facial expression shows his surprise. It is Prohibition. Sonja offers.

"You __are__ in the special section."

"An Irish coffee would be just fine. Thank you."

Sonja leaves with his order. Al shakes his head. He thinks to himself.

"Special section. You can even get a drink at Field's".

Al doesn't know the special section is his table only. Will has arranged for Al to have a real drink with his meal. Bridget, Angela, and Sonja are all in on it. Will selected the strategic location of the table as well. It was reserved for Al. Will's eye for detail which is usually trained on his betting is fully focused on Al Shires.

Al can't help wondering if this is his last meal. While he ponders. Sonja returns with a small fine china plate. Resting on the plate are two small chocolates. Sonja smiles.

"A special Christmas Eve treat for you Mr. Shires. A gift from Marshall Field."

Al samples both chocolates. His order is in. Al checks his newly purchased Lord Elgin watch. 6:10pm. He nurses his Irish coffee. Enjoys a buttered roll. At exactly 6:25PM, Al lets out a scream. He stands up. Doubles over in pain. He is not faking. Sonja and Angela run to him. Bridget keeps all other traffic free of the area. All are __very__ nearby. In broken English, Sonja calls for help.

Hearing the call. Will, dressed in a white Field's restaurant uniform comes running out of the kitchen. He puts one hand around the back of Al. He walks Al out of the restaurant to the men's room adjacent to the Walnut Room.

The two are not the only ones in the restroom. Will has help. One man stands guard. He will turn away any future patrons. The other man holds a carbonated clear drink.

"Drink this. It's the antidote. You will be fine."

They all wait. In five minutes. Al straightens up. He is no longer in pain. Will is in charge.

"Al. Tonight. Al Shires __dies__. Gangland style. Tomorrow, they'll find your body. New clothes. New jewelry. New shoes. New coat. Your wallet.

And, two pearl guns. All under the tree. Your face will be mangled, bloody, and disfigured."*

Al is horrified.

"Relax friend. It's a homeless person. Chicago. Winter. Homeless. They die every day. Get brought to the city morgue. **Unidentified**. Buried in potter's fields. Fifty dollars bought me this stiff. Size and shape. Made to order."*

His helper opens a stall door. The homeless stiff's body is in a bag. Before his beating, he was washed and shaved. Given a haircut. Provided with talc and Musk cologne. The same as Al's. Will had asked Grace casually while waiting earlier in the week. No detail too small.

The stiff would have looked remarkably like Al. Except, his face has been beat to a pulp. Nose broken. Teeth missing. Black eyes. A baseball bat to the head. Multiple times. Violently. Will commands Al.

"Give me everything you bought today. **Everything!** Clothes. Ring. Watch. Socks. Shoes. Give me everything in your pockets."*

Will proceeds to transfer Al's newly purchased wardrobe to the stiff. Will put's the purchase receipts in the wallet with the identification card of Al Shires. Will straps the "Pearls" on underneath the stiff's suit jacket.

He put's Al's wallet in the stiff's back pants pocket including one-hundred dollars of Al's money. Shoes. Socks. Undergarments. Shirt. Tie. Watch. Ring. It all goes on the stiff. He looks good (other than his face). Al's eyes are bulging.

"They'll never go for it. The Coroner will not declare that homeless dolt me."*

"Yes he will. The one-hundred dollars in the wallet are for him. He has a down payment of fifty already. Your body will be discovered tonight by my able assistant. My assistant will hang around to make sure no-one tampers with the body including hungry policemen.*

The Coroner will identify you tomorrow morning. All of the Field's sales staff from every floor will confirm your presence here today. All but the beautiful ladies of the restaurant team you met tonight. This will be their first night. And their last.

Your wallet. The paperwork and receipts. Your guns will be the sealing factor. The identification will be so easy. Even though you're deformed. A dental comparison won't be required. That will be the Coroner's report."

"How will you get me under the tree?"

"I'm on staff. Dinnertime ends. We clean up."

Will speaks to one of his helpers.

"Go tell Sonja her customer is fine. But. He won't be coming back."

Sonja already knows. This is for show in case another patron is watching. Al is incredulous.

"Will. Won't Sonja give this away?

*"They're on the team. She got an extra ten dollars to give you the chocolate. Angela got an extra ten dollars to seat you. Bridget got an extra twenty to manage the traffic. They are all pros. Al. **'Pros'**. Follow?"*

"And my two grand?"

"Your two-thousand dollars in the safe upstairs? That will belong to the finance manager on Christmas day. He'll ease any questions that arise. I was busy yesterday.

Al. One other thing. Some jewelry is going to go missing tonight from Field's first floor. Good stuff. It's the reason you were killed. It keeps the heat off of Frankie and his boss."

Christmas Eve 10PM

*"It's time. Al. Don't **ever** show up again. It won't be good for any of us. This man is going to take you downstairs to the loading dock. There's a dark green Field's truck waiting for you. You'll be driven out of state. Deposited to a train station. You'll be followed by one of my people. Don't look back."*

*"You saved my life. You **risked yours**. I'll never forget you."*

"It's what friends do. Good life."

The homeless stiff's body was forced under the stage holding up the tree. One leg slightly sticking out. Will had one of his men watch the body. If anyone were to come near, Will's man was to go into a rant. Act as though he were discovering the body for the first time.

Will made a quick stop on the thirteenth floor. Mr. Shedd's office. Then, to the first-floor fine jewelry department. He took about five hundred loose, unset precious stones. Diamonds. Rubies. Emeralds. Sapphires. He took finished rings as well. All small items. He wasn't greedy. Nothing large. All good stuff. The best.

He returned to the seventh-floor Walnut room. He stuck a stolen ring in the stiff's jacket. The police will find it. Put two and two together. Will sent his man to report the body. Will left the store through the service entrance and loading dock.

Will was wearing a brown camel overcoat. It had a button-in lining. In the lining were about forty small pockets. Twenty on either side. He looked a little bulkier than when he arrived that day. No-one noticed.

Winter in Chicago. Everyone is bundled. The night before Christmas. The service entrance is crowded with delivery workers getting last minute gifts out to their customers in the famous Marshall Field green cars. It was gently snowing. It would be a white Christmas.

Christmas day 2AM

Will is sitting in Marv's "Chicago Beat" office. Drinking coffee. Smoking a cigarette. Will cannot remember the last time he ate.

"Here's your story Marv. Run it at 6AM as an Extra and every hour thereafter. Get Phil out of his house. Send him to Field's with his camera and a reporter. Get the pics before anyone else. The Coroner will be there this morning. Get him arriving. He knows Phil will be there. He won't squawk. Here's your Extra headline."

EXTRA! EXTRA!
AL SHIRES BRUTALLY KILLED AT MARSHALL
FIELD'S. HE'S THE PRESENT NEATH THE
CHRISTMAS TREE!
Botched jewelry heist suspected as motive.
Coroner to identify body on Christmas morning.

"You know this how?"

"Just a hunch Marv. Just a hunch. Run the headline. You'll be a star! You'll get a raise. I'll see you after the holiday."

Marv did as Will suggested.

Christmas Day 10am
Marv's next headline read.

Al SHIRES DEAD - IDENTIFIED BY CORONOR.
Mutilated face. Positive I.D. New Field's wardrobe. Shopping receipts. Wallet. Hot ice. Valet Parking stub. *All* found on body. *All* dead Al's.

Newspaper updates and Extras would run all day and into the next week. Marv got a promotion. The other papers got the story out the day after Christmas. No-one knew how the <u>Chicago American</u> got the story early. Or, how the <u>American</u> knew the Coroner would go to Field's on Christmas day.

Will sent half of the jewels to Frankie via a secure courier in a Christmas chocolate box mixed among the candy. There was a note. Each letter cut out from old newspaper. Pasted on newspaper.

"When you're out (of candy)...I'm out!"

Frankie really smiled when he saw the jewels. His take on the jewels were worth over five-hundred thousand dollars. He laughed when he read the note. He grinned uncontrollably when he saw the <u>Chicago American</u> Extra! Christmas morning.

*"I'll be damned. Killed Shires. We got Shires' operation. Stole the jewels. Turned over the loot in tribute. No spotlight on us. **That Will.** I'm going to miss him."*

Marshall Field President John Shedd was so upset over the killing in his Walnut room. He never focused on the robbery. Gems he could replace. Lost customers. He could not. Bad publicity. At Christmas!

It took Shedd about two weeks to realize the Tiffany cat statue had been stolen. Its theft was never made public. Shedd could never be sure the cat's disappearance was tied to the Christmas Eve robbery. His office was locked that night. Losing the cat would be a personal embarrassment for Shedd. Better to let the matter drop quietly.

In reality. No actual harm was done to Marshall Field's or the Walnut Room's reputation. In Chicago. If anything. Their reputation was enhanced. The day after Christmas. The shoppers and eaters were back in force. The "Great Tree" remains an attraction to this very day.

Will reported for his normal work shift at the paper the day after Christmas. He stayed with the paper for the rest of his career. His days of collecting were over. He was out. He was safe.

CHAPTER 10

THE MAN IN THE NICE SUIT

"*The first neighborhood Currency Exchange in Illinois opened in 1937 to assist community residents with a variety of financial needs. Over 75 years later, the number of neighborhood Currency Exchanges has grown to more than 350... Our commitment to serving all members of each and every community has never changed.*" - Community Currency Exchange Association of Illinois. 2014

In 1937, the average cost of a new house was $4,100. A new car ran about $760. Gas was ten cents per gallon. Only one or two people on any given block owned a car. If you lived in the city of Chicago, you probably lived in an apartment.

The Great Depression progressed. Chicagoans with a few dollars needed a place to conduct simple banking transactions. Get a loan. Cash a check for a day's work. Possibly, a week's work if fortunate.

Somewhere between banks and pawn shops, currency exchanges appeared on the landscape. Currency exchange fees may have been higher than the banks. But, they were preferable to loan sharks (or worse). Perfectly legal.

Bank loans weren't always available to all citizens. Currency exchanges provided an alternative to pawn shops. You didn't have to pawn your wedding ring or pocket watch to get a loan from a currency exchange.

My Uncle Davey was a Certified Public Accountant. A CPA. Businesses have to manage their finances and pay taxes. CPAs are employed even in the worst of times. At a time when many American males were still unemployed, Davey always worked and was paid relatively well.

Aunt Helen worked crafting jewelry from silver and gold. Selling it to department stores such as Marshall Fields, Goldblatts and Wiebolts. She was good. Successful.

Dad told me Helen made him an initial ring in Sterling silver around the time he entered the Navy. A common design. I thought. Just two letters connected. The band of the ring wrapping underneath.

The ring survived the war. Damaged. The finger band cracked. I never saw him wear it. He gave it to me years later.

When I was an adult. I brought the ring to a jeweler for repair. I was assured the job would be easy. Just weld a little silver on the band to mend the crack. Come back in a few days.

Returning. The store owner approached me. Very friendly.

"We fixed your ring. Where did you get it?"

"It was my Father's. His sister. My Aunt made it. Right before World War II I believe."

"It's no ordinary ring."

"What do you mean?"

"When I first saw it, I assumed it was made by a mold. They're a dime a dozen. You can get one on e-bay or at any mall."

"And now?"

"This ring is stamped "Sterling". It's not. Well. It is. Just not one-hundred percent Sterling."

"How do you know?"

"The ring did not bend as expected when we heated the back. We took a closer look. See the small pock marks and tiny black spots on the side of

the band? That's not tarnish. We realized. This ring is a combination of Sterling silver and steel. We took a picture and sent it to one of our experts.

It turns out. Your Aunt made this ring by hand. She must have melted the steel and the silver together to harden the ring. She'd let it cool somewhat. Carved the whole thing from a solid piece of metal. This was a lot of work. Must have taken a long time. She must really have cared for your Father. This ring was made strong.

It's a one of a kind. Unique. Not valuable mind you. Rings are only worth their weight in their materials. The steel devalues the ring. Less silver you know. Still. I would think it has a high sentimental value for you. What did your Dad do in the War? How'd he break it?"

"In the Navy. He doesn't talk much about the War. I never thought to ask him about the ring. It's always been broken. Ever since he gave it to me. Thank you so much for fixing the ring. And. For telling me this history."

By the late 1930's, Davey and Helen had saved a nest egg. They saw their opportunity to fulfill an American Dream. To own their own business.

They opened a currency exchange in the western suburb of Cicero. They made a little money. Nobody cared. They opened another. They made a little more. Not a word. They opened still more currency exchanges throughout Chicagoland. They were turning a nice profit. They got noticed.

One day, Davey was visited at his currency exchange office by a middle-aged man in a nice suit. He introduced himself. The stranger did not have a discernable foreign accent. He didn't seem to have any accent at all. He wasn't a Chicagoan. Not north side. Not south side.

As Davey thought about it later, the man was non-descript. Average height. Average build. He would have been impossible to describe (to the police).

He complimented Davey on his success. He was calm and respectful. Then he politely said.

"You're going to sell your currency exchanges to my boss."

Rather naively, Davey said genuinely smiling.

"I'm not interested in selling. But, thank you for asking."

The well-dressed gentleman responded easily.

"I wasn't asking. I am telling you. We'll make you a very fair offer."

In 1937, Mario Puzo had not yet created Don Vito Corleone. This was real life. Since prohibition and its repeal, organized crime in all major cities including Chicago was out in the open. Gangsters were celebrities. Often famous business owners. They certainly were followed by name, face, and deed by the many daily newspapers.

Chicago newspapers printed a now-famous picture of Chicago Cub hall of fame catcher Gabby Hartnett signing a baseball at Wrigley Field for Al Capone and his son. When asked how he felt about Capone coming to Wrigley Field? Hartnett reportedly said.

"Why shouldn't he come to my place of business? I go to his."

Clearly Hartnett was referring to Capone. The respectful tavern or speakeasy proprietor. Not Capone. The cold-blooded killer and widow maker.

The newspaper ran the photo of Al Capone at Wrigley Field. It could have been Clark Gable or Charles Lindbergh in the picture. It was Al Capone. Most people of the day were used to reconciling the balance between good and bad in their public celebrities. Gangsters. Actors. Politicians. Pilots. Athletes. Millionaires. They all bled together.

A little unsure of himself and the situation, Uncle Davey kindly said.

"No thank you."

The gentleman replied calmly.

"We'll make our offer clear to you in a few days."

He turned and left.

Uncle Davey and Aunt Helen had two sons. My first cousins are considerably older than me. They were in grade school in the late 1930's.

About a week after the suited gentleman met Uncle Davey at the currency exchange, my cousins came home from school. Each was carrying a hand-written note.

They each said a nice man in a suit gave them some candy and their note as they were walking home after school. The sons each said that the man had kindly asked that they deliver the notes to their Father. Nothing unfriendly or threatening occurred. The sons did not panic when they met the stranger. They gladly accepted the candy. It was a different time. The notes were identical. The notes both read.

"It is time to accept our offer."

Think about the world they lived in. It might have taken a while. Uncle Davey now understood who the man in the suit was. Understood for whom he worked. Understood the consequences of not accepting. Uncle Davey and Aunt Helen agreed. They accepted. Payments were made. Deeds were signed and transferred. Lawyers were involved. It was all very legal.

They sold their apartment home too. Uncle Davey and Aunt Helen left the only city they had ever lived in. The only American city their immigrant parents had ever lived in. The only city where their relatives and friends lived. The only city that housed the only Synagogue they had ever attended. The only city where they had ever gone to school or worked. The only city their children had ever known friends.

And they moved. They moved two-thousand miles away to the Los Angeles suburb of Glendale. They would have moved farther away. The Pacific Ocean prevented this. No one in Glendale knew Uncle Davey and Aunt Helen or their two sons when they moved in. They never saw the man in the nice suit again.

The sons grew up. One was a pioneer in the computer industry. One owned a garage and fixed cars. At first glance, these two careers might not seem similar. Take a deeper look. Both required significant aptitude with complex inanimate objects.

Neither career required social skills nor personal interaction to succeed.

Neither son knew why they moved. Ever. Neither truly made new friends as children or adults. Neither married. Neither had children of their own.

The Glendale house was beautiful. It was in a beautiful neighborhood. The weather was beautiful. Nothing like a Chicago apartment or the crowded neighborhood they missed dearly. It was safe.

Uncle Davey returned to Chicago occasionally for business. He didn't stay long. Aunt Helen returned to Chicago in 1952. Only for a short visit. Only to attend her brother Bernie's wedding. The wedding of my Dad and Mom. Davey was the best man. He wore a nice suit that day.

When Will and my Grandma Goldie retired to Glendale in the mid-1950's, Aunt Helen, Uncle Davey, and their family had already been there over a decade. It took me years before I recognized and contemplated the ironic nature (karma?) of Will's story in comparison to that of Aunt Helen and Uncle Davey.

Will of course being Helen's Father earned his future ease of retirement in Glendale working for the very same questionable human element that made Helen's childhood comfortable during the Great Depression. Then drove Helen and Davey out of Chicago and on to Glendale years later.

I doubt neither Will nor Helen ever gave a thought to this unusual coincidence. Actually, it's more likely Helen and Davey never knew about Will's past. Helen was sheltered I doubt Goldie even knew. Dad knew. On the other hand. Davey had his own secret. Even Bernie did not know.

CHAPTER 11

SANTA CATALINA ISLAND

The Days Leading Up to December 7ᵗʰ. Pearl Harbor Day

While scared out of their minds (and city). The forced buy-out of the currency exchanges left Davey and Helen with a tidy sum in 1937 terms. Money actually was not an issue. They no longer had to work.

Helen went back to making jewelry. Her business floundered until Will and Goldie moved to the west coast. Whenever it seemed like the jewelry business would not survive, Will seemed to find a gem of extraordinary value.

He always said he spent his spare time perusing the antique stores and hock shops. Just got lucky. Just a hunch. Helen knew jewelry. Will's finds were amazing. The sale of one ring with a Will gem provided her more income than the rest of her annual sales combined. How did he do it? Just lucky she thought.

Too young to retire. Davey busied himself with temporary accounting side-jobs. With his ample leisure time, Davey traveled the Los Angeles area. One sporting event after another.

Pacific Coast baseball. He particularly enjoyed when the San Francisco Seals came to town. Managed by Lefty O'Doul. They brought young stars like Dominic DiMaggio and Ferris Fain.

Horse racing at Santa Anita. He saw Seabiscuit lose in a photo fin-ish. Golf. Bing Crosby and Bob Hope hob-knobbing with Sammy Snead and Byron Nelson.

The United States was climbing out of the Great Depression. War was raging in Europe and the Pacific. In his unprecedented third term as President, Franklin D. Roosevelt was slowly moving the psyche of the country from entrenched isolationism to neutral-ity to the eventuality of war.

The term "political correctness" had not yet been coined. It existed without name. Politicians and corporation owners alike faced many complex considerations before the War. Personal self-interest. Public patriotism. Religious affiliation. Religious bias. Private vs. public political beliefs. Delicate balances.

The elite watched as Roosevelt recalled Ambassador Joseph Kennedy from England in 1940. Kennedy. Boston-Irish. Self-made. Rich. Politically connected. Powerful. Alleged bootleg-ger. Assumed Wall Street wolf. Film maker. President maker? Professed isolationist. Appeaser?

They watched Charles Lindbergh. The most famous, admired, and revered American of the early twentieth century. Possibly more popular than Babe Ruth. By preaching "America First" and isolationism, Lindbergh appeared to be losing his mass appeal. Worse he didn't seem to be appeasing Nazi Germany. He seemed to admire them. His influence waned.

The winds of public opinion could do more than impact base-ball or movie box-office ticket sales. If the noise were negative. If the noise were loud enough. **If**, the Senators and Congressmen feared reprisals at the polls. An elite's public misstep could pre-vent the Defense Department from investing in their company or ruin a career or a business.

While the rich were contemplating the fates of country, world, **and** themselves, Davey, Helen, and their sons were settled in Glendale. Leading a rather routine life in California.

Two Months After Pearl Harbor - 1942 February Catalina Island.

No suit nor tie today. Dressed in a heavy dark argyle sweater. Davey wore a lambs-wool overcoat. The trip on the ferry would be chilly (and bumpy). He carried a black grip. Packed with enough clothes for two days. A nice suit for dinner tonight. His baseball glove. Davey wore dark tortoise shell glasses. Round frames and thick lenses.

Davey was a moderate build. About five-seven. Not fat nor thin. Straight black hair nicely combed. Until. The ocean wind blew. Normally, Davey never carried more than ten dollars. On this trip. He had two-hundred. He was buzzing with excitement.

Davey left his Glendale home promptly at 7:30AM. He had set his alarm clock the night before. He didn't need it. He was up by 6AM. He drove his sensible dark blue Oldsmobile Ninety-Eight hard-top, four-door sedan to Los Angeles Pier 31. He boarded a 9:30AM shuttle ferry. Bound for Avalon on Catalina Island. Arrived on time. 11AM.

Davey took a taxi to the Saint Catherine's Hotel. The center-piece of Avalon. The host hotel of the spring training Chicago Cubs. It was luxurious.

He dropped his bags at the hotel. Ran to see the Cubs practice. By now, many of the Cubs knew Davey. He'd been an annual regular. He swelled with pride when a Cub player or coach spoke to him.

This excursion had been a ritual for Davey since he arrived in Glendale. He'd spend the day watching the Cubs practice. Stay one night at the hotel. Chat with the team. Writers. Occasional celebrities. Watch practice the next day. Take the last shuttle ferry back to Los Angeles at 6PM. Home by 8:30PM.

Helen thought him a big child. Davey didn't care. He took photos. Home movies. He came home each trip with signed baseballs, photos, postcards, souvenirs, and baseball magazines for his boys (and himself). He was a big fan. Waived his pennant while they practiced. Even kept score if they had an inter-squad game.

This year. Slugger Jimmie Foxx was in camp with the Cubs. Old "Double X". Next to Babe Ruth. The greatest home run hitter baseball had ever produced. Part of the 1929 A's team that beat up on Davey's Cubs in the World Series.

Yankee pitcher Lefty Gomez once called him *"the Beast"*. On this day, Jimmie did not look very beastly. He looked hung over. His typically bulging muscles looked a little soft. Certainly, he was stronger than anyone else in camp. But, he was moving slowly. Almost glassy eyed. Waiving at ground balls. Watching pop ups. Barely hitting batting practice out of the infield. Not a good sign. Oh well. It was still early. Davey was sure he'd come around.

Davey meandered back to the hotel at 2PM. The morning practice was completed. The ball players stayed behind at the field for a team meeting with manager Jimmie Wilson. This was a quiet time. Davey realized he was hungry. Hadn't thought about food in the excitement of spring training.

Davey ate at the hotel coffee counter. Enjoyed a meatloaf sandwich. French fried potatoes. Apple Pie. A cherry Coke.

There were very few people around. A couple of booths had groups. Probably fans like him. One booth in the back by the bathroom door had a good-sized group. Waitresses were flying in and out of the kitchen to serve them. A lot of attention.

Davey did not pay the busy table much attention. He happily ate his meal. Thought about his afternoon activities. Get back to the practice field about 2PM. The Cubs should be active by then. Maybe they would let him play catch.

Done eating. Davey paid his check. Eighty-five cents. More than he would have paid for the same meal at Andrew's Café in Glendale. It was worth it to be at the Saint Catherine's. He left a fifty-cent tip. This was a large tip for lunch.

Davey wasn't typically extravagant nor was he so wealthy he could afford to burn money. He was aware that the Saint Catherine's hosted the rich and elite. He was not going to be a second-class citizen. Not on his one night of indulgence.

There was something else. Davey was aware. Jewish people had the reputation for being cheap. He disdained this notion. He belonged in any class. With any denomination. He paid his way. No-one would say he was "cheap". That was important to Davey. He was about to discover something else important.

CHAPTER 12

"THE BIG THREE" PLUS ONE:
ADAMS, FRANKLIN, JEFFERSON...
AND *WILSON*?

A few minutes to go before he left for practice. Davey thought it wise to use the hotel restaurant bathroom before he departed. In the back. By the busy table. A white door. It was locked. Occupied. Davey waited outside of the door. He had a full view of the busy table. He recognized each. He observed.

Louis B. Mayer in a crisp dark suit and tie. Smoking a cigarette. Clutching a cigarette lighter. MGM. Metro-Goldwyn-Mayer. Three names on the company letterhead. One iron-fisted ruler. Louis B. Mayer. MGM employed Leo the Lion to introduce its movies. *"Roar!"* MGM boasted their stable presented "more stars than in heaven".

Lana Turner sitting next to Louis B. Mayer. Very little make up. Pink wool sweater. Pearl necklace. Charm bracelet. Grey skirt. Drinking a milk shake. She is ravishing in her natural state.

Legend has it. A sixteen-year-old Hollywood High School truant named Julia Turner was discovered in 1937. In a malt shop on Sunset Boulevard. Sipping a Coca-Cola at the lunch counter. Wearing a simple sweater. Renamed Lana Turner. Mayer selected

Turner to succeed recently deceased Jean Harlow as the nation's next sex symbol. This would make her twenty-one now.

Spencer Tracy sitting next to Katherine Hepburn. They are sharing a bottle of Jameson Irish-Whiskey. Both are wearing plaid golfer's pants with matching cardigan sweaters. Slowing smoking cigarettes. Relaxed. In a hurry to go nowhere. Smiling.

Ingrid Bergman sitting next to Humphrey Bogart. Ingrid Bergman wears a tan blazer with a low-cut beige silk blouse underneath. Around her neck. A small gold cross on chain. Intentionally sexy. She is nursing a vodka and lime. She continues to look back and forth from her drink to Humphrey Bogart. She appears to want to be somewhere else.

Humphrey Bogart is wearing a sailor's polo shirt and blue blazer. A red ascot. He is drinking a beer. Chain smoking. Checking his Hamilton doctor's wristwatch a little too frequently. He too appears to want to be elsewhere.

Howard Hughes. Khakis. Blue Gant broadcloth button down shirt. He reminds Davey of Clark Gable in "Red Dust". Owner of RKO studios. Hughes Aircraft. A number of other profitable industries. Wealthy industrialist. Future recluse. Howard Hughes was very much a public figure in 1942.

Hughes liked to fly his own airplanes between Washington DC, Las Vegas, and Los Angeles. He was handsome. A dare-devil. Set speed records. Often escorted by a starlet. Sometimes, Katherine Hepburn.

Last. Phillip K. Wrigley. An apparent college professor. Smoking a pipe. Engaged in conversation. A book at his side. Recently published. "Berlin Diary" by William Shirer. Known as PK to his friends and the media.

His Father William Wrigley passed away in 1932. PK Inherited the Wrigley Empire. Gum Company. Real estate. The Chicago Cubs. Along with the Cubs, the Los Angeles Angels minor-league baseball team.

As the Cubs' owner. The Chicago press and public thought PK to be disengaged. Inept. As an international-conglomerate-corporation owner. Operating in privacy. PK was brilliant.

PK also inherited an island. His Father purchased Santa Catalina Island in 1921. Better known simply as Catalina. One of eight Channel Islands in the Pacific. Twenty miles off the coast of Los Angeles.

William Wrigley turned the Catalina city of Avalon into a first-class resort. He began the tradition of bringing his Chicago Cubs to Catalina each February for spring training. A practice which PK continued.

The table was quietly having two or three separate conversations. Davey was a respectful person. He would not disturb this august group. Wouldn't ask for a photo or autograph. He smiled politely when they looked his way. He bided his time waiting for the restroom to un-occupy.

As he waited. He heard Howard Hughes and PK Wrigley discussing a tax issue. As it so happened, it was a tax question. He knew the answer. It was an employee issue he'd faced when owning the currency exchanges.

Deciding discretion was the better part of valor. He decided not to interrupt. The restroom door opened. An older gentleman walked out. Davey walked in. A few Moments later. He was done. Exited the rest room.

As he walked past the busy table, a fountain pen fell in his direction. He bent down. Scooped up the pen. Turned. Handed it to Howard Hughes. The pen was plated in real ivory. Real engraved gold. It likely cost three-hundred dollars. Maybe more. In a deep voice. Howard Hughes spoke.

"Thank you."

Davey would not have spoken first. Now he was engaged. He couldn't help himself. He couldn't help aiding others. Even a celebrity. He speaks with ease. As though he were speaking with a college class-mate.

"My pleasure. The tax law you want to execute is U.S. Government Statute Section 11, Sub-section tax code 3.5. It's from 1933. Roosevelt passed it with the New Deal alphabet agencies. Following his first election. It's never been repealed. Employees have more rights. But, so do employers. Most business owners don't know the sub-section exists – for employers."

He smiled. Shrugged an apologetic shrug. That was it. He walked away. Howard Hughes stared at him. So did Louis B. Mayer. The others paid no attention.

Davey walked back to the coffee counter to collect his hat and coat. As he turned to leave. There was Howard Hughes. He was so close. Davey bumped into him as he turned.

"We're you listening to us?"

"No. Well. Yes. Not intentionally. I was just waiting. I guess I heard you. Not many people talk about tax codes. Not here. It caught my ears. I'm sorry. I shouldn't have said anything. It's none of my business. I'll leave you now."

"No. It's OK. Would you like to join our table?"

I would venture to guess that ninety-nine percent of all Americans in 1942 would have screamed *"**yes**!!!"* to that question. Davey hesitated.

*"Well. I **really** want to get back to see the Cubs. It's my special trip."*

Howard Hughes smiled. He wasn't used to be being told "no." On the other hand. This was an honest man. Not star-struck. At least not by money, power, or beauty. Maybe by the Cubs?

"Come sit with us for fifteen minutes. Meet our table. If you want to leave afterward. No problem. We could use your help. Please?"

Davey didn't know Howard Hughes. Only recognized him. If he **had** known him. He'd have known. Howard Hughes **never** said "please". Never asked for help. From anyone. **EVER!** He was asking Davey. He nodded. Followed Howard Hughes to his table. Half way there. Howard Hughes stops. Turns back to Davey.

"I almost forgot. What's your name?"

"David. My friends call me Davey. Please call me Davey."

"OK Davey. Let's go."

"All. I'd like you to meet my new friend. Davey. He's over to watch the Cubs for a few days. I've asked him to sit with us for a while. Would you each be good enough to introduce yourselves?"

As Howard Hughes was pulling a chair up for Davey. Louis B. Mayer did not hesitate.

"Maybe you know me? I'm Louis B. Mayer."

"Yes of course sir."

"My travelling companion today is Miss Lana Turner."

"Nice to meet you Miss Turner."

"The same I'm sure."

"Next to Lana is Spencer Tracy and Ingrid Bergman. They just finished "Dr. Jekyl and Mr. Hyde" with Lana. Did you see it? Did you like it?"

"I did see it."

Turning to the actors and actresses.

"I did see it. I did like it. Very much. Very exciting. A little scary."

They smiled. He wasn't gushing. They believed him. They were genuinely happy. Louis B. Mayer continued.

"Next to 'Spenc' is Kate Hepburn. On her side is Humphrey Bogart. Kate and 'Spenc' are working on a new film. 'Woman of the Year'. It should be a blockbuster. Putting these two together. They've got chemistry. Don't they? Just look at them."

The table appears to suddenly look a little uncomfortable when Louis B. Mayer introduces Katherine Hepburn and Spencer Tracy. Davey addresses the table.

Congratulations on your new movie. I'm sure it will be excellent. I can't wait to see it. Mr. Bogart. I thought you were wonderful in "The Maltese Falcon." So was Mary Astor. Great book. Great movie.

In a polite yet taciturn voice, Humphrey Bogart replies.

"Thank you. You're very kind. What brings you out here?"

"I'm a Cubs fan. I'm here to see the Cubs."

*"No. I sense you're not from California. Nobody is actually from California. Where are **you** from? Somewhere in the Midwest? Cubs fan."*

"That's right. Chicago. Born and raised."

"What brings you to California? Besides the Cubs I mean."

Davey has been very friendly. His smile vanquishes. He looks down at his shoes. He slowly replies. Softly.

"My health. I came to California for the waters."

Bogart frowns. Reacts.

"The waters? What waters? California is a desert."

"I was misinformed."

The table is silent. Bogart is pensive. The table can see that. He speaks.

"Say. That's a good line. 'I came here for the waters'. 'I was misinformed.' That's good. Very good. Mind if I use that in my next movie? What do you think Ingy?"

Ingrid Bergman nods. Strains to smile. She wasn't paying attention. Davey goes on.

"Actually. I had to…"

He stops. Rephrases.

"I sold our family business."

Tries to smile. It's weak. Continues.

"Made a killing. I'm retired. Brought the family out where it is warm. Glendale. Just a few years ago."

His voice trails off. PK steps into the lull. In a very friendly direct voice.

"I seem to be the only one LM didn't introduce."

He rises. Extends his hand to shake. Davey accepts his hand and shakes. He's happy to change the subject.

"I'm Phil Wrigley. My friends call me PK."

"*Yes sir. I know who you are. I go to your park. Root for your Cubs. Root for the Angels. Chew your gum. I'm a big fan. A big customer I suppose.*"

PK smiles and sits.

"*That leaves me. I'm Howard Hughes. I dabble in a few things. Movies. TWA. This and that.*"

"*Yes Mr. Hughes. I know.*"

"*Call me Howard.*"

"*Yes sir. Ur. Howard.*"

Louis B. Mayer addresses the table.

"*We'd like to have a few Moments with David. Do you think you can find something to occupy your time?*"

Davey watches. Humphrey Bogart stands. Doesn't acknowledge the others. Not a word. Walks out first. Never looks back. Leaves the hotel.

Ingrid Bergman watches Humphrey Bogart with a blank look. Just shakes her head. She says aloud to nobody in particular.

"*Ach. This is the last time I follow a man to an island to make love.*"

She rises and leaves. Heads to the hotel elevator. Lana Turner moves to another booth. She'll wait for Mr. Mayer.

Katherine Hepburn is smiling. So is Spencer Tracy. They seem to rise as one. They walk out together. Davey isn't sure. He thinks he sees the two holding hands. Spencer Tracy has the bottle of Jameson in his other hand. They walk up the lobby staircase together.

This leaves PK. Howard Hughes. Louis B. Mayer. And, Davey. All sitting at the table.

There is an uncomfortable silence (for Davey). It lasts about fifteen seconds. Howard Hughes speaks first.

"*Davey. Let me tell you why we asked you to join us. Would you like that?*"

"*Yes Mr. Hughes.*"

"*Please call me Howard.*"

"*OK. Howard.*"

"That's fine. Now. We think you can help us in a business... Let's say a business venture. Before we discuss that. We'd like to ask you a few questions. Would that be OK?"

"I think so. I'm not sure how I can help you. What would you like to know?"

PK: *"Tell us really. Why did you come to California?"*

"As I said. I sold my business. I thought it was a good time to move."

Feeling uncomfortable. Davey is choosing his words carefully. Howard Hughes knows Louis B. Mayer will intimidate him. Interrogate him. He wants the conversation to stay light and easy.

HH: *"What kind of business was it?"*

"I owned a few currency exchanges."

PK: *"In Chicago? How many?"*

"Twenty-three."

Howard Hughes whistles.

LM: *"And you sold them? You are a young man. Are you ill? Your wife? Your children? I assume you have a wife and children. You said 'family' before. Are they well?"*

"Yes sir. One wife. Two boys. All well."

LM: *"Were the currency exchanges failing? Were you losing money? Did you have to get out? You know. In debt?"*

"No sir."

His voice is rising.

LM: *"Let me get this straight..."*

Howard Hughes cuts him off.

HH: *"We'll get back to that Louie. Davey. What did you do before you owned the currency exchanges?"*

"I'm an accountant by trade. A CPA."

HH: *"That's why you know tax law."*

"Yes."

PK: *"How did you come to get involved with currency exchanges?"*

"I wanted to own my own business. Tired of counting other people's money I guess. Follow the American dream. You know.

In the mid-1930's, the U.S. government created a new type of financial institution. The currency exchange. They help people that can't go to banks. That's a lot of Americans. I didn't have enough money to start a bank. Didn't want to. This was perfect. I scraped together my capital. Opened my first store. Took the profit. Opened a second. Kept going. We were a hit."

Davey was talking. He didn't realize he had stood. He was smiling as he described the currency exchange business he founded and built. Than. Small tear drops formed in his eyes. He took a deep breath. He stopped talking. He looked down at his shoes. With a heavy look on his face.

"The Cubs. The Cubs are practicing. I think I should leave now. It was a pleasure meeting each of you."

PK reached across the table. Gently grabbed Davey's arm.

PK: *"Son. I **own** the Chicago Cubs. I'll make sure you don't miss any of the action. I'll make em' practice in your back yard if I want to. **Understand?**"*

"Not really. What is it you want with me?"

HH: *"We're almost there Davey. Hang in there with us. Tell us. We want to know. Why did you really sell your business?"*

I guess it is sometimes easier to tell a stranger a difficult thing than a loved one. Only his nuclear family knew about the man in the nice suit. Will. Goldie. Bernie. Didn't know. Bernie was his best friend. Bernie thinks he just up and left with his sister and money for better weather. His feelings were hurt when they left. Quietly. He spoke the first words he'd been holding in these past years.

"I had to."

Gently.

PK: *"Tell us why Davey."*

"There was a man…My children…Our family…"

Davey related the whole story. It took about a half hour. He was talking to three of the richest and most powerful men in America.

They hung on every word. Davey thought. Certainly, **they** were never bullied. Davey felt ashamed.

LB: *"You've never told anyone this story before?*

"No sir."

LB: *"Is it true? All of it? I'm going to check. I have J. Edgar Hoover's personal phone number. The FBI. You know them?"*

For the first time, mild mannered Davey is angry. And scared. Speaking quickly.

"Yes. __Yes it's true__. Oh my God. You're going to tell the FBI? What is this? What have I done? If they go after the people I sold my business to, those monsters will come after me. They'll come after my family. They'll think I took their money. Ratted them out. I moved to California to get away. __Why are you asking me these questions?__"

Davey was frantic. Yelling at the end.

IIII: *"Shut up LM. You're not calling Hoover. Hell. We've all got his phone number. Stop scaring the man."*

Calmly.

PK: *"You've never told anyone? The police? How about a private detective? Did you tell any of them? Anyone in law enforcement?"*

"No sir. Nobody. Other than Helen and my children. You're the first. Probably the last."

HH: *"Thank you. Thank you for sharing your story. It was important for us to hear it."*

"Why?"

HH: *"We needed to know that you are not famous. Or wanted by the law. Or wanted by gangsters. Not on the run.*

We needed to know we could trust you. We needed to know you are a man that can keep a secret. Forever if need be. We needed to know that you are a man of honesty and integrity. A modest man. Not searching the limelight.

We think you are all of those good things. We can see you are ashamed for giving in to the mobsters. Do not be ashamed. You are a brave man. You put your family ahead of money. You are a good man Davey."

"*Thank you.*"

HH: "*Here is our story. It is not a coincidence that you find us here. The actors and actresses are here as a disguise. They do not know. If the public sees us together here with them as you did, they assume we are here to discuss movie plots and watch a little baseball. Possibly have a little clandestine fun. Isn't that what you thought?*"

"*Yes. I suppose so.*"

PK: "*What if you saw LB, myself, and Howard here without the actors? Think for a Moment. What would you **really** think?*"

"*That's a good question. I imagine I would think you are putting together some sort of deal. A merger. An investment of some sort.*"

LB: "*Good Davey. Fine. Fine. You are right. That's what people would think. Next question. Who comes to spring training? Who **besides** the players and their families? Think boy.*"

Davey paused a Moment. The other three liked his thoughtful consideration. Not a guesser. Not impulsive. A thinker.

"*The newspapers. The press. The writers. The Movie-olas for the theatre news shorts.*"

The conversation was moving faster now. With excitement.

HH: "*And what happens if the press photographs us together? Writes stories about us? Films us?*"

"*Publicity. Speculation I suppose. Stock fluxuations? Deals could die. Competitors could get envious. Suspicious.*"

PK: "*Your almost there Davey. Who else might become suspicious?*"

Davey thought. He had nothing.

"*I don't know. Our government? Worried about monopolies?*"

Beaming with pride.

HH: "*A very good guess. Almost. Not our government. Foreign governments.*"

"*But why should they care about…*"

He looked around the table.

"I mean no offense. Why should a foreign government care about you three? Two movie studio owners and a gum maker? I apologize. Really I do."

Mayer frowns. Wrigley and Hughes smile.

PK: *"It's OK Davey. We appreciate your honesty. You came through our questions with flying colors. You have a keen grasp of perception. **And**, reality."*

"Perception? Reality?

LM: *"Perception. Two movie studio executives and a Gum seller."*

HH: *"Reality. The three of us own the lion's share of raw materials in the United States. Darn near in the world I guess. Chewing Gum is just a step away from rubber. My engineering company runs on steel. Aluminum. Tin. Copper. You name it. We own it. All those movies. All those records. Where do you think plastic and celluloid come from?*

"Oil."

HH: *"Smart man. Why are all of these materials going to be in demand?*

"The war."

PK: *"That's right Davey. We're going to blow Japan into kingdom come. We are going to drive the Germans and the Italians out of Europe."*

Tracking right along. Davey adds.

*"You'll make money **and** protect your assets at the same time."*

HH: *"**That's the plan**. Patriotic. Free market society! When it's all done. We might have to rid the world of those red communist Russians too. I tell you what. Hoover and I are going to rid Hollywood of those SOBs. I can tell you that."*

LM: *"Stay on topic Howard."*

Now Louis B. Mayer is the voice of reason. Davey asks.

How do you keep the world from knowing? Your companies are world famous?"

PK: *"In a word. We're all very much 'layered'."*

"Layered?"

PK: *"Layered. We have our publicly held companies. We have our companies which we make public. Not the same thing. Our companies own companies. Different names. Different countries. Different assets. Hard to track. Hard to trace. Not illegal. Just hidden. Understand?"*

"I do."

Davey was smart. He really did understand.

HH: *"Davey. Who are the "Big Three?"*

"1929 Cubs. Our 'Murderer's Row'. Rogers Hornsby, Hack Wilson, Riggs Stephenson. Each drove in over one-hundred RBIs. So did Kiki Cuyler. Big four?"

Impressed with his own knowledge of Cub's trivia. Davey is beaming. Howard Hughes and his colleagues are not smiling. Davey sees this.

A little flustered.

HH: *"Cubs? RBIs? What? No. Not close. Please try again. **Think.**"*

"Ford. GM. Chrysler?"

HH: *"Getting there. Try again."*

"Roosevelt. Churchill. Stalin?"

Slightly smiling.

HH: *"Nope. Closer. Try again. Last chance. Take a Moment. Think hard."*

It's as though you can actually see Davey's brain straining. The silence at the table is not uncomfortable. The table is willing to wait. Davey is looking at his hosts. One by one. Back and forth. He is saying to himself. Barely aloud.

"Big three? Big three? Big three?"

Pause. He's excited. He's got it. He slams his hand on the table. He looks at each as he says their names. Rising from his seat.

"Big Three!" Mayer! Hughes! Wrigley! Big Three!"

HH: *"**Now** you've got it."*

LM: *"We've been dancing around it. Here it is. We're working for FDR. President Roosevelt. Directly. No intermediary from his cabinet or*

*the military. No-one can know. He has enemies at home as well as abroad.
We may be well off, to say the least. But, we're Americans **damn it!***

*We've spent our lives building our fortunes. We're all immigrants too.
Or came from immigrants. This is our country. We'll be damned if we'll
hand it over to the Nazis or the Commies, or the Japs or anyone else.*

*We meet here to discuss our plans. Nobody gets suspicious. If we get
filmed. We're just out with our movie stars. PK's with the Cubs. Hell, he
owns the island. No-one thinks twice.*

*We're quietly re-tooling our plants to go to war. We're buying the re-
sources abroad. Both for us. And, to keep them out of the hands of the Axis
and the Commies.*

*We need an intermediary. We need one person we trust. We need you.
We need you to be the go-between the three of us when we can't meet. We
need you to deliver personal reports to FDR. Not over the phone.*

*You'll be on my payroll. As far as the outside world knows, you'll work
for MGM. You're an accountant in the movie industry. It will mean some
travel. Your family will understand your cover story. You may **never** tell
them the truth. Even after the mission is done. I assure you nothing we
will ask you to do will be illegal."*

PK: *"We'll provide a way for you to reach us when you need to.
Meetings will be arranged. The war is going to take about four years. We
are **going to win**.*

*We have the natural resources. The three of us will see to that. We need
a quiet go between now. Out of the public eye. That's where you come in.*

*Today. The country still needs the resolve to fight. FDR will see to that.
You will be a hero. But, only you and we will know. It could be dangerous.
You'll never have any glory. No war record. We'll see that you are deferred
for medical reasons. You'll be paid well.*

*We are powerful men. We will protect your family for the rest of your
lives. We'll be watching. You won't even notice us. We'll be there. No-one
can ever hurt you. You'll never be scared again. Never ashamed.*

Howard Hughes jumps in. He is standing. Exhorting.
Transfixed. Loud. Forceful.

HH: *"We three. We are Adams, Franklin, and Jefferson in support of Roosevelt! Our Washington! We see America. We see the future. You'll be on the right side. The American side. We need you to be our James Wilson.*

Hughes is yelling. He's completely in his own world now. Loses a little steam. Recovers. Davey has chills. He is mesmerized. Listening intently. Asks.

"James Wilson?"

In a firm voice. Softer now.

HH: *"Yes Davey. James Wilson. An anonymous signer of the Declaration of Independence. A Judge. No grand place in history. Not in any text books. Continental Congress. He represented the state of Pennsylvania.*

Sat between British loyalist John Dickenson and true American Benjamin Franklin. He worked behind the scenes to defeat Dickenson. Delivered Pennsylvania. Assured all thirteen colonies would unanimously ratify the Declaration. A true American hero. You'll be __our__ James Wilson."

"I didn't know."

HH: *Are you in?"*

Not smiling. Deadpan. Monotone.

LM: *"Or, do we have to kill you now?"*

Davey's eyes are big as saucers.

HH: *"Oh. Louie's just kidding. Right Louie? You are in. __Right__ Davey?"*

They all smile at Davey. They say in unison.

"Or will we have to kill you?"

It is the proudest day of Davey's life. Never scared again. The American side.

"I see what you see. I will be your Wilson. I'm in."

HH: *"Go watch the Cubs Davey. Enjoy yourself. Your hotel and meals will be paid for. See something in the hotel store. Take it home. PK's got the tab covered. Every year you come out from now on. Go home tomorrow as planned. We'll know how to reach you. Don't worry. An agent of MGM will be in touch with you in about a week."*

Davey leaves the three as he is told. He wanders through the lobby. Out to watch the rest of practice. He is in a fog. Back at the busy table.

LM: *"You laid it on pretty thick there."*

Howard Hughes does not respond. He is transfixed by his own words and emotion. He is in another place. PK looks on.

LM: *"**I said**. **Howard!** You really sold that hard."*

Howard Hughes snaps back. As though he was just snapped out of a trance by an illusionist.

HH: *"I meant **every** word."*

LM: *"You're some actor. Maybe you should work for me."*

Serious.

HH: *"I own RKO. I work for nobody but myself."*

LM: *"Is that James Wilson crap true?"*

HH: *"Every word. Ask your buddy J. Edgar Hoover."*

LM: *"How do you know?"*

HH: *"I am a true American!"*

Louis B. Mayer just stared in disbelief.

PK: *"OK gentlemen. I think we got what we came for."*

They disburse.

It all worked exactly as described. Davey never saw the three together except at Catalina or an occasional movie screening in Chicago. Actors, actresses, or ball players were always in attendance. Davey was invisible. The press saw him at each public event. No-one noticed or asked his name.

Davey never told a single person. His work was invaluable. His family never knew. The war took just under four years. Exactly as PK had predicted that day in Avalon.

I only visited Davey and Helen's Glendale home once. By then, they were retired and quite happy with their home and lives.

My favorite room in the house was Uncle Davey's den. Cushy leather chairs and plump sofas. Bookshelves. Baseball pennants. Signed baseballs. Programs. Stuff was **everywhere**.

A framed forty-eight star American flag hung on the wall. It was signed.

"To David. I could not have "walked" without you.
Thank you!
Franklin Delano Roosevelt Washington D.C. 1939"

Autographed photos on every part of the walls. Each personally inscribed to Davey.

"The same I'm sure.
Your Bunny, Lana Turner" (Pictured as Bunny Smith in "Weekend at the Waldorf")
"All 'Gloamin' without you, Gabby Hartnett Chicago Cubs – Catalina 1940"
"We'll always have Catalina, Humphrey Bogart" (Pictured as Rick Blaine in "Casablanca")
"To the greatest Cubs and Angels fan, PK Wrigley"
"You're a great American! Come fly with me! Howard Hughes"
"You outta be in pictures, Louis B. Mayer"
"Davey, Not much meat on you, but what's there is 'cherce". Spencer Tracy" (Pictured as Mike Conovan in "Pat and Mike")
"Davey. You'll always be on my pedestal, Katherine Hepburn" (Pictured as Tracy Lord in "The Philadelphia Story")
"Bless you Davey, Ingrid Bergman" (Pictured as Saint Joan of Arc in "Joan of Arc")

There were many more. Athletes. Movie stars. Politicians. The room was like a museum. I was so impressed. Everything seemed so personal. Uncle Davey was being modest. Or, not telling me the whole story.

*"Uncle Davey, this is amazing. How do you know all of these people? They seem **very** fond of you."*

"Oh you know. You live in a town long enough, you meet a few people. Just acquaintances. See these trinkets on my shelf? This ivory and gold pen belonged to Howard Hughes. The lighter. Louis B. Mayer. The pipe. PK Wrigley. All were gifts.

I have something for you. I'd like you to take it home with you."

Davey took a book off the shelf. It had been next to the pen, pipe, and lighter. He handed me the book. "Coming Through – A Book of Sports for Boys." Copyright 1927. The inside page is autographed.

This book belongs to:
Bernard
"The Rajah"
4205 Gladys Ave. Chicago

It was Dads. He was six in 1927. Dad had given the book to Helen. Helen gave it to Davey. Davey kept it all these years with his most treasured mementos.

Davey saw Bernie when he came through San Diego during the War. He missed his best friend. He couldn't tell him why he left Chicago. Couldn't tell him why he stayed in California. Bernie loved Davey too. He accepted things as they were.

BOOK TWO

The Greatest Generation
Comes of Age

"*Never* let the fear of striking out keep you from coming up to bat."

- Babe Ruth

"*Never, never, never give up!*"

- **Winston Churchill**

CHAPTER 1

THE RAJAH IS DEPRESSED

On April 7, 1896. Benjamin Leiner was born on the lower east side of Manhattan, New York. Twenty-one years later in 1917. Leiner, Or Benny Leonard as he was now called, defeated Freddy Marsh to earn the World Lightweight Championship. Leonard defended and retained his Lightweight championship well into the 1920's.

The greatest Jewish boxer of all time. Leonard is on every writer's all-time greatest "pound for pound" boxer list. He shares space with the likes of Joe Louis, Sugar Ray Robinson, Rocky Marciano, and Muhammad Ali.

April. 1921. Will and Goldie name their blue-eyed baby boy Bernard Leonard. Unlike other religious groups, Jewish people traditionally only name their children in memory of the dead. You will rarely see a Jewish boy named for his living Father with a designation of Junior. Had Benny Leonard been dead, Bernie would have been named Benny. But Leonard was very much alive **and** World Champion.

Today. Naming my Dad Bernard Leonard might not seem like an act of heresy against Judaism. In 1921. **It was**. It was a statement. Will made it known. Bernie was named for a Jewish champion. Will exhorted Bernie.

"Stand up and fight.
If you don't defend yourself, no-one else will.
Stand up for those that can't defend themselves.
Be afraid of no-one.
Be your own person."

Will was proud of Judaism at a time when most Jews were scared or apologetic. Henry Ford demonstrated that it was an era of open anti-Semitism. Many Jews changed or shortened their names. The simple naming of my Dad put a brand on my Father he would wear proudly till his dying day. Dad **wasn't** named to mourn the dead. He **was** named to honor the living. He would be different.

Chicago's Soldier Field was erected during the 1920's. Named to honor the fallen soldiers of past American wars. Sitting in Grant Park. On the shore of Lake Michigan. Stone pillars designed in the style of the great European stadia. Seated over 100,000 people. An architectural marvel.

1927 was the height of the "Golden Age of Sport". The year Babe Ruth hit sixty home-runs. In September, Dempsey knocked down Tunney. Yet, lost the famous "long count" rematch at Soldier Field.

On November 26, 1927. The Trojans from the University of Southern California took on the Fighting Irish of Notre Dame University. An epic football game. 123,000 rabid fans entered Soldier Field to view the team coached by Knute Rockne face their rivals from the west. Decades later, both Bernie and Jack still told this story.

Bernie and his life-long Irish Catholic friend Jack (named John - always called Jack) have a heavy steel sewer lid on their head. The boys are dirty. It is night. They are quietly rising out of the sewer. It is dark where they are. Looking around for police and guards, they carefully make their way out of the sewer toward the light provided by the powerful flood lights of Soldier Field. The boys have snuck into Soldier Field by entering a sewer outside of the stadium.

Soldier Field is so large. Security is so scant. Their biggest fear is not really getting caught. Their biggest fear is coming up somewhere on or near the field. Getting trampled by the players (and then getting caught). They do not get caught. They watch the game from behind the Irish bench bathed in the flood light. Bernie would go through a lot rougher travels than the Chicago sewer system before he married my Mother (and after).

Will raised Bernie as an early 20th century male. Growing up in the Jazz Age with Will meant a fast life. Gambling. Sports. The underworld. All abundant. Will treated Bernie like his brother; Never his son. Will took Bernie everywhere. Will was Bernie's idol.

Will impressed upon Bernie that some heroes weren't perfect. Some drank. Some smoked. Some gambled. Making his way through life would be hard. Doing the right thing should never be hard. Protect your family. Defend your country that provides opportunity. Bernie saw a lot of reality at a young age.

Bernie was influenced by a rich reading life. He indulged in his favorite street-wise fictional characters. Ring Lardner's letter writer Jack Keefe ("You Know Me Al"). Damon Runyon's Broadway gamblers like "Harry the Horse" (made famous in "Guys & Dolls"). Horatio Alger's rags to riches heroes. Athletic virtuosos Frank Merriwell and Baseball Joe Mason. With "Tin-Tin", he travelled the world. "Sherlock Holmes" solved the crimes.

While named for a boxer. Only one hero stood out among the pack for Bernie. His sandlot friends called him "The Rajah" or "Rogers Hornsby". Named for the best right handed hitting baseball player of the day (and of all time).

His Cubs were on a long siesta from their turn of the century "Tinker to Evers to Chance" World Series Championships. Won before Dad was born. William Wrigley of gum fame wanted a winner. Invested heavily into his team and the furnishing of Wrigley Field at Clark and Addison.

The twenties progressed. So did the Cubs. By 1929, the Cubs sported the National League's "Murderer's Row". Led by Hornsby. The real "Rajah". They won the National League pennant. Ready to challenge the Philadelphia Athletics for baseball supremacy.

Like the Cubs, the Athletics had known glory in earlier years. They too had been on a long hiatus from the World Series. Now. Their owner and manager Connie Mack built a club for the ages. With Jimmie Foxx and Lefty Grove, the A's supplanted the mighty Yankees of Babe Ruth and Lou Gehrig from the American League pennant.

Historians generally report that the Great Depression began on October 29, 1929. It's cause, the inevitable stock market crash on Black Tuesday. Bernie will tell you that the Great Depression actually started on October 12, 1929 at 3pm in the afternoon. Goldie allowed Dad to stay home from school. Graham McNamee called the fourth game of the World Series on NBC radio live from Philadelphia's Shibe Park.

The Cubs entered World Series Game Four down two games to one in a best of seven series. By the completion of the top half of the seventh inning, the Cubs enjoyed an 8-0 lead. They were set to win the game. Tie the series.

Athletics bottom of the seventh inning: Another of Bernie's heroes, Hack Wilson dropped a high fly ball in the sun. A Momentous error. The flood gates opened. The Athletics scored an unprecedented ten runs in one inning and went on to win the game.

Two days later. The A's defeated Dad's idol Rogers Hornsby and the dispirited Cubs again to win Game Five and earn the World Series championship. For a young die-hard Cubs fan, this was the greatest pain Bernie thought he would ever endure. He was truly **<u>depressed</u>**.

Regardless of the actual date. The Crash came. It produced panic at home and overseas. Will wasn't a speculator nor stock market investor. While an astute gambler, he thought the market was for suckers. He trusted himself.

He knew more about sports, cards, and horses than he did companies. Will always kept an eye on his surroundings. He observed the people that ran the paper. He observed the people and the companies they reported on. He didn't like any of them. More accurately. He didn't trust any of them.

Will didn't lose any money in the crash. He saved well enough to avoid bankruptcy. They had their apartment home. It was paid off. It was theirs. A valuable lesson Bernie remembered. Will continued to work at the paper which made him better off than many. Still, it was a rough time for the family. It was a rough time for everybody's family.

A Jewish boy celebrates his journey into adulthood at age thirteen.

"Today I am a man."

That's what Jewish boys say at the end of their Bar Mitzvah ceremony. It seems inconceivable today that anyone would think a thirteen year old should be considered a man. I have the Tallis (religious scarf) and cuff links my Dad wore at his Bar Mitzvah.

I have one other thing from Bernie's Bar Mitzvah. I have the "PermaPlate" gold and faux-tiger eye cigarette case monogrammed with his initials he was given as a Bar Mitzvah present from his family. Thirteen years old. Cigarette case. It was a different time. He was going to be a man sooner than he realized.

The "Roaring Twenties" and the "Golden Age of Sport" were over. Bernie would spend his formative teen years in the throes of the Great Depression. Graduated from Senn High School. He worked odd jobs. His favorite was selling peanuts at the Lincoln Park Zoo.

Dad continued to play sandlot baseball with his buddies emulating his hero "The Rajah". Real life Cubs like Billy Herman, Frank Demaree, and "Rowdy" Dick Bartell would come out to play with them. The players lived in the neighborhood. This would never happen today.

Goldie would feed the boys **and** the neighborhood Cubs dinner at night or whenever they needed some home cooking. Word got around. Sometimes, Goldie fed the players breakfast when they were a little worse for wear following a night on the town. Sometimes she let them sleep on the sofa. It was an open door during the Depression.

If grown adults attempted to play with your children today at the playground, how would you react? If these same men showed up at all hours at your house inebriated or hung over, would you be concerned with the example being set for your precious charges? This was the home Bernie grew up in. This was the culture.

CHAPTER 2

THANK YOU TOM BROKAW!

In Chicago, It is a common belief that George Halas invented the NFL. Pretty well invented modern football. In 1940, the Bears whipped Sammy Baugh and the Washington Reskins 73-0 in the championship game.

In 1941, writer Jerry Downs penned a catchy song. It became instantly popular in Chicago. "<u>Bear Down, Chicago Bears</u>" became the signature anthem for the Bears.

<u>December 7, 1941</u>
Will and Bernie were at Comiskey Park. The south side of Chicago. 35th Street and Shields. It was easy to get to. They rode the Halsted Street bus due south to 35th. Walked the six blocks east to the park.

Directly west of Comiskey Park. The Stock Yards. In the summer during Sox games, the whole neighborhood smelled of livestock and slaughtered meat. If, the wind was blowing in the right direction.

Today. Afternoon. December. It was a very pleasant 39 degrees. Little wind. No aroma. Their beloved Bears were playing an "away" game against the Chicago Cardinals. Their cross-town rivals.

The Bears were truly the "Monsters of the Midway". Coached by George Halas. The team boasted future Hall of Famers brilliant Sid Luckman, shifty George McAfee, and the fierce Bulldog Turner.

They beat Marshall Goldberg's Cardinals 34-24. The win was important. This win and their win the following week over Curley Lambeau's hated Packers qualified Halas's Bears to play in (and win) the NFL 1941 championship game. At Wrigley Field. Against the pro champions of the east. The New York Giants.

Throughout the Bear-Cardinal game, PA announcements paged military personnel in attendance. Words of the attack filtered through the stadium.

Bernie and Will walked slowly through the crowd after the game toward their bus stop. Bernie had a Bears pennant on a stick in his hand. Newspaper boys were selling extra editions. The USA had been brutally attacked. December 7th would be forever known as "Pearl Harbor Day". Bernie started.

"It was a great game Dad. I wasn't sure the Bears could pull it out."

"What are you talking about? We had 'em all the way."

*"We **were** losing."*

"Temporary setback. We never gave up. Never lost hope. Sid Luckman's too good. I had faith. You should too."

"What do you think it means?"

"What?"

"This Hawaii stuff. The Japanese. The bombs."

"It means were going to war."

"Me?"

"You."

"I know. It's been coming. Dad?"

"Yes?"

"We've never really talked about the Great War."

"Not much to tell. We handed the Germans what for."

"What did you do – then?"

"Not as much as I wanted. I came over from England. I'm a U.S. citizen now. I was a British citizen when I came over. I can't recall if I was a citizen when the Great War began."

"Dad. Why do you call it the 'Great War'?"

"It was supposed to be the war that ended all wars. Old empires were crumbling everywhere. In particular, Germany and France have been fighting for centuries. England and France too. This time. The French and English joined together to fight the Germans.

We joined in on the side of France and England around 1917. They had been fighting since 1914. I tried to enlist in Canada around 1914 when the fighting started. Then, I tried to enlist here.

Neither would take me. Something about my eyesight. I worked up at Great Lakes in a naval yard. Not a fit job for an able man such as myself. They should have let me fight. War would have ended sooner.

By 1917 when the Yanks finally got in, I had Goldie. She understood. But Helen came. I could have gone back to England to fight. I didn't want to leave Goldie and the baby. I needed to keep working."

"It's not going to be the last war is it?"

"No Bernie. All hell's broken loose over there. This guy Hitler is a bad person. The Nazis want to run the world. They don't like the Jews so much either."

"We're you scared? Back then in 1914. Did you think you'd be scared?"

"Everyone's a little scared. I was what they called a 'cocky bantam rooster'. A lot of bluster. I would never let the other guy know I was scared. Not in the ring. Not when I was riding the track horses. Not when I was facing fastballs at Mills. But yeah, my toes and stomach tingled a little bit. It would have been the same if I had been in the trenches."

"Trenches? Do you think I should go into the Army?"

"Not if it's anything like the Great War. I'd say the Navy. More modern. Cleaner. Better life for you." None of it will be easy."

"Going to the Navy means the Pacific. Right? No chance to kill Nazis."

"Just think about killing someone that wants to kill you. Wants to kill your Mother and Father. Wants to take away your freedom. Wants to rule the world."

"Is it OK to be a little scared?

"Son. You wouldn't be alive if you weren't."

"Dad. What are the odds?"

"What do you mean?"

*"You **know** what I mean. What are the odds we beat the Japs **and** the Nazis? What are the odds I come back alive?"*

*"Japs and Nazis? That's a good parlay. Beating them both **and** coming back alive. That's a hell of a trifecta. You can do it."*

With a smile. He said to Bernie confidently.

"I'd take that action any day. I'd give the odds. My money's on you. I'd pay fifty dollars out to get just one dollar back. That's how confident I am. I wouldn't give those odds on the Bears. And they're going to be the world champions again. Shoot. The Japs and Nazis don't have anyone near as good as Bulldog Turner fighting on their side! No-one near as smart as Papa Bear George Halas or Sid Luckman. No-one as brave as you Bernie. You're a shoe-in."

Bernie smiled. Beamed at his Dad.

"Let's go home and tell Mom."

*"I'm proud of you Bernie. **You're** the 'pride and joy of Illinois' now."*

"You never said that before."

"I didn't have to. I was thinking it."

Like so many Americans, Dad enlisted in the Navy the next day. His path in the Navy was a typical one. Great Lakes. San Diego. Pearl Harbor, Hawaii. The Pacific - Asian theatre.

You might ask yourself. "What does a scared young volunteer bring to war?" Bernie carried two personal items with him through the entire War. First. A United States "Peace" Silver Dollar with the image of the Goddess of Liberty. 1921. "In God We Trust". "E. Pluribus. Unum" (Loosely translated: "Out of many, one"). A gift from Will on the day he departed.

Second. Dad brought his equivalent of comfort food. He brought a small white envelope containing his 1933 Goudey Gum baseball cards.

#211	Hack Wilson	#202	Gabby Hartnett
#204	Riggs Stephenson	#51	Charley Grimm
#23	Kiki Cuyler	#188	Rogers Hornsby
#226	Charlie Root	#67	Guy Bush
#55	Pat Malone	#135	Woody English

All members of Dad's 1929 Cubs. His "Murderer's Row". The numbers next to each name? Not their uniform numbers. The numbers on the back of their baseball cards.

Along with a picture of Will and Goldie, Dad carried this envelope through the entire war. Heat. Rain. Ocean tides. No matter. Little cardboard pieces of home. Right in his pocket. Dad's Cubs might not have won a World Series. Bernie thought they helped him **and** the U.S. win the war.

Letters from home to the south Pacific arrived infrequently. Every letter Will and Goldie sent included at least one Playball baseball card of Dad's heroes. Cubs: Billy Herman, Dick Bartell, Frank Demaree, and Billy Jurgess. Non-Cub stars: "King" Carl Hubbell, "Double X" Jimmie Foxx, "Big Poison" Paul Waner, and "Little Poison" Lloyd Waner. Will made sure to include Jewish stars: Hank Greenberg and "Harry the Horse" Danning.

Bernie started at the bottom. Ultimately, he found his way to CINCPAC. The naval intelligence sector for the Pacific. He was in Admiral Nimitz's command. He greatly admired Nimitz. Thought him fair to his men. He trusted Nimitz. He did **not** trust MacArthur. Thought him too grandiose.

Nimitz was unassuming and orderly. Bernie liked that. Bernie often took notice of a 3x5 note card on Nimitz's desk under glass. Handwritten.

"Objective, Offensive, Surprise, Superiority of Force at Point of Contact, Simplicity, Security, Movement, Economy of Force, Cooperation."

Short. Succinct. Easy to understand. Easy to follow. Pure Nimitz.

Dad rose to the rank of Chief Petty Officer. Dad and his crew participated in securing the Islands. Normalizing them for living after the fighting and capture.

Near the War's end, President Truman warned: If the Japanese did not surrender unconditionally, he would approve the use of nuclear weapons. The Japanese ignored President Truman's warning. Over one-hundred thousand Japanese died at Nagasaki and Hiroshima.

Dad was always respectful when discussing the atomic bomb victims. He never gloated. Never made light of the situation. But, he was never regretful either. The U.S. did not attack Japan. We were attacked. Our allies were attacked.

My Father firmly believed he survived the war (with millions of other Allies **and** Japanese) owing to Truman's decision and his guts to make good on his warning. Bernie believed that conventional warfare would have lengthened the War by at least two years. Possibly longer. The additional human carnage on both sides would have been simply unimaginable if the Allies had been forced to invade and fight on mainland Japan.

He was in the Navy for the duration of the War. The official surrender of the Japanese came on September 2, 1945. Four years of vicious hand-to hand, island to island fighting. Americans and our Allies. Brave and scared. A heroic victory in the Pacific by every-day people.

Bernie actually was not mustered out of the Navy until 1946. Upon his release, he received a form letter from President Truman. He also received a personally typed and signed letter from the Secretary of the Navy that was very special to him.

The Secretary of the Navy
Washington

May 8, 1946

My dear Mr. Rosenberg:

I have addressed this letter to reach you after all of the formalities of your separation from active service are completed. I have done so because, without formality but as clearly as I know how to say it, I want the Navy's pride in you, which it is my privilege to express, to reach into your civil life and to remain with you always.

You have served in the greatest Navy in the world.

It crushed two enemy fleets at once, receiving their surrenders only four months apart.

It brought our land-based airpower within bombing range of the enemy, and set our ground armies on the beachheads of final victory.

It performed the multitude of tasks necessary to support these military operations.

No other Navy at any time has done so much. For your part in these achievements you deserve to be proud as long as you live. The Nation which you served at a time of crisis will remember you with gratitude.

The best wishes of the Navy go with you into civilian life. Good luck!

Sincerely yours,

James Forrestal

Dad left the Navy. Dad kept the letter. He kept a bag of pictures and his discharge papers. He kept the palm sized plastic spiral notebook the Navy gave him listing the medals and ribbons he earned and was allowed to wear.

All of these were in a drawer by his nightstand in his bedroom in our house when I was growing up. He never talked about them. He never took them out.

There are no amusing or compelling stories I can share about Bernie's time in the service. He simply did not talk about it (unless I asked). It was a vacuum of time in his life.

It's like he jumped into a big pool of water holding his breath in 1941. Came out of the water in 1946. Exhaled. Other than holding his breath, nothing else really mattered. He went into the War. Did his best. Survived. Got out. There was **nothing else**.

This surviving generation created two types of veterans: Those that lived the War every day for the rest of their lives and made it a large part of their persona. And, those that buried the War deep in a compartment in their soul choosing to never let it out unless forced. Neither type of veteran is better or worse. Just different people reacting differently. Bernie was the latter. He buried it **deep.**

Tom Brokaw gave name and voice to my Father's era. He named them "The Greatest Generation". I am forever in the debt to Mr. Brokaw for creating this title which became their identity.

He gave voice to brave Americans that were not celebrities. Jimmy Stewart, Ted Williams, and Hank Greenberg (to name three) entered the service with deserved fanfare. Americans like Bernie were ordinary people before the War. After the War, the rest of their lives were spent recapturing their ordinariness ("Normalcy"?). Each was extraordinary in their own right. And of course, many did not return at all.

Bernie was eight years old when the Great Depression hit. His reward for spending his childhood in the Great Depression was World War II. He would spend the next five years in the Navy in the Pacific. He was twenty-five when he was released. Bernie and those like him truly were "The Greatest Generation." They spent the better part of sixteen years struggling, sacrificing. Scrapping.

CHAPTER 3

BERNIE'S "MARSHALL PLAN"

F ollowing World War II, The United States engineered the greatest economic recovery plan in the history of the world. It was called the "Marshall Plan".

The idea: Get Western Europe up and running as fast as possible. Returning from Depression and War to self-sufficiency and prosperity. The plan also intended to strengthen our Allies (new and old). Provide a buffer against Stalin's post-war Communist aggression. A very real threat.

Back on the home front in 1946, Bernie was just beginning to move off the one yard line onto a "Marshall Plan" of his own. He attended Northwestern University in Evanston on the GI Bill. He found full-time work selling (legal) liquor products for Chicago based alcohol distributor Hesher Brothers.

He rarely spoke about the war. He just wanted to get on with his life. It was a good fit. Bernie was a good salesman. Not a glib used-car salesman. He was hardworking and honest. Well versed in sports, drinking, and Chicago. He earned trust. He did well.

Bernie also gambled. I'm not sure if there is a technical or medical term for the "math gene" or the "card playing gene". Will's ability to calculate long columns of numbers passed to Bernie.

Being a good card player and a good gambler takes more than a knack for numbers. It takes a strategic mind. Good judgment. An iron stomach. Much confidence. And, knowing when to say "*when*".

Bernie had it all. He didn't learn these attributes at Northwestern. His childhood experience with Will cemented his intelligence. Bravery and confidence from the Navy provided his muscle. He would **never** be bluffed. **Never** fear losing. **Never** fear another. Bernie channeled his strengths into his ability to play cards. He was stone cold. He was brilliant.

It wasn't just Poker. Bernie was excellent with dice. Shooting Craps. Bernie was a superior Bridge player. Often serving as a practice partner for famous Bridge professionals.

As a boy, Dad and I spent endless hours playing seven or eleven card Gin and his favorite game, Casino. I only won when he let me win. Just often enough to keep me interested.

Back from the Navy. Working steadily for the first time in his life. Bernie could do as he wished. His time was finally his own.

High stakes Poker games began on Friday nights. Ended Sunday morning. Money earned Monday through Friday selling liquor provided his ante and table stakes. His Poker earnings dwarfed his day-job income.

In the PBS mini-series "Baseball", Ken Burns and Geoffrey Ward attribute an anonymous Negro League baseball player from the 1930's Pittsburgh Crawfords team with saying.

"The Crawfords played everywhere, in every ball park. And we won. Won like we invented the game."

Substitute Bernie for the Crawfords. Substitute Poker for baseball. That was Bernie. When he got out of the war, he won at Poker. Like **he** "invented the game".

Conversely, Bernie sparingly bet sports games or matches. When he did bet on a game, he bet significantly less than he wagered on himself playing Poker. As a kid, Bernie had bet pennies and nickels with the gamblers in the Wrigley Field bleachers.

Bernie had never forgotten Will's lessons about the track. Dad had spent enough time around athletes to believe that men **and** horses (actually trainers, jockeys, and owners) could be bought in different degrees. "Eight Men Out" aside, Baseball was the hardest to fix. Boxing the easiest.

Shaving points (Scoring enough to win games. But, not scoring enough to cover the point spread) was prevalent in basketball. It wasn't enough to know which team would win. You had to know by how many points.

College football and basketball? Even harder to figure out. Too many schools. Too many games. Too many gamblers. Eventually the roof fell in when a point shaving scandal was uncovered in college basketball. Around 1951. CCNY, University of Kentucky, Bradley University and others were implicated in the scandal.

The Chicago Stadium, home of many college basketball doubleheaders pulled their pay phones out in an attempt to stop gambling. For years, the Chicago Stadium and other venues banned college basketball doubleheaders.

Bernie's betting on sports was recreational. It was for fun. His gambling with cards or dice – **That** was work. Dad's life settled into a comfortable routine. Work. Sports. Jazz. Casual dating. Occasional travel. Gambling. He had missed a lot of life. He wanted to make up for it. He was living at home. He was making good money. He was finally happy.

CHAPTER 4

VERNA'S GIRL – ANN ETHEL

A nn Ethel's Baby Book...

"Baby was born on Sunday 11/8/25 11AM.
Sunday's child shall never know aught of want or aught of woe."

Mom was born legally blind. This is a legal term. She could see. Just not very well. Better when she was younger. Progressively worse as she aged. She was never allowed to drive a car. She wore prescription glasses and sun glasses all of her life. She wore a man's wrist watch. Larger numbers. Always fashionable.

Mom helped pioneer contact lenses. The earliest contacts looked like mini halves of goldfish bowls. Not attractive. Ann Ethel would not wear them in public. Subsequent versions were wearable.

I spent many days and nights on my hands and knees searching for one of Mom's contacts which had popped out. Typically at Wrigley Field or the Stadium during a Hawks game. Any unexpected nudge would do the trick.

Our whole family was on auto-pilot with Mom. Acted. Never thought. Riding in the car. As Mom got older, we'd say the street signs as we passed. Just talking under our breath. A little louder.

"Barton. Hull Terrace. Austin. Oh. There's the school. (Like it was a surprise)"

If we saw a bill board or a store sign, we'd read it out loud. It was all very unconscious. Subtle. Just did it. **All the time**. Same thing at ball games. We'd quietly play a running commentary.

"Brock leads off first. About a four-step lead. There he goes..."

At restaurants, we'd read the menu out loud. Dad might say.

"The special looks good. A Cobb Salad. But, I think I'm going for a cheeseburger and cherry coke. What looks good to you Ann?"

"I think I'll try the Cobb Salad."

It turns out, I carried these unconscious habits into adulthood. I really had no idea. My wife and I would be driving along. There I was. Calling off the street signs. Worse. I'd read restaurant menus out loud. Even today, I'm continually asked.

"Would you please just shut up?!"

It's hard for me to say how much Mom really saw. People have amazing abilities to compensate for a disability. Mom watched Cubs games on TV and in person. She always knew what was occurring. I'm not sure how much of that came from what she saw. Or, from what she knew through listening and her knowledge of the game. It would be the same when she rode the bus or worked. Understood her surroundings. Never lost.

Even wearing glasses, Ann Ethel was athletic. A fast runner. A good swimmer (no glasses). She learned and practiced in Lake Michigan. She would say. Half kidding. I think.

"I had to be a good swimmer. Teddy and Eileen were always trying to drown me."

She started smoking at age twelve or so. Started drinking around the same age. This was typical behavior. Not hidden at home. Accepted. Expected.

She read incessantly. She held the books up very closely to her face. (Glasses off). The characters were her friends.

I wouldn't say she had a photographic memory. More like a steel trap. She recalled what she read. Referred to her literature friends as though they were people. Cited them in conversation to make a point.

Ann Ethel loved sports. All Chicago teams. Could talk sports with any boy. Often did. She was not shy. Not a tom boy. Not a tough broad. Not loud. Not a wall-flower.

She was raised by my Grandmother Verna to be confident, empathetic, and an independent thinker. Enlightened. She was a feminist by deeds. Not by words. She believed in civil rights before Jackie Robinson or Rosa Parks. She was raised a Roosevelt Democrat. She looked up to Eileen. A very independent woman.

Ann Ethel wasn't glamorous. She was classy. Very little make up. Channel No. 5. Do you know someone who seems to always be well dressed – but not overly dressed for every occasion? Jackie Onassis? Kate Middleton?

Anne Ethel was Audrey Hepburn stylish. Thick black hair. She had a natural full well-proportioned build (a buxom bosom as Bernie said back around WWII). At five feet-four inches tall, she never weighed over 115 pounds a day in her life.

A woman's career path was almost non-existent before World War II. It was still a rough go after the war. Mom was a college graduate. Single. She didn't intend to stay home and wait for a husband to come along. Mom liked to say that she and her friend Alviera, who Mom swore *"practically invented the insurance industry"* worked on Michigan Avenue. Proudly she would tell me with a smile.

*"We **owned** the city."*

Today. Ann Ethel's position in a large corporation would be titled Chief Operating Officer. COO. Circa 1950, she was the Executive Assistant to the Owner/President of an international liquor manufacturer. Headquartered in Chicago. Mom ran the day-to-day operations for the President freeing him up to do what executives did in the late 1940's and 1950's.

It was a great life. From her office (***Her*** office!), she worked with people globally in every time zone. She liked to arrive at the office about nine-thirty AM. Enjoy a two-hour lunch shopping on Michigan Avenue. Work till ten PM. Complete the day with a late date or dinner. Back again the next day.

Ann Ethel was aware her salary was not as high as her male counterparts (which she had few). Ann Ethel was also aware of her era. She made a tidy salary and bonus (more than most men her age to be sure). She lived at home. She was a good saver. Single, smart, pretty, and a good earner. She was happy and content.

She was also a good catch. She could handle her bourbon. She drank a cocktail known as an Old Fashioned which she shortened to "Old Fashion". She never was drunk. Never out of control.

Not a confirmed bachelorette, she was in no hurry to be caught and settle down. Verna had taught her well. She was her own girl. In a word. She was unique. As Bernie would learn. She went "to your head."

CHAPTER 5

TWO RIVERS

Ann Ethel was working for a liquor manufacturer. Bernie was working for a liquor distributor. Same city. Eventually, they were going to meet. And they did. When Eileen and Josef met, fireworks were immediately evident. Not so when Bernie met Ann Ethel. No combustion. No explosions.

It was more like two river tributaries coming together to form one river. The Mississippi and the Missouri. It's impossible to really know where each river ceases to be its own entity. Or, when they become part of a greater singular force. Like the two rivers, two people entering into each other slowly with no path for reverse.

She was confident but reserved by nature. While an untraditional woman, she expected to be courted in a traditional way.

Dad learned about dating from the neighborhood growing up. Nobody had any money. Which is to say, they didn't go out much. They found other ways to occupy themselves. Then. He was in the Navy. Where the "girl in every port" saying was somewhat true.

Bernie was not a Romeo stringing along a bevy of girls as his fleet moved through the Pacific. But Bernie had charm. He liked girls. They liked him. The nature of the War meant you met people... formed short term relationships...and moved on. It wasn't dishonest. It was real. It was comfort. It was perfect for Bernie. He had never had a long-term relationship. Too young before. Too transient after.

Circa 1950. They met at a function at the Palmer House between State and Wabash in the south Loop to promote Ann Ethel's company.

Bernie disdains ties. He wears a blue blazer. Open collar. White Oxford shirt. French cuffs with modest cufflinks in the shape of small gold skeleton keys. No wristwatch. Only the initial ring his sister made for him adorns his hand. Tan slacks and Chicago made cordovan Florsheim wing-tip shoes finish off the workman-like appearance.

Ann Ethel wears a refined off-white business dress and medium close-toe beige heels. Other than her tasteful man's Longines wristwatch, no other jewelry with one exception. Mom wears her trade mark clip-on earrings.

Today, clip-on earrings are somewhat of a novelty. They can be found in abundance at any antique mall. Mom never pierced her ears. More common then. Easily half of all women Ann Ethel's age wore clip-on earrings. All shapes and sizes. All materials. Sold in the best stores. Sold at the five-and-dime. Some valuable. Some not.

Watch an old movie. The phone rings. The woman answering runs her hand past her ear. Removes her clip-on earring. Places the phone to her ear. Speaks. All in one seamless motion. It is nostalgic.

For the record. On this evening. Ann Ethel's clip-on earrings are petite. Fourteen karat gold with a small, real lavender jade stone. Tasteful. Beautiful. They set off her outfit perfectly (per usual).

Unique. Ann Ethel had them made to her design specifications. By Sarah Green. A nice young Jewish immigrant woman just starting her own business with her young husband. A small shop. In Jeweler's Row. On Wabash near the Palmer House.

Bernie approaches Ann Ethel. She is slowly sipping a cocktail.
Smoking. Talking seriously to a business woman. Dad is accompanied by a work colleague. No fancy lines for him.

"Hello."

Ann Ethel isn't interested.

"Go away."

"That's not nice."

"I'm working."

"I can wait."

"Don't."

Bernie and his friend have their drinks and cigarettes in hand.
Ann Ethel didn't notice. Bernie is drinking an Old Fashioned
made with water. The boys take a step back. They stand for a
Moment. Not really put off. Just standing. Dad says to his friend.
Not intentionally loud. Just loud enough to be heard over the din
of the party.

*"I heard last night at the Aragon Ballroom that Frankie Frisch is going
to sign 'Double No-Hitter' Johnny Vander Meer to pitch for the Cubs."*

Ann Ethel, still in conference, pivots. Looks at Bernie and
forcefully states.

*"That's just like the Cubs. Frisch is too old to manage. Vander Meer
is over the hill. He pitched his no-hitters over a decade ago.* PK (William
Wrigley's son and now Cubs team owner) *is wasting his money. If they
want to contend, they should sign Roberts and Simmons from the Phils.
You get your information at the Aragon???"*

Our boy Bernie has traveled around the world and come back
to tell about it (or not tell about it as the case may have been). He
reacts in the only rational way possible. In shock, he drops his
"Old Fashion".

The glass shatters sending ice and liquid everywhere including Ann Ethel's perfect shoes. She doesn't move an inch. She is
unflappable. She stares at him. Not glowers. He stares at her. He
finally gains his composure. Strongly but not shouting, he says.

"*What?* **What**? *Who do you want to manage the Cubs? Pafko? Cavaretta? Hack? God forbid, Durocher. And what's wrong with the Aragon? I saw Stan Kenton last night. Don't you like him?*"

A little softer.

"*I'm sorry about your shoes and the mess.*"

"*Stan Kenton's OK. I prefer big band. Artie Shaw. Count Basie, Jimmie Lunceford, Chick Webb. Have you ever seen Benny Goodman?*"

Switching without hesitation, she continues as if one sentence.

"*I like that Stengel guy but I don't think the Cubs can get him from the Yankees. My shoes are OK. You're not the first person to drop a drink.*"

Sometime in your life, you'll be somewhere. See something. Meet someone. You've never experienced before. You'll have no context. You are trying to find a register. But nothing is coming. It's alien. You'll get a cold sensation.

At that Moment, the man who could not be bluffed got the cold shiver. He had never met a girl like Ann Ethel. He never would again. He knew it. Battlefield calm. He extended his hand.

"*My name is Bernie. I've seen all of those bands and more. Los Angeles, Chicago, Harlem. Stengel is a flake. He'll never win another pennant. The Sporting News says there is a kid managing in the Dodger organization on his way up to look out for. Alston.*"

"*I read that article. I think Lopez has more potential. How did you get into the clubs in Harlem? Weren't you scared? My name is Ann Ethel. You may call me Ann.*"

"*You read The Sporting News? I've been going to Jazz clubs since I was a little boy. My Father took me. I was raised on hot Jazz. I'm not trying to brag, but I have an unbelievable 78 collection. Musicians White and Black are my friends. They take me in where I shouldn't go. I've never had a real problem. I'll call you Ann. May I call **on** you, Ann?*"

Ann seemed more serious for a Moment.

"*Do I read The Sporting News? **I read everything!**"

"*May I call on you?*"

People would say for years about Paul Newman and Frank Sinatra.

"Those eyes. Those beautiful blue eyes."

Ann Ethel saw in Bernie a man that was short, a little chunky, thinning hair, with a round face. A nice smile. But those eyes. Those robin-egg blue eyes. She saw those right away. She also saw what Mae West described. He had "life".

"You may. Why don't you come up some time and see me?"

Ann Ethel smiled. Her favorite Mae West line.

Of course. For all of her Michigan Avenue cool and training from Verna and Eileen, she had not met a boy like Bernie either. Sure. War veterans were everywhere now. Muscle bound and movie star handsome. Each told her their exploits at the Battle of the Bulge or Iwo Jimo – even if they never made it past Great Lakes.

Bernie talked about the Cubs. He talked about his Father. He talked about being a boy. About '78 records. She thought to herself.

"Who says those things?"

In the liquor industry, there was no shortage of salesmen and men in general anxious to spend time with Ann Ethel. She was selective. She wasn't a prude. Sometimes she went along. She enjoyed the dates. But they were just that - dates.

She had no long-term relationships behind her. She had never been engaged. She was not a war widow. Others might have seen her as a spinster. Even felt sorry for her. She didn't see it that way. She was a working girl (in the good sense). Had no interest in stopping. If that meant not marrying, so be it. After all, **she** "*owned Michigan Avenue*".

Josef and Eileen reveled in their oppositeness. They were two halves that made one. They found each other like a lost key and a lock. They could not live apart. They couldn't help anyone else. They completed each other. They were soul mates.

Bernie and Ann Ethel were soul mates too. But they weren't opposites. They might have come from different households (Verna would always believe her family superior to Bernie's.). These two found each other. They understood each other.

It wasn't just love of hobby or mutual interest that made them one. It was a spiritual understanding they would share their entire life. They thought alike. They didn't have to speak. Religion... sports... money... politics... ethics, they were "just so". In perfect harmony. They intertwined. Like two rivers.

CHAPTER 6

"YOUR BOY – BERNIE"

The concepts of love and belonging to another were completely foreign to both Bernie and Ann Ethel. Neither had a plan. Neither had a preconception or a road map.

I don't think you can call what Bernie and Ann Ethel did dating. They managed their lives as they had before. Making room for each other. Ann Ethel now accompanied Bernie to sporting events and Jazz clubs during the week. Dad gambled on the weekend.

Mom worked. But now, went out with Bernie after work. Dinners at Chez Paul, Pizzeria Duo, Irelands, or Ricketts. Magic shows at the Ivanhoe. Of course, sporting events.

Sometimes before work, they met at Lou Mitchell's for breakfast. Sometimes lunch at Millers or the Berghoff. They were still solidly entrenched in their former lives. But, the two lives were coming together. Missing each other when apart. A new sensation.

Dad had been to New York before. Not with too much money. He loved all of it. The food. The jazz. The sports. In late August of 1951, he and a few friends ventured east. He hoped this would be a grand adventure. With cash in pocket, he could do everything he wanted. He packed in as much as possible. Sent postcards.

Front side picture: **Sugar Ray Robinson's Tavern**

Monday August 27, 1951
Dear A.E.
Arrive train about 9am. Grand Central Station. Cab to Essex Hotel. Check in. Breakfast at Lindy's. Looked for D. Runyon's Harry the Horse & Lemon Drop Kid. No luck. Subway to Coogan's Bluff-Polo Grounds. Cubs lose to Giants 5-4 in 12. Giants good. Have all Black outfield. Irvin, Thompson, and new kid Mays. All very good. What's wrong with Cubs? Dinner in Harlem. Sugar Ray Robinson's tavern. He was there. Shook his hand. Saw Duke Ellington at the Savoy Ballroom. – Miss you. - Bernie

Front side picture: **Empire State Building**

Tuesday August 28, 1951
Dearest A.E.
Breakfast. Automat. Walk to Emp.St. Bld. Wow. Tall! See all of NYC. Subway to Brklyn. Ebbets Fld. Double HDER vs. Pitt. Split. Hard to believe Bums ever lose. Furillo, P-Wee, Duke, J Robby, Gil, Campy, Pafko, Cox, Branca. What a line up! Wish Cubs had same. Sure to win pennant in 51. Jack Dempsey's to-night. Then A. Shaw and Helen Forrest at Kelly's Stable. – Miss you & Love you. Wish you were here - Bernie

Front side picture: **Statue of Liberty**

Wednesday August 29, 1951
My dearest Ann.
Saw Ellis Island & Stat of Liberty. Quite a sight. Wonder if Will passed thru here? Back to Polo Grounds. Giants beat Kiner and Pirates. Mays is something. Can do everything.

Just a rookie. Maybe spoke too soon on Dodgers winning flag. Steak at Gallagher's tonight. Saw pictures of Man O'War, War Admiral, Sea Biscuit, & Whirlaway. Saw Satchmo & Ella & 3 Deuces. Highlight of trip. Miss you. Love you. Blue without you - Bernie

Bernie was torn. The little boy in him loved New York. The baseball games by day. The food and Jazz. The post cards told the story. Which each day, he missed Ann Ethel more.

Following his post cards. Post marked August 30, 1951. A three-cent stamp with a picture of the Supreme Court building (that looked amazingly like the West side of Soldier Field) was affixed to a letter addressed to A.E. To my knowledge, it is the only letter my Dad ever wrote to my Mother. On note sized Essex House Hotel stationary.

Ann Dearest.

A VFW convention here. The town is loaded (physically & alcoholically). Didn't have too much trouble getting accommodations and as you can see from the letter, we are staying at the Essex House. Went to the Embers. Red Norvo and his group and Bobby Hacket and his group are there. I met Shelly Mann, drummer from Kenton's band. Spent the evening together. No use going into too much detail. I will give you all of the facts when I see you. If all goes well, I will be home sometime Sunday or early Monday. If per chance you don't go to New Orleans leave word where I can get in touch with you if you go out. The only thing wrong with this vacation is you are not with me. If it's OK with you, I am not going anyplace without you again. I love you very much. Your boy,
Bernie

This should have been the trip of a lifetime. It wasn't. He missed Ann Ethel terribly. He had never missed someone before. Not like this.

It just spilled out on paper. Unplanned. Dad's true feelings. *"I'm not going anyplace without you again."*

Not everyone would have understood the seriousness of these words. Ann Ethel understood. It was Dad's proposal. Heart-felt. Direct. I think he would have rather asked in person. But there it was. Unfiltered. Bernie came home. The letter arrived before his train.

Ann Ethel was waiting at home. She did not go to New Orleans to visit Eileen. As Josef had done years before for Eileen, Bernie goes straight from Union Train Station to Verna's apartment. Still has his travel bag. Needs a shave and a shower. Bernie rings the doorbell. Ann Ethel answers the door. Before Bernie can speak. Ann Ethel says.

"Yes!"

One word. All that is needed. He doesn't have to ask. He knows. She knows. They hug on the apartment landing. Passerbys smile. They have Verna's permission. They have Will and Goldie's blessing.

Will gave Ann Ethel and Bernie their wedding presents. Four small boxes. Four small gifts. At the time, Bernie thought them a little odd. Very generous. But, a little odd. Still, he knew. Odd gifts were his family's legacy. He never questioned his Father.

The first gift was an engagement ring for Ann Ethel. The ring was Colorless. Flawless. Excellent condition. Weighed just over one carat. In short. This stone was perfect. It did not come from an ordinary retail jeweler. The diamond ring was square cut. It was set in 18 karat white gold. There was a matching wedding band.

Neither Bernie nor Ann Ethel knew anything about diamonds or jewelry. The style seemed a little out of date. More of a 1920's design than 1950s. Not that they cared.

If they **had** known anything about jewelry, they would have realized that none of them, including Will, could have afforded this wedding set. Ann Ethel wore the ring every day of her life.

The second gift was for Bernie. It was a twelve-karat gold band with a single large ruby stone faceted with six sides. "Dress Up" was engraved on the inside of the band. Will said it was a good luck token. He'd earned while boxing.

He wanted Bernie to have it. Bernie kept the ring in his cuff link box. He rarely wore it. He loved it. Aside from occasionally wearing his initial ring made by his sister, he stopped wearing rings after World War II. In fact, Bernie never wore a wedding band. When Ann Ethel asked him to wear a wedding band (which was rarely), Dad slipped on the ruby ring.

The third gift was a porcelain cat. It was an antique. About one foot tall. Brownish in color. The cat had apparently faux sapphire eyes. There was an inscription engraved on the underside.

For M.F. & Co
Good luck, 1907
L.C.T

The cat sounded like a muffled maraca. There were things inside making noise when shaken. Probably just old newspaper and ceramic chips Will said.

Will said not to open it unless they were in a dire emergency. Bernie never understood what that meant. Ann Ethel kept the cat by her bedside her entire life. Years later. I kept the cat statue in my office. It's never been opened.

The final gift was an American "Indian Head" two-and-a-half-dollar gold piece. It was a tradition (superstition) in Bernie's family to give a coin at important events. Bernie gave Ann Ethel a Peace dollar when they married. Ann Ethel gave Bernie a Morgan silver dollar. Both carried their coins their entire life. Dad asked Will.

"Why this gold coin?"

"There are two of you. Two dollars. When you have your first child. Two and a half."

Ann Ethel put the coin on her charm bracelet. She loved it.

Bernie and Ann Ethel were married in January of 1952. A Rabbi conducted the ceremony. Bernie stepped on the glass. Uncle Davey came back from Glendale to be Dad's best man. Alviera was Mom's maid of honor. Jack, Josef, Eileen and Aunt Helen made up the rest of the wedding party. Mom wore a beautiful ivory off-white wedding dress. Dad wore a suit and tie. No tux for him. A tie was enough.

The reception was held at a rented union hall. A restaurant was not needed. The liquor was freely provided by Bernie and Ann Ethel's employers. The food was catered by Josef and Eileen who came up from New Orleans. The furniture was supplied by Bernie's best friend Jack who after the war ran (and eventually owned) Harold's Rental in Chicago.

Bernie's friends played hot jazz. With flowing drink, and exotic Cajun delicacies to eat, the wedding was reported to be like none other experienced in Chicago (or anywhere else). Before or since.

The only other note of interest is that Bernie, wanting to impress his new bride took his car to a carwash on the big day. Chicago in January in the best of winters is well below freezing. This day was no exception. The doors and the windows froze making the car an impenetrable fortress on wheels (but clean).

Bernie almost missed his own wedding. Another car was found. We have a picture of Dad behind the wheel in his overcoat and fedora with Mom in top coat leaving on their honeymoon. He looks like Al Capone. She looks like a movie star. The happy couple spent their honeymoon in a cabin at Starved Rock State Park in central Illinois. They came home.

The night they came home Ann Ethel made Bernie an offer of a lifetime. You might say, an offer he could not refuse.

CHAPTER 7

DECISIONS

I t was their first night back home in their north side apartment.
They had already continued their honeymoon. In their small
bedroom, Ann Ethel was relaxing under the sheets with just a
nightgown on. Bernie was standing by the dresser in his boxers
and white undershirt. Casually standing and stretching. Smoking
a cigarette. Very content. In no hurry to be anywhere else. Ann
Ethel starts.

*"I have an idea. I think you should consider. You know. I make a
pretty good salary. The liquor business does not seem to be going anywhere.
I should be working for a long while. Here's what I think. I think you
should stop working. I'll bank roll you. You'll play cards and gamble for
a living. You'll make much more money than you do today. And, you'll be
happier."*

It may have been that Mom became worried that married life
would not appeal to Dad. But, I never had the sense this was her
motivation. If it was, she never said.

Later in life, Mom and I discussed her offer to Dad often and
at length. It seems unlikely she would discuss with her son that she
encouraged my Father, her husband to break the law but did not

151

feel comfortable sharing with me she was doing so to preempt a potentially failed marriage.

No. I have always believed that Mom believed this was the appropriate business move which coincided with what she thought would make Dad happiest. That was Mom. Very smart. Very strategic.

Everyone understands that in 1950's Chicago, as corrupt as Chicago has been known to be, gambling was **still** illegal. Clear? A week into the marriage. This was a whole crate of TNT for an offer. It's Bernie's family that came up through the not-so-legal aspects of society. Nowhere in Ann Ethel's family was it ever reported that any family member was issued so much as a parking ticket (yet).

Mom was serious. Dead serious. She wasn't a silly person. Not frivolous. Not hasty. Dad had shared **everything** with Mom. She came into the marriage with full knowledge of Bernie. She knew how he spent his weekends. She wasn't needy. She wasn't jealous.

Once married. If Bernie was going to lead the gambler's life, she didn't just have to **believe in him** and his ability to succeed ("was he really that good a card player?"). She had to **believe him**. These are different concepts.

Imagine if you were dating or married to someone. They were gone every weekend. Money is flowing in and out. Would you be concerned? Would you believe your spouse? Would you be suspicious?

With cold calculation, she'd watched her own family. She'd watched business in the corporate world. She wasn't Mae West. But, she'd been around the block. She knew what she was saying. She knew what the risks were. She just entered into a partnership. And, **she was all in!**

Bernie was surprised. Not shocked. Just surprised. Being a full-time gambler with a backer was a dream. Being unconstrained from daily work was too good to be true. His Father Will would have been proud of him. It made him smile and pause for a Moment. No ordinary person he.

He might have shared this ambition with Ann Ethel in passing before they were married. He could not recall. It was not something they had ever seriously discussed nor was it a recurring theme in their intimate conversations. His answer was obvious. It was easy. He didn't need time to think about it. He had already thought about it. He knew exactly what he wanted. He sat on the edge of the bed beside her.

"No."

It wasn't that he thought it was a bad idea. It was a great idea. It wasn't that the offer was too good to be true. He knew she meant it and would stand by him.

Ann Ethel had seriously asked. **That** was too good to be true. He loved her for that. And she waited till they were married. She did not offer it like a carrot before they were married. It wasn't part of the package. It wasn't an inducement to get the bachelor to pop the question.

It was her showing her unbound-less love for him. The only people that had ever believed in Bernie and loved him unconditionally this way were his parents. And they had just left him for Glendale.

"No." he repeated softly to himself as though he recognized his life was changing forever as he said this one word.

"No."

As long as I can remember, when denied, Ann Ethel never argued. She didn't plead her case. She thought it beneath her. I only remember her raising her voice two or three times in my life. She asked questions. She was always dignified.

She was used to getting her way. Not by way of being spoiled. She didn't nag or badger. It was that people tended to want to help her. Or, be in her favor. She was judicious with her opinions.

Simply, most times people tended to agree with her. She rarely asked for anything. Now Ann Ethel asked directly.

"Tell me why."

This time, Bernie did not need time to formulate his thoughts. He had his own TNT for Ann Ethel. He hadn't thought the honeymoon was the appropriate place to discuss it. He really only had a few things on his mind for the honeymoon. He was happy that in this regard, it was a very successful honeymoon.

*"**If** I wanted to continue to gamble, I would not have married you. I can gamble. I can do it well. I can be married. I will try to do that well. But, I cannot do both well.*

__If__ I gamble, it will require my being away from __our__ home often. At all hours - day and night. It will mean you will never be able to save or budget. If I need money, I'll take it.

The phone will ring at all hours. Men __and__ women will be calling. They'll leave secretive messages. When the phone rings or someone is at the door, you'll also wonder if it's the police.

When I go out, you'll worry if I will come back. While I am out, you'll worry if I will be robbed or beaten for which I will not be able to call the police."

Still sure of herself. Not arguing but giving Bernie one more chance.

"I'm prepared for all of that."

"I know you are. Or, at least you think you are. From now on, when I stay home, we will stay home together. When I go out, we will go out together.

Even before your generous offer. Even before we were married. I had decided to stop all gambling. That part of my life is over. I choose marriage. I choose __you__."

They didn't hug. They just went back to the rest of their day. A very nice day at home. They never discussed it again. **Never**. Mom was happy. That's all Dad wanted. Dad was happy. That's all Mom wanted.

My Dad was true to his word. Aside from occasional vacations with Mom to places like Las Vegas, he never gambled again. To stop, he was not in need of Gambler's Anonymous. He did not have a sickness. He did something well. He enjoyed it. He got married. He stopped. Never looked back. Never regretted it. If he regretted it, he never said so.

In later years, Dad always described himself as a simple man. From the outside looking in, that's probably how it appeared. Maybe from his perspective as well. But Dad was just a little bit deeper than people understood. We were talking one day. I asked.

"When you first got married, how did you know what to say when Mom asked you about gambling? Gambling was your passion and you were so good at it."

He responded.

"Let me ask you a question. If you bought a gun and brought it into your home and an intruder broke in and threatened you and your family, would you use the gun? Would you shoot the intruder? Would you kill the burglar?"

I was a little confused by the question. It was interesting. But, it didn't seem to be on topic. I responded.

"I guess. I don't know. It depends. I'm not sure."

He said.

"You're wrong. You would use the gun."

"How do you know? How can you be so sure?"

"Simple, the decision to use or not use the gun wasn't made by you when the intruder broke into the house. The decision to shoot the intruder was made when you bought the gun and brought __it__ into the house. See the difference?"

He continued.

"The decision for me to stop gambling and the gambling life style was not made when your Mother asked. It was made when I asked her to marry me. I was surprised she asked me to go on with it but it didn't matter. My

mind was made up long before. I knew what I wanted. I knew how I felt. It was easy to tell her."

Dad chose an interesting example. At no time in our lives, did a gun of any type enter into our home. He was on a roll and I was fully engaged.

*"Truman, Nimitz, my Father. People I admire. They knew this. If you think through and understand your choices beforehand **and** decide wisely. You'll **always** be able to sleep well at night. No regrets.*

It will never be a matter of whether you made the right decision or if the decision worked out. It will always be a matter of how you considered your options and came to a decision. And then, how you executed your decision at the appropriate time.

For at this appropriate time, your adversary will think you are consider-ing your options for the very first time. This will not be the case. This will give you the advantage."

Continuing.

"I'll give you one last example. The great Cleveland running back Jim Brown made a seemingly impossible touchdown run. On this particular called play, he took the handoff at full gallop toward the line. It was an inside run off right guard.

The hole opened momentarily. As Brown approached, it suddenly be-came filled with defenders. Stopping short of being tackled for a loss. He seemed to bounce backwards a step. Untouched, he circled around the line and ran for a touchdown.

After the game, the newsmen supposedly asked him.

'How did you change directions and make that touchdown? You were stopped for a loss. No-one could have made that decision to cut outside as quickly as you did. It was impossible.'

Jim Brown reportedly said calmly and confidently.

'In my dreams, I've run that play a million times.'

See?"

Now I understood why Dad was such a good card player. And in truth, why he was good at everything in life.

Years later after Mom had passed away and Dad was in his mid-seventies, we were talking on the phone. He mentioned in passing that he had joined a community senior's center. That sounded nice enough. Then he said, occasionally they play Poker. I stopped him.

"Dad. Dad!"

"Yeah"

"How much did you take them for?"

"Nothing... Not much... A few dollars... About twenty.

"Give it back."

"OK"

BOOK THREE

Life Gets Real

Karma: "*...Good intent and good deed contribute to good karma and future happiness, while bad intent and bad deed contribute to bad karma and future suffering...*"

- **Wikipedia.org, the on-line "free encyclopedia"**

CHAPTER 1

"DO YOU KNOW VERNA IS DEAD?"

Our mailwoman Audrey delivered a non-descript grey envelope to our house. First class stamp. Typed. Addressed to
me. Inside. A typed letter on grey stationary.

> **January 29, 2003**
> **Dear Nat,**
> **I am writing in regard to the side of your family through**
> **your late Mother Ann Ethel. I will gladly explain in detail**
> **when we speak. I believe the situation will interest you.**
> **Please call me at your earliest convenience. Please feel**
> **free to call collect.**
> **Thank you very much. I apologize for being so vague, and**
> **look forward to hearing from you.**
> **Sincerely, David**
> **Beverly Hills, California**

In this twenty-first century, we are living in an environment of
distrust. Every e-mail, text, and phone call brings an immediate
impulsive negative response. "Am I being scammed?" I also wondered. Do people get letters anymore?

It had been twelve years since my Mom had passed away. Volumes of encyclopedia sized dissertations have been written about Jewish boys and their Mothers. If I fit the stereotype, so be it. I missed my Mom. I know Dad did too.

I did not know David. I don't know how he knew me, Ann Ethel or my address. In the internet era, I recognize that nothing is truly private. I should have thrown the letter in the trash the day it came. It had to be a scam. I didn't.

I also didn't respond. At least not right away. As if removing the letter from my house would sanitize me from harm, I brought the letter to my office. I let it sit on my desk for a few weeks – Just staring at me.

News about my Mom that might interest me? All I had to do was call. It got the better of me. I won't keep you in suspense. It was not a scam.

But on that first call in 2003, I was more than skeptical. I was angry. Some-one had the nerve to use my Mother's name in a scam. I was going to put a stop to it. I called.

"David, this is Nat. I believe you wrote me a letter regarding Ann Ethel."

Monotone with no emotion or recognition.

"Hello Nat."

I was on his speaker phone. He sounded like he was in a canyon and not too close to the phone. I waited. Finally I asked.

"How can I help you?"

It seemed as though he came closer to his phone. He still spoke with no emotion but his voice was clearer.

"Your Mother had a brother. Theodore. Correct?"

"Go on."

"Is that correct?"

"Yes."

"Well, it's actually in relationship to Theodore that I contacted you. Did you call him Ted?"

"Go on."

His voice was taking on a stronger tone.

"At any rate. You have a considerable amount of money coming to you as Ann Ethel is deceased and you are her son."

I called from my office because I worked for a large corporation. I knew if there were any problems in the future, it would easier if David had my work phone number rather than my home number. Anyone in their right mind would have hung up at that Moment. All I could say was *"Go on."*

"In my research, I uncovered some information. It turns out Theodore was entitled to a large estate before he died. He died without a will. It's a long story. We'll get into it. The bottom line is that his estate belongs to you and the survivors of your Mother and her sister Eileen."

This sent a cold shiver down my back. It was clear he knew about Eileen. My Mom. And, Teddy. I responded with some force.

"Any money Teddy had, he got by bad means. I don't want any part of it! He was a very bad person. And, what research are you doing on my family???"

"I'm sorry. Let me step back. I am a writer. I've written episodes for many television series as well as movie scripts. I also write books. I was writing a biography of Jean Harlow when I stumbled on to your family. Actually, I stumbled on to Dorothy. She was married to Theodore."

Quietly I said.

"I know. That was my Aunt Dotty. Everyone called him Ted. He was my Uncle Teddy."

I was softening. Intellectually, I knew this is exactly how a scam is supposed to work. A little bit of personal and public information to set the stage followed by the bite.

The beauty of the internet is that it provides information instantly at your fingertips. Within two minutes, I had "Googled" David. If this was him, he was real. He had a long-established career writing in film, television, and print.

"Do you have information about my Uncle Teddy?"

As soon as I asked the question, I stopped listening. I could hear him talking. I zoned out. I flashed to my Mom. I was a young teen. It was the early-mid 1970's. We were at our home in Evanston.

The phone rang. She answered. She burst out crying. It didn't well up and come out. It exploded out like a burst balloon. It was immediate. She stretched the kitchen phone wall cord through the living room as she paced to the base of the staircase that lead upstairs. It wasn't a long walk. I heard her screaming at the phone. With anger…

"Where have you been?
Do you know Verna is dead?
Did you know?"

Her voice trailed off. Then with some tenderness…

"I've been crazy with worry over you. I miss you. I love you. How are you?"

She didn't shout the last question. She fainted. On the stairs. Just laid right down like she was on anesthesia before surgery. Let go of the phone by her side. No thud. I don't know if he answered.

Side note: *I watched the movie "Castaway" on DVD with my family this week. Many months after I had written this chapter. Helen Hunt learns Tom Hanks is still alive. Four plus years since his plane went down. On the phone. She faints.*

I immediately thought of my Mom. It made me wonder. Why was I able to write about my Mother fainting so casually? One sentence. Two words.

Are we conditioned? All of us have seen movies and TV shows. A central character receives shocking news. Faints. My Mom fainted. How many of us have actually seen someone faint in person? I hadn't. This is still my one and only time.

The level of shock a person's brain takes in to shut down the body must be tremendous. Why didn't I give more attention to writing about this event? I don't know. Thank you Helen Hunt for helping me think about it now.

I yelled.

"Dad!!! Something's wrong with Mom. And someone is on the phone."

Mom was stirring. More like purring I think. Dad checked on Ann. Dad picked up the phone.

*"**Who** the hell is this?"*

"It's Ted."

Dad paused. No emotion.

"What do you want?"

"I need money. How much do you have? Can you wire it to me? C'mon Bernie, you were never a good provider for Ann Ethel, living in that small house with your small job and your small life. You were never good enough for Ann Ethel. Why don't you do the right thing and help me out? You know my sister would want you to."

He'd pushed the right buttons. Dad was fanatical about taking care of Mom. Mom and he were both very happy with their lives. Real or not. They had once lived in the shadow of Teddy's glamour and Eileen's absence in Verna's mind. Dad could have provided a more lavish lifestyle. The cost was too high.

He could not say "no" to Ted. He would not say "no". Ted knew. The 1970's were a very tough time in America. Between, unemployment and inflation, it was the worst economic time America had seen since the Great Depression.

Dad was on the other side of it now. He wasn't a kid sneaking into Soldier Field. He was an adult trying to feed his family preparing to send his daughter to college.

He knew Ted was correct on one score. Ann **would** want Bernie to help him. No matter what he had done. No matter what he ever did. Ann Ethel would always love her brother. He wired Teddy $500. A lot of money for the time. We never heard from Teddy again.

I stopped David from talking. I had not been listening. I asked.

"May I call you back? I have to go to a meeting."

I didn't have a meeting. But I had to get off of the phone. I needed to think. He politely agreed. We selected another time to speak later in the week and we hung up.

CHAPTER 2

WARM MEMORIES OF WABASH AVENUE

My office door was already closed. I started to think back. Everybody loved Teddy. He was the pride of the family. I recalled one time. I must have been about six years old. Mom and I took the EL downtown Chicago from Howard Street.

When we wanted to go somewhere. We walked. Took the bus or took the EL. Dad was at work. It was a weekday. We'd wait for the #7 bus to come down Asbury (which was Western Avenue a few blocks away in Chicago). The #7 turned East on Howard. Took us to the EL.

If we wanted the bus to come fast, Mom would light up a cigarette. She'd get in a few puffs. The bus would come. Every time. She never got to finish. If it seemed like we were waiting a long time, I'd tell Mom to light one. They always came. It was our game.

This day, the EL took us to the south Loop. While called the El for "elevated" train. The Howard Street EL actually went below ground as the north Loop approached. We always wanted to sit in the first car to watch. Once underground. It was pitch dark.

The EL whipped through the darkness screeching. In the 1960's, you could take the Red "A" or Green "B" train from Howard Street. They stopped at alternate stops except the busy ones like Addison on a Cubs game day. In the loop, both the "A" and "B" EL stopped underground at Washington. Right at the basement door of Marshall Field's. Shoppers didn't have to walk outside.

At that time, Marshall Field's Store for Men was located about a block from the main State Street store. That's where we met Teddy. Teddy came from his office. Inside Field's. We passed the giant real Kodiak bear, now stuffed, in sporting goods on the first floor. That's where I wanted to stop.

Up to the third floor. Teddy bought me a full suit of clothes. Just like that. From shoes to an honest to goodness men's fedora hat. Men had not completely stopped wearing hats yet. Kids did not wear hats. I did not wear hats. I didn't have any place to wear a suit. This was an extravagance.

Teddy treated us to lunch at Miller's Tap under the EL tracks on Wabash. Lunch over. Teddy and Mom kissed. Then hugged. I shook his hand. Said "thank you". Teddy went back to his office. Leaving Millers, Mom smiled.

"As long as we're down here. Let's enjoy Wabash Avenue today."

Novice Chicagoans thought State Street was the shopper's paradise. Not Mom. Wabash Avenue. Mom's budget. Fifty-five dollars and change to spend on Bernie's presents. She'd been saving.

The goal was to buy Bernie Christmas presents during the year. Things he would like – but did not need. She'd put them away for later. Little things she could hide in her unmentionables drawer. Off we went. Mom knew her way around Wabash Avenue. We walked. She explained.

"Never buy your Father a shirt or tie for his birthday or Christmas. Never a sweater. Nothing practical."

"Why Mom?"

"Your Father and I lived through the depression. I lived through home rationing during the War. Your Dad spent four Christmases away from home. He got what the Navy gave him for his holidays. What Goldie might have sent. Likely socks or a t-shirt.

Now. He gets angry if he gets something impersonal. Something he might have bought for himself during the year. It sounds odd I know. The gifts don't have to cost a lot of money. They just require a lot of thought. You see?"

I nodded. I confess. I carried this impractical present giving, receiving ritual into my own adulthood. A string of purchasing on Wabash began. We arrived at our first location.

Kroch's & Brentano's. Their flagship book store.

"The Spy Who Came In from the Cold" by John le Carre. Signed hard cover first edition. $8

"Christmas is Together Time" by Charles Shultz. Signed. $4

Mom read about the newly published book signings the week before.

V. L. & A. – The original Abercrombie & Fitch. (The store with all the gadgets.)

Brown and Bigelow - 52 count playing cards. Two decks. Designed for Bridge with score-pad. Brown leather gift box. Each card sported a drawn image of a real American Indian. Rich color. Just the heads in full dress. Each card different. $6

Official Swiss Army Knife. 30 Gadgets. Even a tooth pick! $20 (This was the ultimate useless gift. Dad did not hike or camp. He couldn't fix anything. Had no need for the tools. Still it was something he had always admired in V.L.A.'s window.)

Rose Records

"Hello Dolly" 33 1/3 LP by Louis Armstrong $2 (A little harder to hide.)

Marshall Field's – Wabash side. A quick stop in the basement for a snack. Frango Mints and fresh whole white milk. Up the silver aluminum colored escalator.

<u>Stamp department.</u> A block (4 stamps) of mint 1945 U.S. issued three cent stamps honoring the U.S. Navy. Blue stamps with sailors in their white uniforms. $1

<u>Coin department</u>. 1964 Canadian silver dollar. Commemorating French Quebec. $2

<u>Fields Afar</u>. A pair of special cuff links. Made in Europe exclusively for Marshall Field & Company. A pair of hockey players with stick and puck. Dressed in red jerseys. $7

<u>Toy department</u>. Chicago Cubs ceramic bobble head. In box. Green base. Full color uniform with a brown bear head (Not a white player face) under a blue Cubs hat with a red "C". $5

Wabash Avenue. All in. Fifty-five dollars spent. It was a whirlwind spree. We took the El home. A six-year-old on the El with bags **and** a hat box. Mom with her special presents for Dad. She hid everything when she got home in her lingerie drawer. It was our secret. I kept all year.

Mom gave the presents to Dad at Christmas. Each had its own cryptic gift tag. Examples:

Swiss Army Knife – *"To Bernie from SGT. Swiss cheese – Oh holey night!"*

Cubs bobble head – *"To Bernie from Ernie Banks"*

Canadian silver dollar – *"To Bernie from Jean Beliveau & Maurice Richard"*

Before he opened the presents, Dad had to try to guess each based on the gift tag clues.

The trips downtown were special occasions. Not frequent. Special. Mom and Dad were still doing OK on money in 1964. This day with Uncle Teddy and shopping with Mom is a very warm memory.

Since I can remember. Christmas was always special. Giving really was as good as getting. The thought that went into the presents were wonderfully fun and imaginative. In this regard, Christmas went on all year.

For the record. Dad gave Mom a man's Swiss wrist watch from the original Abercrombie & Fitch. Stainless steel. Waterproof. 17 Jewels. Incabloc (protects the movement from hard shocks). Nice and large. Easy to read.

He also gave her the board game "<u>Monopoly</u>". Yes. He gave a legally blind woman a board game. The houses, hotels, and player pieces were all wooden. It predated the plastic hotels and metal top hat, race car, and dog player pieces.

He replaced the provided dice with his own dice. I'm fairly sure we were the only family on the block playing Monopoly with translucent red dice from the Sands Hotel. Our whole family wore that game out playing it.

CHAPTER 3

TEDDY THE RAT

The warm memory started to fade. Thoughts of Teddy floated back into my mind. I knew some of the story. I'd pieced it together through the years.

Teddy came out of the Army and World War II in one piece. Barely. Family lore had it that he was wounded by shrapnel in Germany. Supposedly, some of the fragments were still in him. And, he wore a metal plate in his head. I don't know if that was true or not. You couldn't tell from looking.

Teddy was handsome. Not movie star handsome. More "believably" handsome. About 5'8 (tall for his family). He was smart. Glib. Very likable. He was just a little crazy. A "good crazy". Teddy could be a charmer. He was never obvious. He was smooth. The war hero stuff was part of his patter. He acted shy. Yet, managed to work his service record into the conversation.

From the beginning, Teddy had game. Ambitious. He was going to move up in the world. Nothing was going to stop him. He wasn't reckless. He was determined. He was a planner. He would take his time and do it right. Like Bernie, Teddy went to college on the GI Bill. His major was finance and accounting.

172

One stereotype of Jews by Jews and non-Jews alike. "All Jews are smart." Sometimes this is offered as a compliment. Sometimes this is offered as an insult. The danger in stereotypes of course is the old adage. "Where there's smoke, there's fire." The true blazing fire comes when a person believes it himself. Teddy was a raging inferno. He surely believed he was smarter than everyone else.

Along the way, Teddy married Dorothy (Aunt Dotty) long before I was born. They did not have kids. Looking back, I have to believe Teddy genuinely loved Dotty. I have no other explanation for their marriage. It didn't fit any of Teddy's later patterns. She wasn't remotely rich. Possessed no political or business connections to ease Teddy's way. She was Pennsylvania Dutch from Lancaster. Not Jewish.

She was plain. She wore more make-up. Used more perfume (different). Dressed more glamorously than my Mom. She might have been a good corporate wife. An asset. Quick to entertain. In control at late night business functions.

As far as I could tell, Dotty was well liked. She was always nice to me. But, she struck me as one of those adults that were just a little uncomfortable around kids.

I remember one year at Christmas, Dotty and Teddy put up an artificial Christmas tree in Verna's house. It **was** white. There was an electric light next to the tree. The light had a circle of four colors in plastic that rotated around. Yellow, red, blue, and green.

The light shone through the colors illuminating the tree in one color after the other. If you touched it, the tree itself felt like jagged little knives. It was made of aluminum or some metal. I was just a kid. And, I knew this was ugly. Probably pretty cool at a night club. Not at Verna's.

Teddy took his good looks, quick wit, book smarts, college education, and war record. Looked for a place to land. He found it. Teddy started as a bookkeeper with the Royce Corporation of

Chicago. Royce made condiments and appetizers such as olives and relish. They did it well. They'd done it for decades. It was a successful, established corporation with nationwide distribution.

Royce was privately owned. There really was a Mr. Royce. He took to Teddy. Teddy took to him. It was a "Father & son" relationship from the start.

Teddy was dedicated. He put in ten and twelve hour days. He worked six days – sometimes seven days a week.

It seemed as though he wanted to learn every aspect of the business – no matter how small or seemingly insignificant. To Teddy, there were no small details.

Mr. Royce was sure Teddy had learned his work ethic in the army. No days off. He looked on with approval and pride. Slowly but surely, Teddy moved up the company ladder. Eventually, he became the Comptroller. His title today would be Chief Financial Officer CFO.

My Grandfather Nat, Verna's husband passed away uneventfully in the 1950's. Eileen, Teddy, and Ann Ethel were married and living on their own. Verna sold the apartment. She bought a small, nice, white stucco house on Campbell Avenue on the north side of Chicago. It was in a Jewish section near Western and Devon. She owned the house. No mortgage. As the apartment had been, it was the focal point for gatherings be it family or friends. Verna enjoyed a full and very satisfying social life on Campbell Avenue. All of her children were happy. It was a happy time.

And then a little cloud formed. Just a little one. We didn't see the storm coming. Nobody did. Teddy was doing well. He was starting to live a very high life. Bernie and Ann Ethel enjoyed many nights out with Teddy and Dotty. Mom adored her brother.

Mom loved Dotty for who she was and for making Teddy happy. Teddy was a little loud for Dad. But, he too loved how happy Mom was when she was around Teddy. And, he enjoyed the night life they all shared.

Teddy had a corner table and tab permanently on reserve at Grassfield's on Ridge on the north side of Chicago. Wherever Teddy and Dotty went, they ended up at Grassfield's to enjoy a steak or drink (or both). It looked like one of those art-deco supper clubs from the movies.

Grassfield's had a Las Vegas type neon sign. At night, the lights appeared like satellites revolving around a moon with comets going by. Very bright and colorful. One day, our family happened to be driving by Grassfield's when my Dad said.

"Look at their sign post. Teddy drove his car into it last night."

The sign post was dented badly but not down.

"Aunt Dotty called Ann this morning. Evidently Teddy had a few drinks last night and plowed into it."

He wasn't smiling. But, he wasn't reprimanding when he told us either.

"No-one was hurt. Mr. Grassfield told Teddy 'don't worry about it'. He'd have it fixed and come back soon."

That was Teddy. We didn't think about it then. In retrospect, how much money **did** Teddy spend at Grassfield's? "Don't worry about it."? "Come back soon."?

The next thing we knew. Verna was moving. "What?" Teddy made **his** offer that could not be refused. He was moving to a more expensive address. The clouds were getting darker. His offer to his Mother was.

*"Sell your house. Give me **all** of your retirement money. Live with Dotty and me for the rest of your life. We'll take care of you."*

This was a hard decision for Verna. Eileen was in New Orleans. Ann Ethel was nearby in Evanston. Visiting less often. She didn't drive. Her kids were getting older. Verna was getting older. Independent as she was, being taken care of her by her son had an attractive ring to it. Her only son. She said.

"Yes."

At 2300 Lincoln Park West, The Belden Stratford Hotel is located on Chicago's gold coast directly across from the Lincoln Park Zoo, Lake Shore Drive, and Lake Michigan. It was built in the 1920's with perfect art-deco décor. It was once a destination for the famous and a residence for the rich.

Teddy and Aunt Dotty moved into the penthouse on the top floor. They had a castle-style wooden drawbridge made at the entrance of their door. Their suite was palatial. The view east from the window of Lincoln Park and Lake Michigan was stupendous.

The hotel was aging. It was still a prestigious address and location. But it was slipping. No doubt they were happy to have Teddy as the latest resident in their penthouse. It had been vacant a while. Teddy was paying top dollar. If he had thought about it, he probably could have struck a better deal. He didn't think about it. Money was for spending.

It was cold and lonely for Verna. She was separated from her friends and family. Teddy bought her a fur coat. It wasn't the same. Teddy and Aunt Dotty were never home. Mom and Dad visited as often as they could on the weekends. She missed her house. She missed Campbell Avenue.

The penthouse of the Belden-Stratford? Fur coats? Nobody said anything. The family wasn't suppressing doubts. Truly, nobody doubted Teddy could afford the splendor. With Verna's bankroll, Teddy had his business connections as well as his salary. Banks must have been lining up to lend Teddy money.

There is someone else that should have had doubts. Mr. Royce. He didn't. Not yet. His company was flourishing on paper. "On paper" would be the operative words.

Since the invention of business, financial records were kept in pencil on paper. Computers hadn't been invented. "Keeping the books" was a big job. It was Teddy's job. It was perfect for him.

Every larger company had overhead, payroll, invoicing, accounts receivable, tax requirements, multiple ledgers, cash accounts, multiple banks and multiple bank accounts. A company needed a sharp person to keep it all straight. Royce had Teddy. He'd put in his time. He knew every inch of the company. Teddy went to work. His work.

Teddy and Aunt Dotty lived in splendor. Then one day around 1970, there was a knock on the door of our house. It was the FBI.

"Have you seen Theodore? Have you heard from him?"

Mom and Dad answered honestly.

"No, Why? What's happened?"

*"We can't say. No-one seems to know where he is. If you hear from him, we **expect** you to call us."*

The FBI left. Mom called Aunt Dotty.

"No. She hadn't seen Teddy in a week.

No. She hadn't heard from him.

No. She didn't know where he was.

Yes. The FBI came to see her.

No. She didn't think the FBI believed her.

Yes. She was scared. So was Verna."

Nobody we know ever saw Teddy again. Eventually, the FBI pieced it together for us. Teddy had been embezzling from Royce. No-one knows how long or how much. He was slow and methodical. He was covering his tracks from one account to the next.

Borrowing from one bank to make a small payment to the next. He made sure Mr. Royce stayed paid and the company kept operating. He was syphoning off funds. Teddy was stealing the money he borrowed from the banks too.

There is no evidence in the beginning that there were other women or other families. I do think Teddy branched out and started to take advantage of women eventually while he was still with Aunt Dotty. Well-to-do women who trusted Teddy and gave him money or valuables.

I think this was all business for Teddy. He needed the money. Needed the network of women for the day he ran. Which, he must have known would come eventually. Dad was not the only one taught to plan for the future.

The aftermath was not **just** emotionally crushing. It was an economic disaster. Aunt Dotty was left holding the bag. All of Teddy's creditors came after her starting with Mr. Royce. The authorities determined that Dotty really was in the dark. No criminal charges were brought against her.

Teddy had stolen or spent all of their personal money. All of their remaining possessions were sold to pay creditors including the Belden-Stratford. She was penniless and homeless. So was Verna.

As much as Mom felt for Aunt Dotty, Verna was her first priority. The Belden-Stratford evicted Aunty Dotty and Verna shortly thereafter. Verna had no possessions left other than her knitting needles. For Verna, it was humbling to say the least. She came to live with us in Evanston.

Looking back, it's not that I blame Aunt Dotty (although I did at the time). She panicked. She said some horrible things to my Father. Her life was crumbling. It was crumbling fast. Rather than embracing those around her, she lashed out. Dotty blamed anyone near her who would listen or tried to help her.

You can see where this was heading. Teddy was the golden boy. He didn't lie or steal before Aunt Dotty came into his life. He didn't have or need the extravagant lifestyle. If he stole, it was to keep **her** happy. It wasn't his fault. It was **her**.

This would be Verna and Ann Ethel's version. Aunt Dotty lashed out at Bernie. Bernie took Verna in. Verna and Ann Ethel circled the wagons. Dorothy was out! To paraphrase Verna. "She was dead to us."

It did not end well. Close friends for so long. My parents and Aunt Dotty did not speak again for years. I saw her at Verna's funeral. Dotty came to our house many, many years later for dinner. It was an attempt at reconciliation. But, there was nothing left. No anger. No words. No rehashing the past. No "good old days". No future to speak about. Mom and Dad had a lot of great traits. Forgiveness wasn't one of them.

It was the last time any of us saw her. Aunt Dotty found an apartment and a job. She worked the rest of her life at a nut and candy store on north Clark Street. It was a meager existence. It was honest. In one of life's ironic twists, David met Dotty many times at her store. He was a young hungry customer.

I called back David and learned the rest of the story.

CHAPTER 4

THE "BLONDE BOMBSHELL"

I was now comfortable that David was not a scam artist. I still did not understand why he contacted me at first. We began to speak regularly and things became clearer. He sent me a copy of his recent book on Jean Harlow. It was objective and caring.

I learned. In the 1930's, Harlow was a star of the greatest magnitude. She graced the covers of <u>Life</u> and <u>Time</u> Magazines. Shared top billing with Jimmy Cagney, Clark Gable, Spencer Tracy, and William Powell just to name a few.

Harlow starred in classic films such as "<u>Dinner at Eight</u>". My personal favorite. "<u>Wife vs. Secretary</u>". Howard Hughes featured a young Jean Harlow in "<u>Hell's Angels</u>".

She was the first true sex symbol of the talkie movie era. She preceded Marylyn Monroe by twenty years. Following a meteoric rise to the top, Harlow died at age twenty-six. Kidney failure. 1937.

It wasn't murder. It **was** a death that could have been prevented with greater care and attention from her Mother and hangers-ons. She was sick for quite a while. She was shooting the movie "<u>Saratoga</u>" with Clark Gable when she died.

Preventative care was not a consideration. The studio knew she was ailing. Her Mother knew. She was on a schedule. A lot of money was at stake. By the time she went to the hospital, it was too late. In retrospect, she died a slow death. To her circle, she died suddenly without warning – or without preparation (this is important).

David's Harlow Bio was the first to ever portray Harlow as anything other than just another vapid, sex-starved, movie tramp; whose demise was expected. Even deserved. Like a soulless girl devoid of morals. It's too bad. David accurately portrayed Jean Harlow as a warm, deep person with a stage persona carefully honed by her ubiquitous stage Mother.

There are many writers in Hollywood. David's impeccable research distinguishes him. Keeps David constantly employed by "A-List" TV and movie executives. How fun it would have been if David could have met my Uncle Davey and his World War II movie mogul friends.

Always on a work deadline. David was generous to me and my family with his time. We began to have regular discussions. Researching Jean Harlow. David ran into an unusual situation. He explained.

"Harlow died and was interned in California. After taxes, any money she had was taken by her Mother and is long gone. Every state has their own laws governing estate transfer. There really are no film right royalties.

Further, while her image is still managed by an agency, there isn't much residual money attached to this either. The bottom line is, for all of her fame and success, there really isn't any money to be had anymore."

I just said.

"OK."

David was nice. This was interesting. I like old movies. I wasn't tracking with how this related to my family. He continued.

"Jean Harlow died intestate (She did not leave a will). *So did her Mother. At the height of her fame and star-power, Harlow invested in a very complicated annuity called an Indian Headright."*

Anticipating my question. David explained.

"Headrights are essentially oil rights on Indian land. They are called 'rights' because the US government way back when secured these oil rights for Indian tribes that had been dispossessed from their land. This one was in Oklahoma. I guess outsiders were allowed to invest in them."

"Oil wells?"

"In essence. Here's where it gets interesting. Harlow designated herself, her Mother, and her childhood friend Ruth as beneficiaries of the Headright annuity. Ruth outlived Jean and her Mother – both of whom died without wills.

Ruth married Johnny. Johnny was a pretty famous bandleader at the time and friends with Jean Harlow. Johnny was born in Lancaster, Pennsylvania. Dutch Country. Care to guess the name of Ruth and Johnny's adopted daughter?"

"No idea?"

"Dorothy."

"Teddy's Dorothy?"

"Teddy's Dorothy. Want to know something else? The Indian Headright Annuity hasn't been touched since it was created nearly eighty years ago. I doubt Jean's Mother, Ruth, Johnny, or Dorothy knew it existed. Jean Harlow died prematurely and suddenly without instruction or direction for survivors."

He continued.

"__Eighty years__ of oil production. Proceeds going into an annuity. Earning interest year after year. Bank accounts that age eventually become bank property if dormant or unclaimed over a given timeframe.

The Annuity of the Headright can never expire. The oil is still on Indian land. Any money made from the oil goes into the annuity. Only the owner of the annuity can claim the money."

"So what are you saying here?"

"I'm saying that while I was researching Harlow, I stumbled onto this Headright. I've been using my own money and lawyers these past four years to figure out which state or states the estate would actually be adjudicated.

And, while I was doing my day job, I was trying to figure out and contact the actual beneficiaries of this estate. This is how I came to find you. You sir, through Dorothy are an heir to the estate of Jean Harlow."

For emphasis. He added.

"__The Blonde Bombshell!__"

"Because of Aunt Dotty? I'm not related to Dorothy - Aunt Dotty in any way."

"The law is funny. And, there's more to the story I think you'll want to know. Theodore..."

"Teddy."

"Teddy left Dorothy and Chicago in the 1970's for good which was the last she ever saw of him. Right?"

"I think."

"He was her husband. What happens when a husband goes missing for a long period of time? Say seven years or so."

"I don't know. The wife starts over I guess."

"More accurately, the wife legally declares their husband dead. That's what Dorothy did. She declared Teddy dead. There was no reason to think otherwise.

The local Chicago police and local FBI. The creditors. They had all stopped calling Dorothy years before. No-one in Chicago believed Ted was alive or questioned Dorothy when she declared him dead. She had no money. It was over for her.

We wouldn't be speaking today if this is where it ended. Teddy dead. Dorothy or her decedents collect the Headright Annuity."

"But we are talking. Why?"

"Because Teddy wasn't dead. Not dead. Alive!"

"Son of a..."

"That's right."

"And you know this how?"

"It wasn't easy. The local authorities stopped checking on Dorothy. They knew she was not a part of the puzzle. Still, the national authorities had no evidence he was dead.

They kept looking. They knew he was living day to day. He got out of Chicago with some money. But, not enough to live under the radar for the rest of his life. He was going to surface. And he did."

"Where?"

"Eventually, New York City. It was a big city. Are you ready for this? When they finally caught him, he had been getting treatment from a VA Hospital. He was still taking advantage of his veteran benefits. While the FBI was looking for him, another branch of the government was making him better. There were no computers to tie the two together."

"Incredible"

"After some doing, my attorney was able to get me access to his criminal record. He was wanted in about eight states including Alaska. He was once even suspected for murder although there were never formal charges. Mostly, he was wanted for con jobs right up to the day he really did die."

"Wasn't he an old man by then? Who would let themselves be conned by Teddy?"

"Older yes. By the early 1980's, he was old. And, he was also dying. When they caught him in New York City, they interviewed a number of ladies he was currently seeing. Each one said the same thing."

"Which was?"

"Ted is charming. Ted is my friend. Ted has money. He doesn't need mine. I would gladly give him money if he asked. He makes me happy. I don't believe the bad things you are saying about him."

"Everything he had ever taken was gone. Spent. By the time he was caught and went in front of the judge, the VA doctor confirmed he was terminally ill. There was nothing to recover. There was no current complainant. The judge allowed Ted to go home and die. And he did. Shortly thereafter."

"And Aunt Dotty?"

"She died three years before Ted. Without a will!"

"Which means?

"According to the applicable laws, the estate and Headright Annuity traveled through dead Dorothy to living Ted. Ted died without a will. His estate, which was nothing other than this Headright traveled to Ted's siblings."

"Eileen and Ann Ethel."

I said aloud to myself.

"Both of whom are also dead. Which means..."

"Eileen's children RoseAnne and Bobby and my sister and I are next in line."

I finished his sentence.

"Yep. Want to hear something ironic?"

"Sure."

"Ted wanted to be rich. If Ted had just worked his job and never stole, never left Dorothy, and the Headright had been discovered, he would have been richer than he could have ever imagined. As it is, he died penniless. And, he never knew."

"Karma" I said.

The aftermath proved to be far less interesting. The estate traveled through the courts of various states for years. Every court has lawyers somewhere nearby looking for a client. By the time the estate ran out of states, there were dozens of legitimate heirs to the Headright Annuity.

What might have started out as a windfall turned out to be little more than a breeze. Very little money was left. It didn't matter. Learning about my family. Meeting David. The money was secondary. I was probably the only person sad to see the whole affair come to an end with the payout. The journey was far better than the destination.

David was a prince through the whole thing. He had the connections and knew what to do. We made him an equal partner on whatever we earned. I doubt he made enough money to even cover his legal expenses. We never stepped into a court room. He took care of everything. It was part of his exacting research. He was determined to see it through.

I count David among my closest friends. We have never met in person. He knows about my family intimately. I trust and admire him. He is a man of his word.

When it was all over, I sent David a monogrammed cigar humidor for his office. It was an antique. Ann Ethel had kept it all those years. She gave it to me. It contained one old black and white photograph. The monogrammed initials and photo. Teddy. His humidor.

CHAPTER 5

EVANSTON

Evanston, Illinois is a Township. Thirty-six square miles. Not very large for the nearly 80,000 people that live there. Lake Michigan to the east. Affluent Wilmette and Baha'i Temple at Sheridan Road on the north. The Chicago River borders on the west. South Evanston abuts Chicago at Howard Street.

Evanston is most famous as the home of prestigious Northwestern University. Home of the purple and white "Wildcats". Bernie's school.

Bernie and Ann Ethel were living happily in an apartment in Chicago on the near north side at Pine Grove and Surf. That would be just east of Broadway. Just north of Diversey. Walking distance to both Wrigley Field and Lincoln Park Zoo in opposite directions. Just a couple of blocks from the lake.

They were married in 1952. They had my sister in 1954. They lost a baby at childbirth in 1956. I was born in 1958 at Cuneo Hospital in Chicago. After the lost child, Mom was told she would never have children.

I was a surprise. I was a Caesarian (Breach) baby. Julius Caesar was the first breach baby. Hence the name Caesarian. I was born on March 15th. I always thought it kind of cool that on the day

Caesar died (The Ides of March), I was born the way Caesar was born. No-one else thought that was very interesting.

I was months pre-mature. I was scheduled. I was born on a Saturday. I know this for a fact. Bernie worked Monday through Friday. He was free on Saturday to drive Mom to the hospital. I stayed in the hospital for a while getting bigger (I was palm sized at birth). Then I came home.

Even though I was really small, there was no place to put me. Bernie and Ann Ethel had a decision to make. Move. Or carry me around for the rest of my childhood. They decided to move.

With the exception of Dad's time in the Navy, neither Bernie nor Ann Ethel had ever lived anywhere other than Chicago. Further, they had never lived in any type of home other than an apartment.

They weighed their options. They could afford a larger apartment in the city. They moved us into Evanston. Western Avenue in Chicago is one of the longest continuous streets in the United States. Going north, Western turns into Asbury when it hits Howard Street.

Just a few blocks from Howard Street off of Asbury, we moved into a townhouse. Instead of going up, these houses went across. Four two-story square houses connected by side walls. Sideways apartments.

If you were not watching the street signs when you passed Howard Street, you could not tell you'd left Chicago. There was one exception. Evanston was the home of the WCTU. The Women's Christian Temperance Union.

Evanston was dry. Bone dry. Every third store front on the south side of Howard Street seemed to be a bar, tavern, liquor store, or restaurant.

We ate pan pizza at Gulliver's on Howard. The most famous tavern was Biddy Mulligans in Rogers Park. Where Evanston and Chicago met near Howard Street and Sheridan Road. About a mile east from our house. A Jazz bar. Dad took me to hear Muddy Waters. Son Seals. Koko Taylor. B.B. King. No cover charge. Draught beer cost twenty-five cents. Twelve-ounce paper cups.

The townhouse had three rooms on the first floor. Kitchen. Living room. Service bathroom. There were four rooms upstairs comprised of two bedrooms, a full bathroom, and a storage room. My room was the storage room.

My parents never needed much room. The brilliance of this move is that it allowed my sister and me to attend the Evanston Schools. With the lake front, the north shore, and all of those people in Evanston, it was actually a very wealthy suburb. Just not where we lived.

The funding and quality of the school systems were amazing. It likely cost them twice as much to live in Evanston as Chicago. Bernie and Ann Ethel made the sacrifice. Made the move.

That was Bernie. Not a big talker. He always knew the right thing to do for his family and others. Moving for better schools seems obvious today. It wasn't in 1958.

After they got married. Bernie left Hesher Brothers and the liquor industry. He went to work for Mr. Bruin at S. Bruin Incorporated. A bruin is a baby bear – Or a **cub**. This could not be a coincidence.

Bruin was a wholesaler. In plain English. A re-seller. In the 1950's and 1960's, independent stores needed a way to get their goods. This is where the wholesalers came in. It was before franchises and national stores owned their own supply chains.

Bruin sold candy, tobacco, Coke syrup, shaving supplies, and so on. Anything you could buy in a local drug store. Think of it this way, Hershey's Chocolate Corporation did not send a truck to the local paper stand to deliver one box of candy bars. They needed Bruin.

They needed wholesalers to get their goods to market economically. Bruin bought the goods in volume at wholesale pricing.

They put a markup on the products. Sold the products to the retail stores for less than the stores would pay directly to the manu-facturer. The store than sold at list price. Everyone made money.

Dad made a commission on everything he sold. He was good. He was very good. In an era when bubble gum sold for two pieces for a penny, Dad sold over one-million dollars' worth of candy.

This isn't the Uncle Teddy story. Bernie was honest to the day he died. His customers trusted him. It was a dream job. Just as his Father had done before Bernie was born. He drove to about twenty stops a day on the north side. Of course, Dad's clients were not bookies (I don't think). Each day. A different set of stops. No office for Will. No office for Dad. Always on the go.

The great sidelight of his job were his lunches. Celebrities were not removed from the public yet. No paparazzi. No camera phones. Dad ate his lunches at hot dog stands and diners across the north side.

Ate with the likes of DePaul basketball coach Ray Meyer. All time Cub great Charlie Grimm. Northwestern football coach Ara Parseghian (pre-Notre Dame). 1961 Stanley Cup winner coach Billy Reay of the Black Hawks. 1963 NCAA basketball champion-ship coach George Ireland of Loyola. And, a host of other sport-ing types through the years.

At each store, he'd spend a few minutes talking sports and poli-tics with the owner. Then, he'd leave the owner. Go to their inven-tory room. Review their stock. Write up their order. Move on. When I was young, I asked him.

"Why did the store owners let you write up their orders every week? You could have ordered a ton of everything."

He told me.

*"They trust me. When I review their inventory and place the order, I save them time and money. Sure, I could take advantage of them. **Once.** But that would be it. If I stuck them with inventory that couldn't sell, I sure heard about it. But that was not too often."*

He smiled. That was Dad.

The candy manufacturers used to give Dad boxes of candy as samples. Dad would bring them home and ask me and my friends to try the candy to see what was good.

The young kids in the neighborhood used to stick their hands in Dad's suit coat pocket and pull the candy out. Dad let them. He loved it. I guess that wouldn't happen today. He brought home boxes of baseball cards with all of that thick chalky pink bubble gum too. Dad was very popular.

The winters in Chicago can be brutal. Bernie never missed work. Never. If he was sick or the weather was bad, he just plowed right through.

That noted. There was one time Dad did not go to work. January 26, 1967. "**The Big Snow**". This was the worst blizzard in the history of the city. Everything was paralyzed. No-one worked. Mom sent Dad to the El Store to buy supplies. Dad trudged through the snow. He came back two hours later with a six-pack of coke and a frozen pizza. This is one of the few times I heard my Mom yell at Dad. Everyone in the neighborhood heard it.

When Mom had her first child, she stopped working. She was a stay-at-home Mom. Dad was the provider. If she missed Michigan Avenue, she never said a word. Bernie and Ann Ethel were living the life they both wanted.

When they moved to Evanston, Mom became perfectly suburban. She was in the Oakton PTA (Parent Teacher Association). Ann Ethel was a **very** fast touch-typer. She averaged between eighty and one-hundred words per minute on a manual type writer (not-electric). It seems almost impossible. Legally blind. Fast touch-typer? It's true. She didn't look at the page till she was done typing. There were rarely errors.

On nasty weather days, the school sent office staff to our house with typing requests and carbon paper. Mom would whip through it while they waited. Before copiers. Cleaner than mimeograph machines. They loved to make the trip. They could share coffee, conversation, and a cigarette with Mom while they waited.

She didn't just type. She helped the principal's office. She put her business skills to work. Unpaid volunteer. Only worked if asked. Didn't want to get in the way of the paid office staff. She was a welcome addition.

She bowled with the Oakton Elementary School Mothers at the Howard Bowl. Averaged about 125 per game. Couldn't see the pins. It was a big night at dinner if Mom made a "turkey" (three strikes in a row) or picked up a seven-ten split that day.

On the other hand, Mom was not exactly June Cleaver ("Leave it to Beaver"). Mom was not a good cook. She wasn't raised to cook. Made no real effort to learn.

Any attempt to make meat ended in a meal you chewed for a considerable time before spitting it into your napkin. We became experts at moving our food around our plates to appear eaten. I'm sure we were not the first.

We also became proficient at finding food that didn't cost much. So, Mom didn't **have to** cook. Mexican mini tacos that came in aluminum tubs. The inside of the taco was bean paste (I still eat them).

John's frozen pizza. Mom cut it with our house scissors. Chicken Noodle Soup. Macaroni and Cheese (from a can). I was out of college before I learned everyone else ate Macaroni and Cheese from a box. A box?

In an attempt to dignify us, Mom served an appetizer before each dinner. Juice in a small cup. Crackers and cheese. We ate as much of the appetizer every night as we could. We couldn't take the main course. I don't think Mom ever figured us out. I don't think she cared. By the way, she didn't spend much time cleaning the house either.

Since Mom did not drive, we walked to school. I don't know anyone whose Mothers drove them to school. On the first day of kindergarten Mom walked me to Oakton Elementary School. That was it. I was expected to find my way back. For the rest of my school days, I walked the four or five blocks to school (and back). Quickly, my friends and I learned the shortcuts through the alleys and the walkways next to the apartments.

What did Mom do all day? I'm really not sure. She read constantly. She listened to the Cubs on WGN TV and radio. She did not watch soap operas. Later, Verna watched "<u>General Hospital</u>."

I came home from school for lunch **every day**. Ate peanut butter and jelly **every day**. Mom ate her cottage cheese with French dressing. Drank her Diet Rite Cola. And, she smoked her cigarettes which Dad also brought home from work.

From the time I could walk, she took me on the EL to the Cubs home game every Friday. Friday was Lady's Day. She got in free. I was under age. I was free. She packed a lunch. For the cost of the EL, the scorecard, pop, and Cracker Jack if I was lucky, we enjoyed a great day for less than a dollar or two.

This was the early 1960's. Before Leo Durocher. The Cubs were bad. We had fan favorites. Ernie Banks. Billy Williams. Ron Santo. The Cubs usually hovered around last place. They only drew about eight-thousand fans to each game. Wrigley Field held thirty-eight thousand. We had our run of the place. The upper deck was closed off. Not enough fans.

We arrived about 1pm for a 1:20pm start. Sat wherever we wanted. Usually the old grandstands which ran right behind the box seats. Third base side. The Cubs' dugout side. Every game was a day game. The Cubs did not install lights in Wrigley Field till the Wrigley family sold the team to the Chicago Tribune in the 1980's.

Note: The first night game at Wrigley Field was August 8, 1988. 8-8-88. Playing the lottery? Stay away from this combination. It poured rain. The game was postponed after a few innings. Fate?

Once I went to school, Mom enrolled me in morning kindergarten so we could still go to the afternoon games. It broke her heart when I went to first grade. Mine too. All day school. We still had our summers.

So many books have been written about Fathers taking their sons to baseball games. Of course, we all went on the weekends too. But, Dad worked weekdays. It was just me and Mom.

CHAPTER 6

1968

1968 exemplified America's cultural change from black and white to color. The year sent the country on a new course. A year before "Woodstock Nation". In 1968, the stage play "Hair" opened on Broadway. Not with a "cast". The play's ensemble named themselves "the Tribe".

The young talented Broadway Tribe included a young actress. Diane Keaton. A nude scene. Outrageously good music. "Hair" challenged traditional senses. America was ready. Tony nominated. Grammy winning "Hair" brought music, clothing, hairstyle, drug use, the War in Viet Nam, civil rights, and the generation gap mainstream.

You didn't have to like "Hair". But, you couldn't avoid it. The "Age of Aquarius" was everywhere. "Hair" was **the** soundtrack for America's most explosive year since the Civil War.

1968 is the year when our nation's maximum force hit the proverbial fan. By the start of 1969 and into the early 1970's, the energy still roared. But, the collective resolution was on its way. After 1968, the steam was coming out just a bit.

Thursday April 4, 1968. Approximately 6:30pm

<u>Through my eyes as an adult...</u>

In Evanston, Mike's Rexall Drug Store is located at the corner of Dodge and Church Streets. The drug store is next to a record shop and a barber shop. It's across the street from Evanston Township High School. The neighborhood is a mix of Black middle class and Black blue-collar workers. Smaller than those in north Evanston, houses are mostly brick with nicely trimmed lawns.

Mike and Bernie have been doing business together for over a decade. Before Bernie, companies and salespeople did not want to do business with Mike's Rexall. Mike is the owner and the pharmacist. He is Black. He is slightly younger than Dad by a year or two. He is a World War II veteran. Earned his college degree on the GI Bill. Mike and Bernie never discuss the War.

By 1968, there are still no fast-food franchise restaurants in this neighborhood. Occasionally, Bernie and Mike would enjoy lunch together at Leon's down the block from Mike's.

Conversation always centered on their families or sports. Mostly sports. The up and coming Cubs. Those great Sox pitchers Peters, Horlen, John, and Wilhelm. The declining Bears. Butkus and Sayers. An aging George Halas. The new Bulls. Or, Bobby Hull, Stosh Mikita and the Black Hawks.

These days, everyone at Mike's was talking about the Evanston Township basketball team. Named the Wildkits - In deference to Northwestern's "Wildcats". It was an exciting time for the locals. Wildkit starter Bob Lackey was on his way to play for Al McGuire at Marquette. Just a few weeks earlier in March. The orange and blue Wildkits won the Illinois state basketball title.

This day, Dad got to Mike's later in the day. Mike was waiting for him at the door.

"You might not want to come in."

Entering with a smile.

"Why not? I know I'm late. I'm sorry. You're not mad at me are you? I have some nice new things I think you'll want."

"You don't know."

"Don't know what?"

"Martin Luther King was shot in Memphis today."

"When"

"About a half hour ago I think. It just came over the radio."

There are damp tears in Mike's eyes.

"I'm sorry."

With some force in his voice.

*"**You** don't have to be sorry. You didn't do it. You are my friend."*

As he speaks, Mike puts his hand out on Bernie's shoulder as if to steady himself. Bernie quietly stands still. Let's his friend gain his composure. He doesn't speak. Mike shakes his head and says aloud but not really to Bernie.

"You are my friend." It's almost a whisper.

"Do they have the guy that did it?"

"I think so."

Crystal walks into the store. She's eighteen. A senior in high school. Tall. Pretty. Black. Athletic build. Big afro. Big smile. Short shorts. Pink sleeveless shirt. Basketball in one hand. Stack of Motown and Tamla 45's in the other hand with her thumb in the middle to hold them together. She works for Mike after school. She's going to attend Southern Illinois University on a basketball scholarship in the fall. Mike and Bernie are proud of her.

"Hey Mike. I'm here."

Mike does not respond. She does not notice. In a very flirty voice.

"Heeeey Bernie. Bring me any candy? You listening to James Brown and Aretha yet?"

They have nearly the same conversation every week. They like each other. Bernie's watched her grow up like a proud Uncle. It's clear she doesn't know about Dr. King. Dad responds as he does every week. With a little less enthusiasm.

"Candy is on the counter for you. Try the "Sprees". They're new. I think you'll like them. You hear Louis Armstrong or Billie Holiday yet?"

Mike leaves Bernie for a Moment. He escorts Crystal into the backroom. He tells her the news. Mike returns to Bernie. A Moment later, Crystal returns from the backroom. She is no longer smiling. She is sniffing. Composing herself. Trying to. Her eyes are damp. A little redder all of the sudden.

She walks up to Mike. They hug for about thirty seconds. She turns to Bernie. Bernie is standing still as a statue. He does not speak. Crystal leans in and gives Bernie a strong hug. She is hanging on. Dad puts his hand on her back. She is easily five inches taller than Bernie. He takes her in. All of her weight is on him. All the while, Bernie is looking at Mike. Mike is looking back. Neither have an expression on their face. Eventually. They break. Crystal asks Mike.

"OK if I go to the back and work inventory?"

Mike nods. He knows. Crystal hates inventory. She always wants to be out with the customers when her friends come in from school. Not today. She does not want to see anyone. Very few friends will be coming in today.

More people come in and out of the store. All are Black. Some are regulars. They recognize Bernie. Usually, they asked Bernie about the Cubs or his kids. Today, they don't speak. They don't smile. They nod. Dad nods back.

Some going into the store are not regulars. They see Bernie. He is White. He is wearing a white shirt, sport coat and tie. He's carrying a note book. He's talking to Mike. The assumption by the strangers in the store – Dad is a cop. This is not a good day to be mistaken for a White policemen in Mike's. They stare hard at Bernie. They are not intimidated. They are angry.

Over the radio, the announcer reports.

"Dr. *Martin Luther King has just been pronounced dead at St. Joseph's Hospital.*"

Mike says.

"*It might not be safe for you to go home just about now. You can stay here in the back room. Call your wife. Go home when things cool down. Even come home with me if you want.*"

"*Thanks Mike. I'm going to go home. I've been through worse. I'll get home OK.*"

"*Bernie.*"

"*Yes.*"

"*You'll put an order through for me? The good stuff my people will buy? Make sure it gets delivered? People are going to be scared.*"

"*I'll bring it myself if I have to.*"

Mike is nervous. Agitated.

"*Bernie, before you. They wouldn't call on my store. Wouldn't deliver to me. Didn't think I would pay. Didn't think coming here was safe for a White man.*

"*Mike. I'm a Teamster. The only reason I pay my dues is so the truck drivers will deliver my orders. They **have** to deliver my goods. Like I said. If they won't, I'll go to the warehouse. Get the stuff. Deliver it all myself.*"

"*Bernie. See you next week?*"

"*Yeah. See you next week. Maybe we can go to Leon's and listen to an inning of the Cubs.*"

"*Bernie.*"

"*Yes?*"

"*Be careful.*"

It goes without saying (almost). Mike's order was delivered on time. As scheduled. Without incident the following week. Bernie saw to it.

As if this day could not get any more difficult. When Dad got home, I had a friend over. A Black friend. His name was Willie. Dad had to drive him to make sure he got home OK. Just a middle aged White man driving through a Black neighborhood (again) on the day Dr. King was assassinated.

Later he told me, he was a little more worried this second time. Things seemed out of control. Even in Evanston. His home town. But, he did the right thing. He got Willie back with his family. His parents were worried about their child. They were happy (with Bernie).

Monday April 8, 1968 8:45AM
Through my eyes as a fourth grader...

School Monday started on time. Friday had been a waste. We had a substitute. Not that I was complaining. It was like a day off from school. A holiday. Lots of art work. Long recesses. It's as though they didn't know what to do with us.

Oakton integrated this school year. As a kid, it wasn't a big deal to me. I was used to seeing different looking people in our neighborhood. The sports got a lot more interesting on the school playground. The Black girls were as good as the boys **and** faster. That was different.

I guess the city wanted more Black kids at each elementary school. So, Black kids were bussed to "White" schools. We were told. If you were for integration, you were for equal rights. If you were not for integration, you were for segregation. (It was years before it dawned on me to ask what the Black families actually wanted). My Dad had told us. Truman desegregated the military. Our family was for integration.

On Monday, our teacher was back. I guess he was not feeling so well Friday. His first name was strange. It was Leather (Pronounced "Leether"). He was young compared to the other teachers. **He** was a man. That was different for Oakton. And he was Black. That was really different.

I could recite the names of every member of the Chicago Cubs starting line-up. I was on pretty good footing knowing that LBJ was

President. I knew that the Vice President was Hubert Humphrey. He wanted to be President. I knew George Wallace was Governor in Alabama. My parents did not like him. He wanted to be president too.

I watched the Huntley-Brinkley report with my parents. I knew Dr. King had been killed. I knew a lot of people were angry. I did not know who Dr. King was. Why he was killed. Why people were mad. I had never seen anything quite like this. When President Kennedy was killed. People were sad. Not mad. This was new.

Leather came into our room. We had been with Leather since the fall. Having a man teacher was special. He was awesome. He treated us like men. Straightened us out when we goofed off (which was a lot). Played sports with us on the playground at lunch or recess. Lost his temper now and then. Laughed with us sometimes. We liked Leather. We respected Leather. He had our attention.

On Monday mornings, he would typically come in. Turn his back to us. Start by writing words we had never heard of on the blackboard. Every week, we were learning new words. This Monday, he came in and did not turn his back. He did not write on the blackboard. He stood and waited. Waited till the class settled down without saying a word. Just waited.

He said these words slowly but forcefully.

*"We are going to stand and have a minute of silence for the Reverend Doctor Martin Luther King Junior who was **murdered** last week in Memphis, Tennessee."*

He did not say "died". He did not say "passed away". He said **"murdered"**.

I did not know what a minute of silence was. It is unlikely I had ever been silent for a whole minute in my life other than sleeping. Over the weekend, I had seen a lot of the riots and the *"I have a dream"* speech on TV. But, I really did not understand Dr. King's importance.

The minute of silence: My friends and I. Fourth grade boys. We stood up. We laughed. We jostled each other. Pretty much acted like the ten-year-old idiot boys we were. Leather knew us. We were his class. All day. Every day. We were his boys. He'd seen us goof around before (all the time).

He went **nuts!** He yelled at us. Right there in class. He'd yelled at us before. But nothing like this. He was shrieking. Spit was coming out of his mouth. His voice was changing tones. He was beside himself. And, he was beside us. It was a rage. Right in our faces. Didn't touch us. But he wanted to smack us good.

I had never seen him like this before. All I knew is that this minute of silence thing was pretty important. We cried. He cried. I know why we cried. We were scared. I don't know why he cried. Maybe he scared himself.

Post script: On his campaign trail for the Presidency. Bobby Kennedy was scheduled to address a largely Black audience in Indianapolis the night Martin Luther King Jr. was assassinated. Aware of King's death. RFK decided not to cancel his speech. He addressed the crowd.

> *"I have bad news for you, for all of our fellow citizens, and for people that love peace all over the world, and that is that Martin Luther King was shot and killed tonight...*
>
> *...the vast majority of White people and the vast majority of Black people in this country want to live together, want to improve the quality of our life, and want justice for all human beings who abide in our land. ...*
>
> *...Let us dedicate ourselves to what the Greeks wrote so many years ago: to tame the savageness of man and make gentle the life of this world.*
>
> *Let us dedicate ourselves to that, and say a prayer for our country and our people."*

- Robert Kennedy (Speech excerpts)

Friday June 7, 1968 8:45AM

Through my eyes as a fourth grader...

The school term was just about over. In another week or so, I'd be a fifth grader. Oldest in the school!

Two nights ago, someone shot Bobby Kennedy. He died the next day. I knew who Bobby Kennedy was. My parents wanted him to be President. They liked his brother John. I knew what this meant. It meant another minute of silence.

We really did like Leather. We wanted him to like us. We talked about it on the playground. The school year was ending. We wanted to go out on a good note. Have him be proud of us. Show him we had learned something.

Sure enough. Friday morning. Leather walked in. Faced the class. Asked us to rise from our desks. Asked us to participate in a minute of silence in memory of Robert Kennedy who was assassinated this week.

We stood. We stood straight. We stood with serious faces not saying a word. Not **daring** to say a word. We did not jostle. We did not joke. We stared at Leather. We wanted his approval. We were going to get this right.

He asked us to sit. He moved on the with the lesson plan. I think I saw him shake his head. He never said a word about it. Didn't compliment us. **Nothing**. It wasn't like him. We were confused. We should have asked. We didn't. The school year ended. We said goodbye to Leather but something was not right. He was friendly. But, he was not passionate. He seemed tired.

Through my eyes as an adult...

I have always assumed that Leather thought we acted badly when a Black man was killed. Acted respectfully when a White man was killed. It wasn't like that. It was **him** that we liked. Respected. He made a big impact in our lives. He helped to form our opinions on Life. We never got a chance to tell him. **Never thought to tell him.**

1968 played itself out. Andy Williams sung "<u>The Battle Hymn of the Republic</u>" at Bobby Kennedy's funeral. Chicago had its infamous Democratic Convention. Richard Nixon won the Presidency. Riots continued in Black communities all over the country. The War in Vietnam made its way into our living room through TV. While the Detroit Tigers were winning baseball's World Series, Tiger All-Star Willie Horton (A Black Man) ventured into his rioting neighborhood of Detroit. Horton attempted to preach peace and non-violence. Still wearing his Tigers jersey.

Much of the turbulence (and excitement) would spill into 1969 and beyond. The first moon walk. New York Mets. Woodstock. Kent State. Watergate. All still to come. But, the steam was escaping. The anger was out. Not over. But out. The hippies had played out. The war had played out. The generation gap: Out.

People that never admitted being against the war in 1964 were coming out against the war. People that were taking drugs in 1966 were starting companies in the early 1970's. Long hair became main-stream. No-one cared. When the troops came home from Viet Nam. There were no parades. 1968 wasn't a "tipping point". It was middle ground from which all energy began to exhaust itself. The middle ground was coming for our family as well.

CHAPTER 7

"CHRISTMAS EVERY DAY"

The years went by. The 1970's moved in. It seemed like the economy got a little worse each year. Dad was getting older. Words like "inflation" and "unemployment" were creeping into the daily language. The cost of everything was going up.

Health dangers were coming out on smoking. People were stopping. Even Bernie had quit cold turkey a few years before (Cigarettes, cigars, and pipes). Larger chain stores were using their own suppliers leaving less business for Dad. It all added up to leaner years and more stress.

Bernie and Ann Ethel were Depression kids. They could handle tight times. They were not extravagant. They were used to being on the one yard line. Adult stress is different. It's different when you are looking after others.

And then, Teddy left. Where could Verna go? She came to live with her daughter Ann Ethel. There was nowhere else to go. Bernie knew it. I loved my Grandma Verna. Having her come live with us was Christmas every day for me. I loved her cookies and little pancakes. **She** could cook.

For everyone else, it was a nightmare. There was no room. There was no money. There was no privacy. She slept in my sister's room. It was not a good situation.

At a time when money was tight, Dad paid for everything for Verna. Food. Clothes. Medical attention. Spending money. Eventually, her funeral and gravestone. This wasn't even Bernie's Mother. Occasionally Bobby pitched in. He was the only relative. Verna had raised Bobby. He hadn't forgotten.

This meant that Bernie's own family went without. As a young boy who loved sports, I was pretty easy. One time, a Ted Williams baseball glove from Sears. A baseball magazine in the spring and a football magazine in the fall. A soccer ball. A new Cubs hat now and then. I spent my days outside playing on the Oakton playground.

It was hardest on my sister. She wasn't a jock like me. Young girls need things. They don't need their Grandmother in their bedroom.

Verna was proud. She was resentful of the situation. She loved Bernie. But, she couldn't bring herself to show her appreciation. It had been too much. She had been independent all of her life. The family matriarch. **Betrayed**. By Ted. **Her son!**

We were raised on Christmas. Both Mom and Dad believed Christmas was an American holiday. Jewish or no Jewish. There was no way their children were going to miss out.

They believed Hanukah was a religious holiday. We did not give or get Hanukah presents. We lit the Hanukah candles. Recited the Blessing. I love this tradition. My family continues it today.

"Blessed are Thou our Lord our God. King of the Universe. Who has granted us the lights of Hanukkah."

Christmas was very important to us. It was a small house. We had stockings and candy canes. The stockings were hung with thumb tacks on our bedroom doors upstairs. We didn't have a fireplace. No tree - No place to put it.

From Thanksgiving on. Mom wrapped presents. She did not try to hide them. They were stacked all through the downstairs living room. Every nook and cranny.

Presents weren't expensive. But, they were never essentials. Not things someone would buy for themselves or needed. Instead. A toy. A book. Pack of Hockey cards. Always something different. A fun treat.

We ate dinner in the living room to watch "<u>A Charlie Brown Christmas</u>", "<u>Mister Magoo's Christmas Carol</u>", and "<u>Hardrock, Coco, and Joe</u>". All on our Zenith black and white TV.

On December Twenty-Fifth, we came downstairs to a wonderful Christmas of cookies (one of the few things my Mom made well) and presents. We opened them one at a time. Each looked on. From the time I can remember till Verna came, this was our tradition.

Verna's first winter at our house. Christmas neared. There were no wrapped presents in the living room. The night of Christmas Eve. There was a rubber red, white, and blue ABA (American Basketball Association) basketball, a pair of grey sweatpants with a small Chicago Bulls logo, and a book on the couch. The book was "<u>Mr. Clutch</u>" by Jerry West. I asked Dad.

"What's this?"

"We're not having Christmas this year. These are for you."

"What do you mean we're not having Christmas?"

He didn't say another word. He just left the room. The conversation was over. I still have the book. There was no money. This was different than the Great Depression. This was a defeat for Dad. He felt it. He felt he had let us down. Of course, he hadn't. But he felt that way.

We never really got Christmas back. Never exchanged presents at home in the years that followed. No Christmas cookies. No Christmas TV specials eating in the living room. Christmas was just another day.

It wasn't too many years before I stopped thinking about it. By the time high school came, it was just another day off from school during Christmas break. A little bit later. Just an excuse to go out with my friends. Maybe share a few beers.

It was tough on Mom. She was squeezed in between it all. Teddy leaving. Verna coming. Dad silently angry. Her daughter outwardly angry. I was young enough to be an observer of it all. Bernie never said a word. He would always do what was right.

Through the 70's. Goldie died of natural causes in California. Will would follow. Verna would be next. Their generation was born before the Wright Brothers. They lived long enough to watch Neil Armstrong walk on the moon (On a television set!).

My sister went off to college. Fewer people in the house. The tension at home eased. Bernie was nearing retirement. I would go to college. Still fewer people in the house. Dad would retire shortly after. Bernie was ready to spend his golden years with Ann Ethel.

CHAPTER 8

THE PERCOLATOR

For the first twenty years or so of their marriage, Bernie and Ann Ethel were in a good routine. Bernie worked all year. A vacation in the summer for two or three weeks. They were good savers and good travelers. Bernie and Ann Ethel piled the kids into their car or a plane. Travel was cheap. Gas was cheap. We crisscrossed North America.

The 1970's meant less travel. But, Dad thought about it. When Bernie dreamed of retirement. He thought about endless trips around the world with Ann Ethel. Married all of those years. He was still in love.

My sister married after college in 1976. She moved out of state. I moved out of the house after college in 1980. Bernie and Ann Ethel were alone in the house in Evanston. Dad retired. He didn't like not working. He took a position with the Evanston Police Department as a crossing guard at Oakton Elementary School. Where his kids had gone to school. It was perfect. Up early. Three walks to school at morning, lunch, and school's end. The rest of his time for Ann Ethel.

My Dad and I talked for a few minutes each night on the phone. Mostly about the Cubs or other sports. One day he says to me.

"There's something wrong with your Mother."
I said.
"You're crazy. There's nothing wrong with Mom."
"I'm telling you. There's something wrong."
Pause.
"What makes you think this?
"She didn't put out the breakfast set-up for me this morning."
If you didn't know the situation, you wouldn't think this a cause
for alarm. Still, I asked.
"Maybe she just forgot."
We both knew better.
"She didn't forget"
"How can you be sure?"
"I asked her.
'Why didn't you put out the percolator?'
She said.
'I didn't know where to find it.'
That's what she said! What do **you** think?"
Let me explain. The townhouse in Evanston only had two real
rooms on the first floor. One was a kitchen. The house did not
have a dining room. We ate at the kitchen table.

Dad sat at the head of the table. Behind him was the kitchen
sink which he could turn and reach. Mom and I sat on one side.
Behind us was the stove. You could reach it while you were still sitting down. It was a very small kitchen.

Owing to Dad's work schedule. Every weeknight, Dad went to
bed early. Mom stayed up to read or watch television. Dad got up
early to go to work. Mom slept in and stayed out of his way.

Every night. I mean **every** weeknight since 1958, Ann Ethel
took out two pieces of bread so my Dad could make toast in the
morning. She prepared the percolator with coffee and left it on
the stove along with a match for Dad to light the pilot light.

When Dad was done making his coffee. He left the pot on the stove. The one and only small, steel, silver percolator Dad had ever owned since his Navy days. It was always on the stove. **Always!**

I knew he was right. I blew out a puff of breath.

"She couldn't find it?"

"She couldn't find it."

"What are you going to do?"

"I don't know." I've started to quiz her. Simple questions.

'What's my name?'

'What's our phone number?'

You know. Like that. Sometimes she knows the answers. Sometimes she doesn't. I'm taking her to St. Francis (Hospital) for testing."

I had sold newspapers as a kid at St. Francis. It was just down Mulford on Ridge.

"OK Dad. What can I do?"

"Nothing. Let's see what happens."

People didn't seem to know what Alzheimer's disease was then. She took a number of tests. Took a lot of test medicine. The slow march to the end moved on.

Day by day. No better or worse than any other critical disease. It was horrible for Mom. It was horrible for the care taker, Bernie. We don't believe she ever really knew. Her disposition was always cheery. His life became hell.

One day, I snapped. I was married. We lived next door to a family in Woodridge. The Mother of the family next door, her Mom had terminal cancer. She was the main care giver. It had been excruciating for her and her Mother.

One day we saw each other in our driveways outside of our houses. She said innocently.

"You're so lucky your Mom has Alzheimer's. She doesn't know. She's not suffering."

I went off. Right there in public. I was distraught. I had so much pain and anger built up over my Mom. I just let it out on this poor neighbor who was suffering in her own right.

"Lucky! Lucky! **Lucky???** *How do you know what she feels? How* **dare** *you?"*

I said a few other choice words I'm not proud of. I was horrible.

At first, Dad took Mom everywhere. Even went on a driving vacation to Alaska. The disease moves slowly. Dad judged people on how they reacted to Mom. If Mom was welcome, they were his friends. A lot of people stopped calling.

As Mom got worse, she couldn't control her bladder. Not much fun for a host inviting them over. Not much fun for anyone. Still, Dad kept to as normal a routine as possible. Kathy's Mother always made my Mom comfortable and welcome. Right to the very end. I always think so highly of her for that.

Eventually, Dad sold the house in Evanston. I had to clean every room. This was a house stuffed to the ceiling with artifacts, personal mementos, books, pictures, and so on.

Mom had completed hundreds of complex jigsaw puzzles while in the Evanston house. She had to stare at the pieces from about two inches away. Very close. She glued the completed puzzles together. Hung them on the wall. Cardboard paintings. Down they came. Out in the trash they went.

As a child, I rarely cried when I was scared or in pain. It's the same as an adult. It's the little things that set me off. Not blubbering. Maybe a line in a movie or in a song. Water comes into my eyes. I make that little snort noise.

I was by myself. An adult. Almost done cleaning. I'd been there all day. I stopped. Sat on the floor in the living room. Quietly cried for about two minutes. It just came out. All of Mom's pain. Dad having to leave. It crashed back.

I think it was the book shelf that set me off. Off of the break-front shelf. One by one. Coming down. Old friends. Half were about sports. Half were about life. An eclectic group. Some serious. Some funny. Some child-like. A sampling of titles.

- William Saroyan – "The Human Comedy"
- Lawrence Ritter – "The Glory of Their Times"
- John O'Hara – "Appointment in Samara"
- Joe Palmer – "This Was Racing"
- William Shirer – "Berlin Diary"
- Chas. Schulz – "Christmas is Together Time"
- James Jones – "From Here To Eternity"
- Eliot Asinof – "Eight Men Out"
- Ludwig Bemelmans – "Madeline"
- Alexander Johnston – "Ten and Out!"
- Ring Lardner – "Round Up"
- Roger Kahn – "The Boys of Summer"
- Leon Uris – "Trinity"
- Jim Bouton – "Ball Four"
- W. Churchill – "The Second World War"
- David Wolf – "Foul - Connie Hawkins Story"
- A. Doyle – "The Original Sherlock Holmes"
- J. Thurber & E. Nugent – "The Male Animal"
- Charles Addams – "Black Maria"
- Warren Brown – "The Chicago Cubs"
- Damon Runyon – "Omnibus"
- Red Smith – "Strawberries in the Wintertime"
- Louis Armstrong – "Swing that Music"
- Dashiell Hammett – "The Maltese Falcon"
- John le Carre – "The Spy Who Came In From the Cold"
- Douglas Wallop – "The Year the Yankees Lost the Pennant"

I kept a few small mementos. A cut-glass jar of Verna's with an engraved Sterling top. Filled with old Mardi-Gras doubloons. An antique porcelain cat with faux sapphire eyes from my Mom. My

Dad's jewelry box with cuff links and old rings. Mom's cigarette case. All of Dad's Navy stuff. A few other things. Disposed of the rest. Keep – don't keep. I went a little crazy. It would have been easier to walk away from almost all of it. I couldn't.

Other than blowing up at neighbors and occasionally crying at my Dad's house, I mostly kept my emotions tucked in. It was a long road. The day my Mom did not know me or my name was the **worst** day of my life.

Dad had it worse. He moved to an apartment in the western suburbs to be near me so I could help. He took care of her every step of the way. Fed her. Bathed her. Changed her. Diapered her.

Near the end, he couldn't leave her alone. He was landlocked to their apartment twenty-four hours a day except when I came over to give him a break. He never put her in a home till three weeks before she passed. Ann Ethel was no longer able to chew and swallow food. Dad could no longer feed her. He'd nursed her for years. We knew the end was close. Dad said to me.

"When I'm dying, read me the sports page. I did that for Ann Ethel."

"It's a promise. It will be a while. It's a promise."

1991. I got the call from the home when Mom passed. I had to tell Dad. You know what he said?

"I should have put her in the home sooner."

This was **the** "Greatest Generation." This is the man who sacrificed years for his wife. True to the words of Queen Elizabeth, he stayed through the "blitz' of nursing Ann Ethel. She died. He felt guilty. He hadn't done enough. This was his first thought. Of course there was nothing **anyone** could do. He had done all there was.

CHAPTER 9

"BLUE" TO "CUBBY BLUE"

Dad was living about six blocks away from me in an apartment complex when Mom passed away. He was very "blue". Understandably shaken. He was disoriented. His life had been in Evanston. Then, his life was taking care of Mom in Woodridge.

Now, she was gone. He was healthy. He found himself with free time. He started coming over to our house around dinner time. Staying for a few hours each night.

The doorbell rang. 7:00PM. I thought I realized what was happening. I wasn't sure. I took a gamble. I swallowed hard. Dad was at the front door.

"Dad. You can't come in."

"What's wrong? Is someone sick? Are you going out?"

"No. Nothing like that. You can't come in. You can't come here every night. You have to get back out there and restart your life. You can't do that here."

"Ann just died. You're kicking me out?"

"Yes. I love you. It's for your own good."

"I'm a big boy. Don't you think I know what's for my own good?"

"No."

"Go to hell."

He turned. Did not look back. Got in his car. Drove away. I felt about three inches tall.

I was used to talking to my Dad each night on the phone. We had always been very close. I didn't call him. He didn't call me. A week went by. Our house phone rang. Dad's voice.

"I'm still mad at you."

"I know."

"I'm going to do what you said."

"OK."

"I'm going to start over."

"Good."

"We'll talk tomorrow?"

"We'll talk tomorrow."

"Nat."

"Yes?"

"I love you."

"I love you too."

With the spirit and fortitude oft described by Tom Brokaw, Bernie fought his way back from his "blue" time of sadness which followed his love's passing. It took a while. The life in his mind and body came back. He wasn't ready to cash in yet. It was hard.

Bernie had spent so much of his past years indoors taking care of Ann Ethel. It was as though he was now re-acclimating to sun light itself. He was stiff. He began to date. Seek out new friends. Play cards. Join seniors clubs.

May 6, 1998

Bernie is one of 15,758 fans at "Beautiful" Wrigley Field. "The Friendly Confines". It's a misty cool day. Slight breeze. Overcast. It's sweater and jacket weather. He's wearing his "Cubbie blue" jacket with a red "C" in the Cub's traditional circle logo. Of course. He is wearing his blue Cubs hat.

The game starts at 1:20pm. Bernie is with a few friends from the Woodridge senior's center. The senior's center provides a small bus to drive them both ways. Bernie and his small group arrive about 11:30am to watch batting practice.

They'll have a leisurely lunch of hot dogs, Cracker Jack, Frosty Malts, and Coca Cola. All before the game starts. He's sitting in the lower boxes on the third base side. He's about twenty rows up from the Cubs dugout. As game time nears, Bernie fills out today's line ups. In his paper scorecard. He bought at the park.

The Cubs face a very dangerous Houston Astros team. Led by the "Killer B's". Bagwell and Biggio. His Cubs loyalty tears him between unending optimism and a gambler's sense of reality. It's not a great Cubs team. As he has been for every Cubs game he has ever watched, Bernie is "Cubbie blue" optimistic. **They will** win today.

Bernie has seen his share of games up close. He doesn't miss much. There's something different about these Cubs. Same with the Astros. The players seem bigger. Balls in batting practice are flying out of the park (out of the park!). Vicious. Not just the boppers. Everyone is hitting the ball 350 to 400 feet. Still. It's just batting practice.

Bernie particularly likes the development of Mark Grace and Sammy Sosa. First baseman Grace reminds Dad of Charlie Grimm of his beloved 1929 Cubbies. A great fielder. A smooth hitting style.

Since coming over to the Cubs from the cross-town White Sox, Sosa has become a fan-favorite. His home run, RBI and strike out numbers grow each year. Sammy takes a toe-hold and swings with all of his might on every pitch. When he connects, the ball sails.

Sitting close to the field, Bernie notices something he hadn't seen on TV. Sammy has put on **a lot** of bulk. Looks solid. Muscle. Could be a good sign. Mostly, Dad loves to watch Sammy run. He hustles on every play. He plays every day. He's a gamer.

Opening Pitch

The game starts on time. Bernie watches everything. The Cubs have a rookie pitcher. Six foot five inches tall. Kerry Wood from Texas. Just twenty years old. This is his fifth start in the major leagues. He does not appear nervous. Dad is keeping score. Wood strikes out the first five batters he faces.

Dad does not mark his scorecard with the universally accepted language. Dad has his own system. Instead of "K" for strikeout. Dad simply marks "SO". Instead of "BB" for walk. Dad puts down "W". "1B" for single. "2B" for double. And so on.

Bernie cheers with the crowd as the Cubs push over a run in the second inning on a sacrifice fly ("SAC"). In the third inning, the Astros scratch out a hit. Dad knows he won't be seeing a no-hitter today. Dad continues to score the game. It's moving at a very fast pace.

There is a very pleasant looking woman about Dad's age sitting in the box seat next to him. She has a full head of well-tended grey hair. She is wearing slacks and an overcoat. And a Cubs hat!

She's been there since about 1pm. She has been talking off and on with a few gentlemen friends she arrived with. Mostly just watching the game. From time to time, she peers in Bernie's direction. He's a grown man keeping score.

Fifth Inning

While the Astros are batting, the lady says to Bernie.

"Do you think the Cubs can win today?"

Dad never looks at the lady. He just keeps his head straight ahead. Keeps working his scorecard. He is polite when he answers. He's not bothered. Questions about the Cubs are his favorite topic.

*"Yes I do. This kid can **pitch**. Wood. My first time seeing him. What a delivery! Like Dizzy Dean. He just winds up and brings the heat. He's got a big tall curve too."*

There is excitement in Bernie's voice. He has passion. The lady continues to engage Bernie.

"Do you come to a lot of games?"

"Not so much anymore. I live too far away and don't like to drive in the city anymore. When I lived in Evanston, I used to come all the time with my family. When I was younger, my Dad took me. Do you come to many games?"

"I'd like to also. But's it's hard. I still drive too. Like you, I won't drive down here. No, I came with a group. These gentlemen I am with are veterans. I belong to a VFW and POW group out in Aurora. I like getting out and doing things. They take me everywhere."

Dad is still watching the game. He starts to make side glances to the lady next to him. Very polite.

"I like to get out too. It's not easy. I live in Woodridge now. I know where Aurora is. Is that where you live?"

"No, I'm in Lisle. The VFW Hall is in Aurora. Sometimes we meet at a restaurant near there for breakfast. The boys always invite me."

"May I ask about your husband?"

"He's gone now. Been a long time. He had a rough go after the War. He was a POW. We had a great life together. But, I need to get on with mine. He would understand."

"My Ann Ethel has passed too. Alzheimer's. It's a disease. Bad. Ann passed a while back. 1991. It's taken me a while to get back on my feet."

I'm not sure. But, I think this is the first time Bernie has said the word "Alzheimer's" out loud. He has a comfort with this lady.

"I'm sorry"

"I'm sorry for you too. I should have said that."

Seventh Inning Stretch

Bernie and the lady sing "Take Me Out To The Ball Game". It ends. They laugh. Turn toward each other.

"I'm Bernie"

"I'm Ruth."

"Would you like to have lunch with me sometime Ruth?"

"I would like that very much."

"What else do you like to do?"

"It doesn't matter. I just want to go places. Get out of the house. See the world. I walk forty-five minutes every day. I'm restless. I feel like I am making up for lost time. Do you know what I mean?

"I'm the same way. Some of our friends have moved to Arizona. Sun City. I'll never do that. Never move away from my son. Never go where people are just old. Why do I want to be around old people? All they talk about is their illnesses."

Ruth laughs. She writes down her phone number on a piece of paper she takes from her purse. Hands it to Bernie. The game ends. Kerry Wood strikes out twenty batters. Quite a feat. Ties a record. The Cubs win. Dad wins too.

CHAPTER 10

"YOUR PLACE IS HERE."

From that day forward, Bernie escorted Ruth all around town. They fell in love. It didn't take long. Seniors are different. They know what they want. They have dignity. No game playing. They are far more direct with each other. It was a passionate love. Different in some ways than the love they had experienced with their former spouses.

It was the love that age, comfort, companionship, and respect brings. They took care of each other. They made love. Neither wanted to ever marry again. They moved into an apartment in Lisle together.

They shared one other thing. Dad's service in World War II. Dad only shared with Ruth that he had spent his time in the Navy. In Asia. No details. Standard Dad. Ruth had been involved with the VFW and POW support groups for decades. Dad didn't have to talk about the service. Ruth understood.

Bernie had always steered clear of military celebrations. He never joined a VFW. Never marched in a parade. Never wore his old uniform "just to see if it fit".

He was proud of his service to his country. What he had achieved in the Navy as part of his team. Their contribution to the total effort. But, he always believed he'd lost a big part of his life. He never wanted to go back and re-live the War. He always wanted to move forward.

Ruth's husband Russell was in the army. In Europe for the duration. He earned a combat infantry badge and three battle stars. Captured. He had been a POW in Germany.

Surviving a POW camp in any war is a special type of hell. The POWs that came back alive (or partly alive) from war weren't gloating, they needed help. They needed support. Ruth was there. Always.

Ruth's husband spent his post-war years working for Western Electric. He earned additional money repairing watches. His hobby and occasional side job. Many years later, Ruth gave me a Hamilton pocket watch her husband had repaired. I opened the watch to see its inner workings. The watch is engraved.

Hamilton Watch Company Lancaster, PA
I love the watch. What it meant to Ruth. What she means to me. A small bizarre, coincidence. The watch was made in Lancaster, PA. The very same birthplace as my Aunt Dotty.

They raised a beautiful family together. All grown up now. Years after her husband passed away, Ruth continued to attend POW meetings and veteran's breakfasts. Bernie began to accompany her each month.

At the military gatherings, in his modest way, Bernie did not feel as though he belonged. This was Ruth's crowd. They knew each other. Cared for each other. Relived a lot of the same memories.

Bernie and Ruth were at a monthly veteran's breakfast in Aurora one morning. Ruth was at a table with her group of about fifteen. Bernie was alone at the counter of the diner reading the sports page and sipping his coffee. He was content. From the table came a booming voice.

"Hey Bernie. What's your story?"

"What do you mean?"

"Well you come with Ruth every month. But, you don't sit with us. Did you sit out the war?"

Others might have gotten mad. Not Dad. The group was staring at him. He gave them a long look. He slowly walked over from the diner's counter.

With a strong voice yet little emotion (No "I told you so" in his voice). Bernie gave them the "Reader's Digest" version of his service in Asia. Dad was in the service for over five years. He summarized it in less than seven minutes. Ruth had not heard it before.

Always modest. Very uncomfortable talking about himself. The table including the loud one stared in hushed silence as Bernie talked. Some had seen what Bernie had seen. Some had lived what Bernie had lived.

When Dad finished, the loud one got up and hugged Dad. He put his arm around Bernie. He was choking up when he said.

*"From now on, you are sitting with us. **Your place is here**."*

Ruth smiled. She said under her breath aloud to no one in particular.

"God resists the proud, but gives grace to the humble." (James 4:6 New Testament)

The loud one was a Marine. World War II veteran. A Purple Heart and Silver Star recipient. He had earned the right to be loud. He was impressed with Bernie. He should have been.

From that day forward and with Ruth's help, Bernie felt more comfortable about his service time. He let a little out of his very deep compartment. He sat with the boys and Ruth on their monthly breakfast visits. He marched in holiday parades. He accompanied Ruth to her POW meetings. On Veteran's Day, he spoke at River Woods Elementary School in Naperville. My family was in the audience.

I believe the country changed after "<u>The Greatest Generation</u>" was published. Friends and strangers started asking Bernie about his experience. They were saying things like.

"What was it like?"

Or.

"Thank you for your service."

This had never happened to Bernie. No-one had ever told him "thank you". In truth. For anything. He wasn't waiting for it. He didn't expect it. It made him feel very good.

CHAPTER 11

THE RAJAH RETIRES

Part One - Separation

One day. Something Yogi Berra might have said hit me.
"It's funny how you don't think about things sometimes." (I don't
think Yogi actually ever said this.)

I am the keeper of Dad's things. I have all his old pictures, letters and so on. Everything that had been in his night table stand
all those years in Evanston. He was about to turn eighty-five. I
asked him.

*"Dad. All these years, I've had your Naval discharge papers and the
book the Navy gave you showing which medals and ribbons you earned
and can wear. It just dawned on me, I've never seen your medals. What
happened to them?*

*"I brought them home. I gave them to Goldie. I don't know. I never
asked. I guess she threw them out."*

The only medal Dad still had was actually issued by the government of China in 1995. Dad and many others were honored with
a medal by China to commemorate the Fiftieth anniversary of the
liberation of China from Japan during World War II.

He hadn't given his earned Navy medals a second thought. For
his eighty-fifth birthday, we gave Bernie a surprise party. You can

order replacement medals from government approved agencies. We ordered all of his medals and ribbons.

We prepared a shadow box with his Navy medals, ribbons, naval uniform stripes, and pictures. We gave him a Navy ring engraved with CINCPAC and his rank. We prepared a cigar box with little trinkets like stamps, coins, postcards, and so on from the War years. His eyes were damp. He didn't cry. But he was happy.

Dad's health started to slip. It was inevitable. His age was gaining on him. He wasn't like Ann Ethel. His legs started to fail him. Very lucid otherwise. He became confined to a wheel chair. Angry to be confined. He tried to be philosophical.

"Every great baseball player...Willie Mays, Joe DiMaggio, Mickey Mantle, Ernie Banks. They all knew. It's time to get out when the legs go."

Ruth was amazing. She took care of Bernie as Bernie had taken care of Ann Ethel. I looked up the origin for the name "Ruth".

"Vision of beauty. Companion. Friend."
Nothing could have been truer.

By then, they were sharing an assisted living apartment in Naperville. After a couple of years, the administrators contacted me requesting I attend a meeting with Ruth, Bernie, and their medical staff. It was their professional opinion that Ruth could no longer take care of Bernie. It was taxing her health. Ruth's family agreed with this analysis.

We met. My feeling is that everyone in that room cared deeply for Bernie and Ruth. I felt none of the lack of compassion you so often hear about with care facilities. Clinically, I am sure the administrators and medical team were correct. However, there were two people in the room that disagreed. Bernie and Ruth. I argued.

*"I know you are looking after my Dad and Ruth. I can't thank you enough. We have all spoken before. I understand Dad's medical condition. I have no reason to believe you are mistaken. Your point of view. A very valid one. Is that taking care of Dad may harm Ruth. It **might**.*

Here's my point of view. I've asked Bernie if he wants to move. He does not. OK. That's understandable. I've asked Ruth if she wants Bernie to move. I've asked her if she understands the potential strain caring for Bernie might put on her.

*Ruth assures me she does understand. She tells me she does **not** want Bernie to move out. So I have to tell you, these are two consenting adults.*

They pay their fees to stay here. They do not pose a threat to any of the staff or residents. I think they are an asset to your community. They have taken care of their original spouses. Now, they are taking care of each other. I don't want you to split them up until Ruth tells me differently."

I'm not sure if it was reason or passion that prevailed. They were allowed to stay together. Still. Life does not get easier with time. About a year later, I got a call from the administrator.

"Ruth had been taken to Edward Hospital. Would you please go over there? She is asking for you."

"Of course. What's happening?"

"We only know that she was dizzy and fell down."

"I'm on my way."

I got to her room. She was awake. She was tired. In good spirits. Cold. I gave her my jacket. The doctors thought it was likely an incorrect mixing of her prescription medicine. They were going to keep her overnight for observation. Thought she would be fine in a day or so. This was the case.

While we were in her room. Ruth held my shirt sleeve. Warmly. Sincerely.

"I can't take care of Bernie anymore."

She wasn't crying. A very stoic person. She was very matter-of-fact. Very intelligent and proud. Knows her own mind. Knows what she can do. We've always been able to speak with each other directly. I asked her.

*"What do you want me to do? What **should** I do?"*

"I don't know. You'll have to tell the administrators."

"I'll go tomorrow."

The next day. I met with their facility care administrator. She explained. Bernie would be moved from assisted living to a full-service nursing home. Literally a block away. Everything was set. Now we had to tell Bernie. Another group meeting when Ruth came home from Edward Hospital.

This was a short meeting.

"I'm not going."

"Dad. You have to go. Ruth can't take care of you anymore."

"She doesn't need to do that much for me."

"Dad. You can't stand. Can't bathe. Can't get to the bathroom on your own. It's time."

"I'm not going. You can't make me."

To that the administrator replied gently but firmly.

"Bernie. We can forcibly remove you if we have to. I don't want to do this. We have a moral obligation to Ruth. We also have the legal authority. We feel Ruth is in harm's way. She has expressed it.

We have a good room for you. If you don't take this room now, we might not have a place for you in the future. You'd have to find another place to live. We have a long waiting list. We're making an exception to move you now. Please come along."

He and Ruth were in an excellent facility. Ruth and I did not want him to leave. If he moved as they directed. Ruth would be able to visit and look after him. If he refused. If he was put out. We did not have another facility for him. He required too much attention and physical strength to live at our house.

Dad was entrenched. Paranoia was seeping in. He was certain Ruth and I had conspired with the facility to have him removed. An indication that his sanity was not completely where I had thought it was. We had to trick Dad to go to the nursing home.

"Let's just go see it. What could it hurt?"

He never really agreed. I would say he relented. Once there. We gave him the news. He wasn't going back. Ruth brought over his clothes. This was probably the worst day of my life.

He told me in no uncertain terms. I'd stabbed him in the back. Complete with pantomime stabbings. At that Moment. He **hated** me. We'd argued before. We'd never had a generation gap. No argument was ever lasting. This was different.

I left that day weaker **and** stronger than I had ever felt in my life. **Strong**. I knew moving Dad was the right thing to do. For him. For Ruth. **Weak** (in the knees). I also knew he was going to die there. He knew it too. I also knew our relationship had taken a turn.

Part Two – Making Peace

"I am ready to meet my Maker. Whether my Maker is prepared for the great ordeal of meeting me is another matter."

- Winston Churchill 1949

For a while, I was no longer any different than the staff he hated at the home. Just another person telling him what to do "for his own good". He didn't want any part of them. He didn't want any part of me. I had to wait it out. When I was at my office. I was getting calls daily from the home.

"Come help us with your Father...
He's in the lobby.
He hasn't eaten.
He's trying to leave.
He won't take his medicine.
He's propositioning a nurse."
Or my personal favorite.
"Come help us with your Father. He thinks he is going to Kentucky."
Kentucky? Really? I have no idea where that came from. It was a common theme. He was sure he had a furnished apartment outside of the home. Sure I'd hidden the keys. He didn't. I hadn't.

Bernie's diagnosis was Dementia. He had good days and bad. On the good days, he seemed twenty years younger. He was never happy to see me. Never smiled when he saw me. I visited every day. The best I could say was that he was becoming less angry. Thawing out a bit. One day, he was awake. Lying in bed. Out of the blue. **<u>Very lucid.</u>**

"Do you know what I did in the War?"

"Only small bits. You've never really wanted to talk about it. I didn't want to pressure you."

"I know. And I appreciated it. I think you'll enjoy this. First a question."

"What is the 'Green Light Letter'?"

All fans of baseball history know the answer. I knew.

"Commissioner Landis wrote to President Roosevelt right after Pearl Harbor. Asked if baseball should continue. Roosevelt wrote back. He said 'yes'. It's known as the 'Green Light Letter'. How'd I do?"

"Very good. Next question. What was one of President Franklin Roosevelt's jobs before he was elected President?"

I had to give this one more thought. I offered.

"He was governor of New York. I believe he was also the Secretary or Assistant Secretary of the Navy. Yes?"

"Yes that's right. The Navy. He had a passion for the Navy. He had a passion for baseball too. Final question. Out of all of the recruits the Navy had following the Pearl Harbor bombing, do you know why I was selected for CINPAC?"

"I hadn't really thought about it. I know you're a pretty smart guy. I assumed that was the reason."

"Thank you. But no. That's not it. I was selected because I had a unique skill. At least they thought so."

"What was it Dad?"

"You know I've told you about your grandpa Will. His ability with numbers. I was a pretty fair card player. I had the gift Will had. I chose to use it differently than Will."

"I know"

"When I volunteered for the Navy, I was interviewed when I got to San Diego. I was given an aptitude test too. They had my test results. The officer conducting the interview asked.

'Bernie, what does a sailor bring to war?'

I didn't know the answer. I had never been a sailor before. I wasn't sarcastic or sassy. I reached into my pocket and pulled out an envelope of baseball cards. I handed them to the officer. I didn't say a word.

The officer didn't seem surprised. Didn't comment. He took the cards and lowered them under his desk between his legs. He could see them. I could not. He looked up at me. Asked.

'Can you tell me which cards were in your envelope? Can you tell me anything about the information on the back of each card?'

Well. There must have been something like twelve or fifteen cards in the bunch. I don't recall. I started by successfully naming each. 'Hornsby, Root, Hartnett' and so on. Then, I picked a name. Told him what I remembered.

'Hack Wilson. Card #211. 5'6 and 185 Pounds. Bats and throws right handed. Brooklyn Dodgers. Born Elwood City, Pennsylvania. With Cubs 1926-1932. Best season. Hit 56 home runs and .356 batting average with Cubs in 1930.'

I rattled off a few other card backs. The officer stopped me.

'You enjoy baseball?'

'Yes sir I do.'

'You have a pretty fair memory. A pretty good grasp of numbers as well?'

'Yes sir. I believe that is true.'

'We have a job for you. You'll be notified.'

That was it. I went through basic training in San Diego. About eight weeks later. I was shipped off to Pearl. When I got there. My orders were waiting. CINCPAC."

So many questions. I knew the "Green Light Letter" was a real thing. I was reasonably sure everything Dad had said about Hack

Wilson's baseball card was true. I couldn't believe he was recalling this all so vividly.

"Dad. Why did they want you? What did CINCPAC want you to do?"

"My job was to develop a code. A code that could be transmitted or printed for all to see. Out in the open. Obvious. Overt. Not encrypted. Right in front of Japan's prying eyes.

It would carry important information. It had to be in plain language. It couldn't look like gibberish or code. Had to look like something you'd see every day. Want to guess what I did? Why they wanted me?"

"I want to guess. But, I have no idea."

"You know that during the War, "<u>The Sporting News</u>" was provided free of charge by their owner Mr. Spink to any serviceman or woman that wanted it?"

"I do recall reading that."

"I devised a code that appeared in print - a baseball game box score. Minor league games. Sometimes I would include brief game descriptions or playing conditions.

'Oakland' meant Okinawa. 'Miami' was Midway. 'Idaho' was Iwo. I'd work locations, troop movements, losses, wins into the box scores. 'Extra innings' was a prolonged battle. A 'trade' or 'injury' might mean we lost a sailor. 'Cloudy skies' meant Japs in the air. 'Raining' meant we were under fire. Everything had a meaning. Player's names. Hits, runs, errors, innings, fast balls curves. Everything.

I'd transmit my daily box scores to '<u>The Sporting News</u>'. '<u>The Sporting News</u>' immediately sent my messages on to the War Department and Forrestal's office at the Navy. In the off season, I made up winter ball or spring training games. It only took me five or ten minutes a day. Every day.

'<u>The Sporting News</u>' printed my box scores every week. The information wasn't fresh by the time it hit the printed paper. That was just for appearances in case my messages were being captured. Which, I'm sure they were.

I always wondered what the people from those cities thought if they saw those box scores. No-one ever questioned it. No-one at CINCPAC knew I was doing it except my captain and Admiral Nimitz. I sent my box scores the entire time I was in the Navy. Each with a message provided by my Captain. The rest of the time, I was just a sailor. Doing as I was told.

The box score codes were all in my head. Never written down. At least not on my end. If we were captured, there was nothing to find. My Captain and Admiral Nimitz swore me to secrecy. I've never told a soul. Until now.

Not Will. Not Ruth. Not even your Mother knows what I just told you. I never told the boys at the veteran's breakfast. I swore I would take it to my grave. I kept my promise. I just wanted you to know."

It didn't matter if the story was true. It had been months. Dad was talking to me again. Like the old days. So clear.

"Dad, who's idea was it to use baseball for this purpose?"

"That's a good question. None other than Franklin D. Roosevelt himself. He was one smart politician. Evidently, he worked it out with Landis and Spink. They were old friends. The "Green Light Letter" was for show."

"Did they know they'd use box scores for code?"

"No. They just knew baseball could provide a cover. It was up to the Navy to figure it all out. Roosevelt was a Navy man. He trusted Forrestal. Forrestal trusted my Captain. My Captain knew what he was looking for. They found me and my baseball cards. A lot of it was luck for me. Smart Navy interviewer.

Using box scores was my idea. Jack and I used to use shorthand codes when we were little boys. You know. The way kids do.

'Jack. Game time. Hit a triple in the 7ʰ inning. I'll drive you in.'

'Game time' was 2:20PM. A 'triple' meant. Get three friends. Meet at DePaul. '7ʰ inning' ...'Seminary'. Say them both fast. They sound alike. DePaul was a seminary. Get it? 'I'll drive you in'. I'll bring a bat and ball. It was silly. It was fun."

"How did they know how to translate your codes? It was all in your head."

"Who do you think was on the other end of my transmissions?"

I thought for a Moment. The light went on.

"Jack?"

"Jack. He was in the War Department in Washington. He travelled to St. Louis. That's where 'The Sporting News' was published. He trained their staff. All hush-hush."

"Dad. I am so glad you told me. Thank you. I love you."

"Thank you."

He closed his eyes and went to sleep. I kissed his forehead. Left the room.

The night before. Dad thought his fictional girlfriend was driving him to dinner at the Steak House in Old Town, Chicago. He waited in the lobby of the home waiting to be picked up. The home called me. Asked me to come talk with him. Try to get him to eat. He'd refused dinner.

The Steak House had been closed for over twenty years. Dad did not have a girlfriend other than Ruth. He had dreamed it all. He believed it all. His Navy story? Dad had never lied to me before. I knew **he** believed it. I didn't know what to think. It seemed so real.

A few days later.

"Do you know why your name is Nat?"

My birth-name is Nat. It is not Nathan nor Nathanial. I was sure I was on solid ground with this one. I said.

"Sure. Grandma Verna's husband. My Grandfather. He died before I was born. His name was Nathan. I was named for him."

"Nope."

"Come on."

"I'm not kidding."

"So tell me."

"I guess you are old enough to know this now."

Where had I heard that before?

"So tell me."

"There was a movie."

I cut him off. With disbelief I said.

"Oh my God."

He never missed a beat.

"There was a movie. It was called "The Lost Weekend". It won a bunch of Academy Awards. Ray Milland was in it. Ronald Reagan's wife was in it. What was her name?

Milland plays a drunk guy. He's a writer. He wants to trade his typewriter for a drink. He can't stop drinking see. He goes to this bar called 'Nat's'. Nat was the bartender. The movie was pretty good. I really liked that name. It stuck with me."

"The movie sounds like a lot of laughs. Is this true?"

He just nodded and smiled.

I really like old movies. I looked up *"The Lost Weekend"*. I had never heard of it. Sure enough. It won four Oscars. Ray Milland was the lead actor. The actress was Jane Wyman. She **was** President Ronal Reagan's first wife. I watched it on cable TV one night. It was pretty sad. Dad's memory was working pretty well that day. Maybe I **was named** for a movie bartender.

We were down to the last few days now. Every day. I brought the newspaper. Read him the sports section. Some days he was lucid. Other days. He just laid there. Sometimes I just talked. Experiences we had shared.

"Dad. Remember meeting all of the Hall of Famers at the Otesaga Hotel in Cooperstown? Buck Leonard remembered Will. Mom met Casey Stengel and Stan Musial. I got all of those autographs.

Remember the silver dollars you used to give me? College. A Winston Churchill dollar from England? 'Never, never quit' you said. The moon landing Ike silver dollar when I got married?

*Do you remember the British silver dollar Will sent **you**? There's an inscription in Latin. I wrote it down.*

'MDCCCLI. Civium Industria Floret Civitas. MCMLI.'

I wrote down the translation.

'1851. By the industry of its people the State flourishes. 1951.'

Remember the 'Big snow'? The Pizza?"

He was lying there. Not moving. He was on Hospice now. They were taking care of him. It had been a few days since he had eaten or woken up. His eyes were closed. I really was not sure if he was sleeping or in a coma. I read or talked no matter what.

One day. I was reading to him about the new salary of a young baseball player. It was something crazy like Fifteen-Million dollars a year for an average relatively untested ballplayer. I said.

"Can you believe that? Fifteen-Million dollars for that guy!"

He opened his eyes. Lifted his head slightly. Tried to turn toward me. Said with a strong voice.

"That's more than I make in a year."

He closed his eyes. He laid back down. Those were the last words I ever heard him say.

You have a lot of time to think when you are talking to someone who's not talking back. Once I was an adult, we resurrected the holidays. Every Christmas and birthday, we'd try to outdo each other. The gifts were sometimes valuable. But really, they were more often personal or obscure. Not worth very much except to us.

One year, I was traveling on business in Florida. I stopped into a baseball card store. Hollywood Collectibles. It was a weekday. I think I was the only customer in the store. Very quiet.

I was looking at a Louisville Slugger baseball bat. It wasn't autographed. It was a store model. Brand new. Never been used. About thirty years old. It wasn't valuable. The clerk came over.

"Can I help you?"

"No. I'm just looking."

"Do you collect bats?"

"No. Not really."

"What catches your interest about this bat?"

"It's a nice old store model. 33 inches. Roberto Clemente model."

"Do you collect Clemente items?"

"No. It's the same bat my Dad bought me for Christmas when I was in fifth grade."

As soon as the words came out of my mouth, I looked up at the clerk.

"I'll take it."

I gave it to Dad for Christmas.

Our last Christmas together before Dad really went south, he gave me an autographed Cincinnati Reds model baseball bat. Manufactured by the Cooperstown Bat Company. Signed by Pete Rose.

Years after the Rajah, Dad liked Rose. He wanted me to be a fighter. We both liked Rose's famous line.

"I'd walk through hell in a gasoline suit to keep playing baseball."

Rose had the gambling gene too. It was a shame Pete couldn't control it like Bernie. In Will and Dad's day. Speaker, Cobb, even Hornsby were known (or alleged) gamblers. Pete was just born too late.

Pete Rose was a tough guy. A gamer. Winner. Great teammate. Never the best on his team. He made those around him better. He took limited natural gifts. Crafted a Hall of Fame worthy career. The same could be said for Bernie.

A few days later, I was at the Memorial Day parade in downtown Naperville. My daughter was in her middle school's marching band. I got the call.

The man who had lived through the Great Depression. Fought in World War II. Took care of his family. Took in Verna. Took care of his friends. Took care of his wife. Passed away at age ninety-one.

Memorial Day of 2012. Very fitting I thought. Now. He will meet his maker. He will apprise himself quite well.

A week after Bernie passed away, I received a catalog from a prominent auction house in the mail. One of their categories. "*Remnants of The Sporting News Archives*". Most auction lots were of old baseball photographs.

One auction lot: "*The Sporting News goes to War*". A grab-bag of hundreds of documents and photographs. Typed and hand-written correspondence between the owner Spink and Judge Landis, President Roosevelt, and a number of other dignitaries including

Ty Cobb and Babe Ruth. The auction lot sold for many thousands of dollars. Too rich for me. Included in the lot was a thick black spiral notebook. Stenciled on the cover page.

DEPARTMENT OF THE NAVY
Unidentified: Minor League Teams & Leagues
Abbreviations & Box scores.
South Pacific. CINCPAC. 1942-1945.
Confidential – Jack & Bernie

I threw my head back. Smiled and laughed out loud. For the first time in a very long time. Laughed **really** hard.

Mom passed away some twenty-one years before Dad. At Dad's funeral. We had a vase with white lilies near his casket. When I was a boy, Dad gave me a copy of "The Spell of the Yukon" by Robert Service. I framed one of its poems titled "Unforgotten" next to the lilies. It reminded me of Bernie and Ann Ethel.

I said to myself.

"Goodnight Rajah. Wherever you are."

POST SCRIPT

A Recent Conversation At Home

Kathy: *"What's it called?"*

Nat: *"The one-yard line."*

Kathy: *"I wouldn't read it. I won't like it. I don't like sports. I don't like books about sports."*

Nat: *"It's not about sports. It's about life. About faith, courage, and determination. A little divine intervention too. It just has some sporting references. It's sort of a memoir. More 'memoiresque' actually. Although. I'm not sure that's actually a word."*

Kathy: *"I don't care. I wouldn't pick it up. Not with that title."*

Nat: *"The title comes from a poem in one of my Dad's old books."*

Kathy: *"Well. That's OK I guess. Maybe I'll read it. You better change the title."*

Nat: *"I love you."*

Kathy: *"As it should be."*

ACKNOWLEDGEMENTS

My writer friend David really was the "straw that stirred the drink". He got me thinking about Mom. Teddy. The family. David was definitely the catalyst. I didn't realize it till my Dad died years later. It was all stirring inside me.

Bernie died in 2012. I always thought if I wrote a book, it would be about Bernie and Will. I've thought about 'unique talent' as a potential story since the 1980's.

Once I started to write, the book spilled out in a torrent. What started as a retro piece on Will and Bernie evolved into an emotional - and I hope powerful story about people with courage. I'm often asked if these stories are true. Some are. Some are not. As a volume, these should be treated as fiction. Hopefully – Enjoyable fantasy.

This collection of stories meanders from present tense to past tense. This is intentional. People don't think in linear terms. At least I don't. Our thoughts move in and out. These stories are somewhat chronological. Not completely. It doesn't matter.

Like most narrators, I am the least important person in the stories. I'm here to carry the story from one page to the next. This is not an autobiography. Information included by me or about me is only there as it relates to others.

I was very fortunate to have the enthusiastic encouragement, help, friendship and guidance of Jessica Bolvin, Professional teacher, Naperville, Illinois. Her support early in the book's genesis was immeasurable. I would also like to thank Kelly McGroarty, Professional teacher, Naperville Illinois for her generous willingness to read an early draft and provide honest feedback.

It may be obvious. Maybe not. My literary influences are named in the "percolator" chapter – the books on the breakfront bookshelf in my parents' house.

The last acknowledgements are easy. I could not have written this book without the love, support, nurturing, and guidance of Kathy, Annie, John, Bernie, Ann Ethel, Verna, Eileen, Bobby, Yvonne, Ruth and our friend, David. Thank you. I love each of you.

Nat

THE ONE-YARD LINE - J.W. Marson
"Coming Through! A Book of Sports for Boys" Copyright - D. Appleton and Company. Published with the approval of the Boy Scouts of America, 1927

It's easy enough to play with a will
When the breaks are all on your side,
When the scoring is easy, and going is good,
With everyone hitting their stride.
A fellow can keep his courage top-notch
And feel that the prospect is fine;
But give me the chap with courage to scrap,
Backed up to the last one-yard line.
For life is a game that tests every nerve,
And tries all the powers of will.
Sometimes it comes easy, sometimes it comes hard;
When easy, there isn't much thrill.
But when in life's battle the going is rough,
And weaklings would whimper and whine,
Just give me the chap who had courage to scrap,
Backed up to the last one-yard line.

AUTHOR BIOGRAPHY

Born on the North Side of Chicago and raised in Evanston, Nat Rosenberg fell in love with and married Kathy, a beautiful Southside Irish woman. Since neither was willing to move north or south, they compromised by moving west settling into the Chicago suburbs. There, they happily raise their Korean-American children, Annie and John.

Influenced by his family, Nat's stories combine real events with family lore and pure fiction to create inspirational, character-driven explorations of what makes America and its people so special. *The One Yard Line* is his first work of fiction.

Made in the USA
Middletown, DE
10 September 2017